Tom Anderson was born in Blackpool in 1947 and has lived in London since the 1960s. His short story collection *The Last Days of Dad* was published in 2018. *Downturn* is his first novel.

DOWNTURN

Tom Anderson

Published by Tombuktu Books 2020
Copyright Tom Anderson 2020
All rights reserved.
ISBN 978-1-9999926-2-0

to the rank and file

Contents

Part One
October 1982

1. Happy Returns

'Jesus F. Christ,' said Maloney.

He changed back into first. They must have gone a hundred yards at least.

'What is it?'

'The exhaust. It's hanging off again.'

Simon listened to the sharp metallic clunks as it knocked the ground beneath them.

'Marvellous,' he said.

They crawled onward, peering through the windscreen for a parking space. Car lorry, car motorbike, car van, caravan, car Land Rover, car Invacar, car abandoned, car with *Nuclear Power No Thanks* sticker, car occupied but going nowhere, van occupied with man doing paperwork. Unbroken lines of metal and glass on a street built for horse-drawn cabs. As they turned to the left at a T-junction, a smell of petrol began to seep through the interior. Simon wound the window down until it stuck halfway.

'I have this strange horror of dying on my birthday,' he said.

'I'll fix it. Same thing happened last weekend coming back from Birmingham. I had to get out on the hard shoulder... fucking great juggernauts thundering past.'

'You mean you take this thing on the motorway? Is that allowed? This *crate*? This *deathtrap*?'

'It runs like a dream most of the time.'

Simon leaned his head against the window. If it ran like a dream, it was a bad dream. But what did he know about cars? Nothing. Except this one was a Viva, fourteen years old according to Maloney, bought 'dirt cheap' during the summer. No service log, doctored mileage and a broken passenger door.

'Here we are...'

Simon sat up and squinted at a school coming up on their left. The whitewashed No Parking letters were partly obscured by two other vehicles but there was enough space for Maloney to back into. When he switched off the engine, they sat for a moment in blissful silence.

'What do we do now then?'

'Simple, Simon. I get out and tape the exhaust back up again. If I can't, we're fucked.'

1

He twisted round and grabbed a roll of duct tape from the back seat, then leapt out and vanished to the rear. Half a minute later, his head popped up again on Simon's side.

'Can you throw the blanket out. It's filthy under here.'

Simon pushed it through the window, then slumped back into his seat. This, or something like it, always seemed to happen on his birthday. It had seemed innocuous enough. Take the morning off from the Institute, meet Maloney at the Finsbury Park bookshop which was only ten minutes walk from his current abode, get the stencils made, drive to Maloney's 'Centre' and spend half an hour cranking out the Branch Newsletter on their duplicator. But the Bookshop's stencil machine was out of action and they were now stranded in the back streets of North London.

Last year, he'd spent part of the day with twenty or so comrades on a fascist hunt. It was known that the Front had split into different factions after the election and one of the factions was rumoured to be meeting at a Camden pub. The comrades, none of whom Simon knew, had gathered on the pavement just before high noon. At first, nothing much happened except for hostile looks from some of the punters as they arrived and an invitation to 'fuck off back to Russia.' They were all white, but whether they were fascists or just pissed-off pubgoers was hard to gauge. Were the comrades wasting their time? Had the mole got it wrong? Then just after the quarter hour, the door of another pub across the main road had swung open and four men marched in disciplined style twenty yards along the pavement, over a Pelican crossing and twenty yards back towards them. No-one mistook these fuckers. They were muscular hardmen, part of the Front's 'protective force' bearing down with contemptuous confidence. The tension erupted into shouts of 'fascist scum' accompanied by gobs of spit and push-and-shove scuffles before the bastards somehow got into the pub. Word went round that *one of them had a knife!* And Simon had slipped away amidst all the excitement.

The year before that had been less dramatic. His birthday had fallen on the day of an anti-cuts march through South London. It had rained on and off and Clapham Common had turned into a quagmire under several thousand pairs of feet. He remembered the long trudge through Stockwell, Vauxhall and along Millbank, holding the Branch banner with Don Gable most of the way, then speeches in Parliament

Square before slow, shuffling dispersal. The year before *that* was Thatcher's first year in power and his last in the SWP. But that was far back enough. In the playground a few yards away, the cries of small children were piercing the autumn air.

He decided to get out of the car, but the door handle went down without effect. He pushed and shouldered the door, leant sideways and kicked it, put his arm through the window but could only just reach the outside handle with his fingertips. After that, he lacked the will to clamber over the driver's seat. Instead, he watched the school children through gaps in the railings as they ran back and forth, circling, pushing, confiding and mocking, as he'd done once in another place, another time. He did the calculation and felt a pang of fear: *twenty years*, more or less. How could so much precious time have gone by? The window seemed to sigh as he wound it back up. He looked around the car. On the back seat sat a stack of *Workers' Struggle* and a pile of leaflets promoting a march in support of Solidarnosc. Next to them...a box of badges, a scarf, some tools, a dried-up oily rag and a traffic cone. Turning back, he bent forward and picked up a couple of books that his feet had been grinding into the floor. One was a London A-Z which he dropped down again. The other a paperback copy of Trotsky's *My Life*. He opened it halfway through and began to read:

'The twelfth hour of the revolution was near. The Smolney was being transformed into a fortress. In its garret, there were a dozen or so machine guns...'

A minute or so later, Maloney resurfaced. He flung the blanket and duct tape into the car, then stood in the road dusting himself down.

'That should hold it for a while.'

'Oh, good.'

Back in the driver's seat, he cleaned his silver-framed glasses on the front flap of his shirt.

'What's the book?'

Simon showed him the cover.

'I found it on the floor.'

Maloney started the engine and began to manouevre the car out into the road.

3

'It must have slid off the seat. I don't normally keep books on the floor of my car. Not the classics, anyway.'

They set off again.

'I tried reading it a few years ago when I was in the SWP,' said Simon.' Didn't get very far. It seemed to be all about his childhood on some farm in the Russian steppes...'

'That's only the first few chapters. It follows his life from student to Commander of the Red Army. His exile, the 1905 revolution, his relationship with Lenin, the 1917 revolution, the rise of Stalin... Absolutely essential reading. I'm about to use it for a Workers' Struggle educational class, otherwise I'd lend it to you.'

'An educational class. Does that mean you've actually got some new members?'

'Don't be cynical, Simon. There are people who want to join us.'

'How many members have you got now, then?'

'I don't know. Not exactly. Over a hundred, easily.'

'*Over* a hundred. *Easily.* That's progress.'

'Simon, we've had this discussion before. We're not like the SWP recruiting anything that moves. We look for people with some kind of record in union branches or community action groups. Now do something useful and find the A-Z.'

Simon picked up the tattered copy from the floor again and held it aloft.

'Okay. Hold on to it. We might need it soon. Jesus, look at the fucking traffic. What's going on this morning?'

They'd reached a junction with the main road and Maloney kept the car rolling forward, ignoring the honking horns until someone let him in. After that, they trailed along behind a bus and Simon gazed at the shops as they crawled past. Last week's headlines were still in the evening paper stands. PRINCE WILLIAM NEW PICTURES, POUND SINKS AGAIN. A queue stretched out of a Post Office along the pavement.

'Look at that,' he said. 'And it's not even giro day.'

'Every day is giro day now. They can't send out three million cheques at once.'

'True. Maybe you should try recruiting there? That's where the workers are these days.'

4

'No, we're active in the claimants unions because they have a structure and some unity and anger and potential power. We don't trawl along queues just on the off chance.'

'I've seen the SWP leafleting outside post offices.'

'So have I. It's a waste of time. Just leaves a mess on the pavement.'

'Well at least it keeps the roadsweeper in work.'

Maloney shook his head.

'Simon, you're a liberal really. Your politics are fatally undermined by sentiment. If you're serious about revolutionary change, you have to ask yourself *where are the levers of power?* There are no levers of power on the road sweeper's barrow.'

'Oh, yeah? What about the winter of discontent? All that rubbish piling up in the streets? Anyway, I can't be serious about revolution, obviously, because I'm not a member of Workers' Stuggle.'

'The real levers of power are with the workers who provide essential goods and services to big business. Oh, fuck. Look what's coming up in front.'

Simon looked. They'd managed to overtake the bus, but a mounted policeman now came into view about twenty yards ahead. In navy raincoat and peaked cap, perched high and straight-backed in the saddle, he was cantering steadily past parked vehicles while the cars ahead pulled round him one by one. Even from behind, Simon could sense the smugness of authority.

'This could be serious,' he said. 'He'll be looking at your car, checking it for faults, noting the registration number and the stickers - oh, you haven't got any stickers.'

'Car stickers are petty-bourgeois, Simon. Anyway, the modern-day police officer has a lot on his mind. He'll be checking the pavements for anything suspicious, looking for tax discs on the parked cars... we'll only get a glance. As long as I don't have to brake, we'll be fine.'

It was their turn and they moved out smoothly into the middle of the road. Simon had a view of the dark brown flanks of the horse and a booted leg in the stirrup as they passed by. He glanced back and as Maloney had predicted, the policeman was looking away from them at the pavement.

'Looks like we're safe,' he said. 'Though he could easily catch up with us in this thing.'

'You won't see them chasing anybody along the street. It's more about being a deterrent. And exercising the horses, keeping them fit for demos.'

'Yeah, that's where I first saw police horses - some demo or other.'

'Grosvenor Square '68 in my case.'

'Of course, you go back that far. March or October?'

'March. I didn't get to the October one. Apparently, that was peaceful on the whole and ended up at Hyde Park. The Maoists and a few anarchists did go to Grosvenor Square and tried to charge the embassy, but it was well defended. Stupid fuckers.'

'They haven't changed much, the Maoists.'

'They never will. They're Stalinists, basically. They taunt us with chants about ice picks. Who on earth would want to live in a society led by those bastards?'

'Indeed. Anyway, what was the March demo like?'

Maloney paused.

'How did we get onto this? Oh, the horses, the mounted police. They charged the people up at the front and then pushed the rest of us back.'

'Whaaat?! You mean you weren't on the front line?'

'Simon, I was eighteen, still in sixth form. I came up to London with a friend to see what it was all about...and to see Vanessa Redgrave. We couldn't quite believe that a famous actress would get involved in a street demo.'

'And did you see Vanessa?'

'We did. And Tariq. We saw them by the National Gallery as a matter of fact, just as the march was setting off up Charing Cross Road. We followed it on the pavement at first, then when it got to Oxford Street, we joined in.'

'So did you get Vanessa's autograph?'

'Very funny, Simon. We were naive but not that naive. Actually, we were very naive - we thought it was supposed to be a peace march. Then we realised they were chanting about Ho Chi Minh and victory to the NLF...'

'Oh yeah.'

'Then we turned into a side street which led to Grosvenor Square. The police had blocked it off at the end and people kept piling in. It was a crush but everyone knew the police line would break. Sheer weight of numbers. I remember a small child being passed over people's heads for safety, but towards the front. No question of retreat...'

'Wow!'

'When they gave way, we ran into the square and that was it. Battle commenced. We were overawed by it, me and my friend - I have to admit. We stayed at the back. I remember one guy being led away with blood pouring from his head and other people lying on the grass looking dazed, but we didn't see much of the actual fighting. I remember a young copper wandering around without a helmet, looking shell-shocked, and somebody throwing a tin can that bounced off his head. He turned round and said - *All right, who's the wise guy?* We just laughed. As if anyone was going to own up. Then the police horses moved forward through the square and this Inspector started lecturing us from the saddle, telling us the march was over, go home, we'd no right to be there and so on. Arrogant bastard...'

Simon was impressed. He'd never heard Maloney reminisce quite like this before.

'As if he owned the place...'

'Well the police do, more or less. Foot soldiers of the state - they can go anywhere. Just check the A-Z - we're looking for Grosvenor Avenue.'

'Grosvenor Avenue!' yelled Simon. 'What a fucking coincidence. Hang on...' He pushed his finger across the map. 'Next left. Can you Adam and Eve it?'

'Calm down. Anything called "Grosvenor" is probably owned by the Duke of Westminster. He owns half the fucking country. He's richer than the Queen.'

They turned into a long straight road lined with plane trees, their leaves now the light green, almost yellow, of autumn. Behind the trees were substantial Victorian houses interspersed with small blocks of modern flats.

'That didn't say Grosvenor Avenue.'

'Keep going. It leads on to it.'

And it did. Soon they were parking outside a large semi-detached house with a huge pile of rubbish bags and old furniture almost obscuring the basement windows. Maloney leaned across the car and showed Simon how to jiggle the handle and thump the door so that he was freed. Then they climbed the entry steps and found that the black front door opened at a push into a large hallway. A sign in hand-coloured letters directed them up a flight of stairs to an office on the first floor. Here, behind a desk and a large typewriter, sat a woman of refined features and advanced middle age with greying hair sprouting over a purple headband. She gazed up at her visitors with a perplexed unhappy look on her face as if second thoughts about volunteering had already come to the surface. Nevertheless, she answered Maloney's questions with measured concentration.

Yes, she believed there was an electrostencil machine somewhere, but she was sorry, she had no idea where it was kept or how to use it. On second thoughts, it was probably in the workshop but that was locked and she had no means of access. She was sorry, but everyone else was out for the morning on the local nursery campaign march. If they could come back that afternoon?

'No, we have a meeting this afternoon.'

'Oh dear. Well I'm terribly sorry, but I'm just holding the fort.'

They returned to the car.

'Middle class dabblers,' said Maloney.

'They do their best. Where now?'

Maloney dug a crumpled piece of paper from his pocket and studied it.

'Hackney People's Centre, Balls Pond Road. I've never been there before, but I'm told they have a machine. If that's no good, there's a women's centre we can try in Islington.'

'Can I tell you about *my* defining moment?' said Simon as they drove off. 'On the road to revolutionary awareness...'.

'If you must. This place is only around the corner though.'

'Grunwick.'

'Grunwick? A beautiful word.'

'11th August 1977. No - 11th July. Three months after I started at the Institute.'

'Don't remember the date. Was that the National Day of Action?'

'Probably. I'd heard about it on the news and heard you move a motion of support at a Branch meeting, so I went along. I was supposed to be meeting a friend outside the tube station, but I couldn't see him - there were so many people milling about. After a while, I just let myself be swept along in the crowd. It was an amazing feeling. Fists in the air, everybody chanting - *the workers, united, will never be defeated*. The miners marching behind their banner. The mounted police were there too, but we just kept on going. We came to that road around the back - I forget what it was called but it led to the back gates...'

'Chapter Road,' said Maloney. They'd stopped at traffic lights and he drummed impatiently on the steering wheel. 'I was there every morning during that period. No, wait a minute - not Chapter Road, that was at the front...Cooper Road.'

'Sounds familiar. Anyway we filled that road completely and the police didn't like it. They sent in this long line of coppers to defend the gates - forty or fifty of them threading their way through the crowd in single file. And of course everyone was jeering at them and jostling them...and I was stood in the midst of this huge mass of people, not actually doing anything, just watching these coppers struggling past a few feet away. And suddenly one of them got pushed quite hard, lost his cool, swung round and hit out at the nearest person - which happened to be me. He hit me once on the jaw and once in the stomach. Then he went on his way. People shouted at him and someone checked that I was okay, which physically I was. They weren't hard blows - he was off balance. But inside I was stunned - well, I was shocked that I should have been attacked by - you know...'

'The long arm of the law?'

'Well, yeah. It's a criminal offence isn't it to assault someone?'

'And that was what got you into revolutionary politics?'

'The whole experience, but that in particular.'

'You're a romantic, Simon. A couple of lame punches and you're ready to storm the Winter Palace. The police are always attacking people - didn't you know that? Look at Blair Peach - killed from behind by a copper...'

'Hmm...'

'I became a revolutionary socialist after studying Marxist ideas and after meeting certain people who lived by those ideas. Anyway, we're almost there now - as you can see...'

They'd turned on to Balls Pond Road and were heading towards what Simon knew to be Dalston Junction. Following Maloney's gaze, he saw a building hard to miss on a stretch of highway marked by boarded-up windows, hoardings and all-round decrepitude. Built in the shells of two former shops, the entire frontage was painted bright yellow and a large multi-coloured sign announced its name.

9

They found a parking space further along the road and this time Simon managed to fight his way out of the car unaided before pursuing Maloney along the pavement.

The ground floor of the building was given over to a bookshop and coffee bar, while a staircase at the side led to the local law centre, a counselling service and various function rooms above. The bookshop counter acted as a reception desk for the whole place and behind it sat two nice young people with new wave haircuts. After listening briefly to Maloney, one of them smiled apologetically and shook his head.

'I'm sorry but we can only let you use the electro-stencil machine if you're having your work duplicated here as well. Unless you're a registered supporter and even then you need to book in advance.'

The girl sitting beside him echoed the word 'sorry', hunching her shoulders, her eyes shining in sympathy. Maloney stared from one to the other in disbelief.

'But you're the Hackney *People's* Centre. How *exactly* do you serve the people?'

'Well you see, the Law Centre and the other community groups based here have first call on our facilities.'

Simon wandered off to scan the book shelves. When he returned after two minutes of pleading and haranguing by Maloney, a look of prim obstinacy had settled on the boy's face while the girl had turned her back. As a last gesture, Maloney pulled some leaflets about the Solidarnosc march out of his carrier bag and slapped them down on the counter.

'Well at least stick some of these up somewhere. On your notice board...'

'In your window,' said Simon.

The boy looked at the top leaflet.

'Sure,' he said. 'I'll have to pass it by the Centre Manager-'

'Okay, well don't ring us. We'll be engaged in the struggle. That's the class struggle by the way, in case you haven't heard of it...'

They walked out onto the pavement where Maloney once more pulled the scrap of paper from his pocket.

'We'll just have to try Eden Grove. It's a women's centre. Never been there before but one of our female comrades has worked with them. Just off the Holloway Road...'

'Eden Grove - sounds promising.'

Simon checked it out in the A-Z while the Viva did a stately five-point turn in the Balls Pond Road.

'It's near Paradise Park as well. That must be a good sign.'

'There's no such thing as a good sign.' Maloney nodded at the yellow building as they drove past it. 'Look at that one. People's Centre...it means fuck all. Purveyors of first aid and political pap - that's all they are.'

'Actually, you missed a chance back there. You could have said something like we're part of the solution, you're part of the problem.'

'Too clever-clever, Simon. It would have washed over their heads anyway. They were still in nappies when Cleaver came up with that one.'

Simon felt aggrieved.

'So far today, you've called me a liberal, a romantic and now *clever-clever*. Why d'you have to take your frustrations out on me?'

'Oh, come on Simon. If you're going to be a revolutionary, the first requirement is to grow a thick skin. Even thicker than the skins of the ruling class and its legion of lackeys. There isn't time for bourgeois hysterics.'

'*Legion of lackeys. Bourgeois hysterics*. You could write the Little Red Phrasebook.'

'And cynicism is the flip side of romanticism. You should know that one too.'

'You drive me to it, Tony. You drive me to it.'

'Look, Simon, you're not a liberal *yet* - okay? But that's where you could end up because you're not anchored in anything. Being a revolutionary socialist is about being guided by a clear set of Marxist ideas and principles. It's not based upon an emotional reaction to injustice, though that might be a starting point. And it's not just about attending pickets or going on marches and demos. It's more like this - a day to day grind of holding the line, trying to make small advances like publishing a newsletter or organising a meeting, trying to build class consciousness against all the odds. It's always been like this - back in the sixties and before...'

'But that's going to take forever. It sounds as if we're going round in circles. Or cycles. When is the revolution *actually going to happen?*'

'It will happen when capitalism finally starts to collapse. When the working class are thrown out of work and the poor have to start scavenging for food. I can't predict when that will occur because capitalism itself is unpredictable and because it doesn't just depend on what happens in this country. It has to be an international development as Trotsky said. But in globalising itself, capitalism has done us a favour by creating interdependency. Economic collapse in one country will have a chain reaction in other countries. And in the UK, Thatcher is doing us a favour by basing all her policies on the free market. People will see how unstable that is, how it's never going to deliver a fair and just society - and isn't intended to. The post-war consensus has collapsed? Good! It was never anything more than a shield against revolution for the right and a failure of nerve by the left.'

'But the working class are being thrown out of work while we speak. Three million unemployed while we fart about trying to get electro-stencils made for something that'll be read by two hundred people. And what do the opinion polls say? Tories well ahead.'

Maloney waved his hand dismissively before returning it quickly to the steering wheel. They were toiling around the Highbury Corner roundabout by now, switching lanes with a horn beeping in the background, grinding past the tube station onto Holloway Road.

'Yes, but that's the Falklands effect. Her ratings are slipping already - she'll still be kicked out whenever they get round to calling an election. The point is, the Parliamentary Show is irrelevant to the interests of the working class. Whoever replaces her won't be up to the job. Anyway, how far have we got to go? Is it on the left or the right?'

'How far have we got to go? Is it on the left or the right? D'you want me to consult Trotsky or the A-Z?'

Maloney laughed.

'Good one, Simon. You really should join Workers' Struggle. We could do with a comedian in the ranks, I'll admit.'

'You've already got comedians in the ranks. You just don't realise it.'

He opened the street atlas again and began to leaf through its grubby pages.

'Failing that, why don't you rejoin the SWP?' said Maloney. 'At least it would be a commitment. Seriously...'

'A commitment to what though? I can't just blindly follow the party line in an organisation where there's no real open discussion. Here we are...Holloway Road...Eden Grove. It's on the left. What's this street?'

He squinted at the black and white sign coming up.

'Okay, it's the one, two, third on the left.'

'You'd still be doing some good. And you'd have more contact with the real working class than you do at the moment.'

'Nah, it'd be like taking two steps back, then going round in circles again. All they really want you to do is sell papers and go on demos to advertise the so-called Party. Hand out leaflets and placards, chant slogans and recruit.'

'That's better than being a floating socialist, picking and choosing your causes. Anyone who commits himself or herself to a revolutionary socialist organisation, I'm prepared to call a comrade - even if I have disagreements with their policies.'

'I'm a union comrade, Tony. That's as far as it goes at the moment.'

'A union brother,' said Maloney. 'There's a difference between *brother* and *comrade*.'

He changed down into first again and they crawled into Eden Grove which seemed unlikely to live up to its name. A redbrick corner pub followed by council flats stretching down one side and some kind of disused warehouse along the other. Bins, strange graffiti, Arsenal posters in windows and an England flag acting as a curtain.

'Hmm,' said Simon. 'I have a bad feeling about this.'

'Front territory?' said Maloney. 'That runs through my mind when I see the England flag, but they're no big deal around here. This is solid Labour territory. Well...until Cunningham fucked off to the SDP.'

He braked abruptly outside the disused building.

'Something tells me this is it. The window grilles for one thing.'

When they stood on the pavement, it became obvious that this was it. Posters in the arched windows, each bearing the women's liberation clenched fist, spoke of abortion rights, childcare, male violence and self-defence classes. Simon felt tense. The feminists that he knew were sisters in the main political struggle. This looked hardcore.

The door from the street pushed open and allowed them into a corridor, but the door into the women's centre was locked. Maloney rapped on its glass panel and they watched as a woman rose from

13

behind a desk and walked towards them. Short black hair, black trousers and a dark blue denim jacket, unsmiling, she half-opened the door.

'Yes?'

In stream of consciousness sentences, Maloney explained their mission, their problems, their desperation and the fact that his comrade Ruth had worked with the Centre on this project and that.

'Oh, Ruth - yes.'

The voice softened. The door opened wide and they entered a large L-shaped room with desk, meeting table, a dozen or so chairs and a bank of shelves stacked with books, pamphlets and leaflets. Another woman was seated at the table sorting through paperwork. She paid no attention to the two men who were led past her into the little rear annex. The electro-stencil machine sat on an old workbench against the wall.

'Do you need me to show you how it works?'

Maloney peered at the buttons.

'No, I should be okay.'

He slipped off his jacket and began to roll up his sleeves.

'The duplicator isn't working at the moment if you wanted to use that. We have a woman coming to service it this afternoon.'

'It's okay thanks. I can use the duplicator at our Centre.'

The phone started ringing at the desk in the main room and the woman went to answer it. Maloney got the machine going.

'Simon, did you happen to notice that kebab place just before we turned off the Holloway Road?'

'Vaguely. Does that mean you're hungry?'

'I've had a single piece of toast...'

'Okay, I'll go. You don't mind paying though, do you? Given it's my birthday...'

Swearing softly, Maloney dug into his pocket and pulled out a couple of crumpled pound notes.

'I'm not sure they'll want you to bring food in here though.'

They hesitated and looked into the main room. The black-haired woman was talking on the phone, the other woman still sat at the table with her back towards them.

'I'll wait till you've nearly finished.'

'That's wasting time. Go and ask.'

14

The woman at the table seemed to have heard this and turned around. Simon strolled towards her as casually as he could.

'We were just wondering if we could get some food from that kebab place around the corner and bring it back here.'

'Sure, no problem - as long as it's vegetarian.' She looked at her watch. 'They should be open by now.'

She had a soft transatlantic accent, fair frizzy hair and rather cherubic features. Simon liked her grey jacket with striped epaulettes as well.

'Do they do vegetarian?'

'Well we got halloumi and salad kebabs there once. I'm sure if you ask nicely...'

'Okay. Er...can I get you-'

'No, we're fine thanks.'

'Okay. Which part of the US are you from, by the way?'

'I'm from that part of the US known as Canada.'

'Oh, right. Sorry...'

At the Golden Kebab, where a fat hunk of meat turned succulently on the spit, they made two warm pita bread envelopes of halloumi and salad which Simon carried back to Eden Grove. The black-haired woman let him back in and he perched on a table where he could see into the main office. They ate quickly and for the most part in silence as Maloney finished off the stencil making. Two mugs of tea had been produced, Simon's decorated with the words *When God Created Man She Was Only Practising!* while Maloney's merely said *Sisterhood Is Powerful*. The two women spoke to each other from time to time, but their conversation was inaudible for the noise of the machine. When it stopped, Simon was struck by the atmosphere of calm diligence.

Maloney wrapped an elastic band around the stencils and they went over to the desk.

'Thanks for that. How much do we owe you?'

The amount was so small that Maloney asked if they could make a donation.

'Sure, if you think that's appropriate.'

'It's on behalf of our union branch if you could let me have a receipt.'

The woman scribbled something on the back of a leaflet.

'That reminds me. If you could possibly take a few of these...'

15

He pulled some Solidarnosc leaflets from his bag and handed them to her. She studied them carefully.

'Yes, of course. After all, it was a woman worker who started the whole thing...'

Maloney's eyes registered alarm. Simon watched him struggling to recollect.

'Ah, yes...yes...Anna...Anna?...'

'Anna Walentynowicz. She was a crane operator.'

'A female crane operator?' broke in the Canadian woman behind them. 'It almost makes you think Poland isn't so bad after all.'

'Almost.'

The two women smiled at each other.

'Unfortunately, it's not quite that simple,' said Maloney.

The black-haired woman held up her hand to interrupt.

'It's okay. Ruth explained the Workers' Struggle position to us some time ago. We'll circulate the leaflet.'

'Okay. Well thanks again.'

They were ushered out into warm sunshine.

'Well, she certainly caught you napping, didn't she?'

'I'm kicking myself, Simon. Hard.'

They got back into the car. The engine spluttered and died, but fired up after Maloney pulled out the choke.

'They were quite helpful really,' said Simon. 'I didn't get the impression they see us as the enemy. More as...irrelevant.'

'They're separatist feminists, Simon, but a relatively mild version. Separatists see all men as oppressors, or potential oppressors, regardless of economic status, position in the hierarchy, etcetera.'

'Yeah, I know that. But those two let us in, let us use their machine, didn't rip us off. They even made tea for us as if it didn't matter. They indulged us but kept control - did you notice? There was almost something matriarchal about it.'

'Matriarchy's just the opposite of patriarchy. Their basic position is they're willing to work alongside men on specific issues, but they won't let themselves be absorbed into any organisation that's run by men, which I suppose Workers' Struggle is.'

'And every other group on the far left. Gosh, that was another impressive five-point turn.'

'Whilst explaining the protean nature of modern feminism.'

'Oooh, *protean*.'

16

They edged out of Eden Grove back onto Holloway Road.

'Talking about women, is your latest going to be there tonight?'

'Molly? Yes, hopefully.'

'How long has that lasted now?'

'Depends when you regard it as starting. A few weeks...'

'And Lizzie?'

'Should be there.'

'Joe?'

'Joe. Ronnie. Matt. Everybody who's anybody.'

'Okay. I'll be late but I'll get there,' He looked at his watch. 'Shit - it's gone twelve already.'

He had got the car up to third gear and they were approaching Highbury Corner.

'Listen, Simon. I'll have to drop you here.' He started to pull over. 'The Committee meeting's supposed to start at two, right? I'm not going to make that. You need to go back to the office, ring around and reschedule for two-thirty.'

Simon sighed. He'd been looking forward to seeing the anonymous but fortified headquarters of Workers' Struggle.

'Okay.'

He'd begun to walk along the pavement when two short blasts of a horn sounded. He went back to the car. Maloney was leaning across and winding down the window.

'I didn't realise your horn actually works.'

'Simon, listen. I've run out of money.'

'That's a shame.'

'Lend me a fiver.'

'Fucking hell.'

'I'll give you a cheque tonight.'

'No way.'

He peeled a note off the roll in his pocket and handed it over.

'I want one just like that with a black line running down it.'

'I'll see what I can do. Oh - and Simon?'

He was winding the window back up but paused a couple of inches from the top.

'*Yes?*'

'Many happy returns.'

2. Matters Arising

That afternoon Simon took the stairs down from Reception into the Institute's warren of meeting rooms. He knew the basement well. A low-ceiling maze of carpeted corridors and closed doors, it had an air of intrigue at times when voices leaked out from meetings or seminars and isolated words hovered in the enclosed air.

At the start of the maze was an open area with hot and cold drink machines and a table where silver trays of food would be left if ordered. It was deserted now, but a slew of used plates and cups lay across the table. Simon pulled down a plastic cup from the hot drinks machine and poured himself some coffee from a thermal jug. Then he picked up a couple of curled sandwiches and made his way to the small meeting room booked for the afternoon.

For five minutes, he had perfect peace to sort out paperwork, then one by one the Committee members arrived. Good old Don from the Post Room, sweet Marie from Typing, superwoman Lesley from Accommodation, besuited Bashir from Accounts, Vince from Reprographics in his black leather jacket and Bash Street Kids t-shirt and two or three others. And at 2.33 just after Simon had checked his watch, Maloney barged through the door, dropped his carrier bag and a box onto the table and disappeared again with a promise of 'back in one sec'.

'What's going on, Simon?'
'Why are we starting late?'
'What's in the box?'
'All will be revealed.'
'I bet he's gone to get some of the leftovers...'
And indeed, Maloney shouldered his way back into the room carrying more curled sandwiches, a thermos jug and a small stack of plastic cups.

'Oh, Tony, there'll be no cups left in that machine.'
'I'll rinse them out and leave them next to it.'
'You're not that house-trained and it's me who'll have to get it refilled.'
'We do have refreshments coming at 3 pm.'
'Ah well, you didn't tell me that, Simon.'
'And something else.'

'Ooh, something else...'

'Oh Simon, I've just had a thought,' said Lesley. 'Is it your birthday?'

'Damn, how did you guess?'

'I remember it from last year. We went on that march, didn't we? And you bought us a drink afterwards in that pub on Whitehall.'

'Actually, that was the year before.'

'Gosh. How old are you then?'

'Twenty two.'

'Ahem?'

'Twenty five.'

'Keep going.'

'I don't think you are being totally sincere, Simon,' said Bashir. 'You started one year before me after going to university and doing other jobs...I remember you telling me when you recruited me to the union and that was four years ago.'

'You really do think in numbers, don't you Bashir? All right, I'm twenty nine, but you've all got to swear an oath of secrecy about that or no cake. There, I've given it away.'

'I'll swear an oath,' said Vince.

'Actually, Simon, you don't look it.'

'Thank you, Lesley.'

'Twenty nine today,' sang Marie in a quavering falsetto. 'Twenty nine today...'

Simon covered his ears.

'Look, brothers and sisters,' said Maloney. 'This is all very jolly, but we have important business to get through.'

'Quite right,' said Simon. 'Has everybody got an agenda and minutes? Are you all sitting comfortably? Lesley, is your pen poised? Then let us begin.'

And they began. Apologies were recorded, minor amendments made to the minutes of the last meeting and Item 3.0 Matters Arising got underway. They were still on Minute 3.2 Promotion Procedures when the refreshments arrived. After banter and cake consumption, they worked their way through agency staff, annual reports, flexible working hours, new technology, training, the air conditioning system and soft toilet paper. By four o'clock, they had reached Item 4.0 The Cuts.

'Okay,' said Maloney. 'The position is as follows. As you know, the O&M study went ahead without our agreement, although a small number of members have co-operated. Members who either don't agree with our policy, or work in Personnel and feel they can't refuse, or are just too frightened to say "no". We've taken up two personal cases of members who've been threatened by their managers. On the plus side, two people have joined the union because of our campaign.'

'Can I just say,' interrupted Vince 'that it's all very well us not co-operating...but Reprographic management have just been telling the auditors what we do and giving them so-called facts and figures.'

'I know, I know. And I've spoken to Imogen but she's stuck. Their Branch is divided on the issue and she doesn't want to lose members.'

'Well some of our members feel it's better to participate so that the right information can be-'

'No, no. Our policy of non-cooperation is correct and was agreed at the last Branch meeting. We're still entitled to see a copy of the draft report and can challenge the facts and figures then. I want to get onto another little exercise that management are conducting and that is...to estimate the cost of making one fifth of staff redundant.'

'What?!'

'Exactly. I can't say how we got to know about this, but trade union side challenged management at the GPC last week and they admitted it. Initially, they said that it's to address future pension commitments. We just laughed at that. Then they said that because of the threatened cut to next year's grant, they're looking at various ways to make "efficiency savings".'

'Well we thought something like this would happen,' said Lesley.

'We did, but what we didn't realise is how seriously they're taking it. In the past, they've tried to fight their corner with the government or at least fudge their response. Now they clearly mean business - or have accepted that Thatcher means business. Bull is a Thatcher lover anyway. He makes no secret of that at meetings.'

'But every fifth post - that's 20%, that's *250 posts*,' said Bashir.

'That's ridiculous,' said Don.

'Kenworthy has said since that 20% is a worse case scenario,' said Simon. 'But 10% is the bottom line and that would take out 125 posts.'

'They might just about be able to manage that without compulsory redundancies,' said Lesley.

'They might,' said Maloney. 'But fewer posts means fewer jobs for the unemployed and fewer promotion chances for our members. We have to make it clear from the start that 0% is the only acceptable figure.'

'This isn't just our fight, of course,' said Simon. 'Cuts are being planned across the whole public sector.'

'Will our NEC campaign for no cuts?'

'They'll use that slogan, Vince, initially at least, because that's Conference policy. But they won't stick to it. The real campaign will have to come from the branches.'

'And what about the other unions?'

Well, the Executive Society are opposed to cuts and have a mandate for strike action "where necessary", but you know what they're like. They get queasy if the boat rocks too much. Imogen does her best with them locally - she'll get about 50% out if there's action. As for the Professionals, well - they're quite militant here as you know. They see themselves as under-resourced already and they'll be pissed off at the prospect of further cuts. But they can't strike without HQ backing and that doesn't look very likely. Let me give these out...'

He stood and opened the box.

'Take enough for your members and a few extra for notice boards.'

The pile of newsletters was passed around the table. Under the union masthead, the headline 250 STAFF FACE REDUNDANCY was etched neatly over two columns of type on plain white paper.

'Basically, this sets out what we know. They wouldn't discuss their methodology, but our information is that Finance are going through a print-out of staff selecting every fifth person, then working out the cost of making them all redundant. That will give management a ball-park figure to put to the Department as a likely saving.'

'But it will cost them a fortune to make that many staff redundant. Where's that money going to come from?'

'It may seem a lot to you, Vince, but not to the government. The Institute will have a reserve fund for things like this and if that's not enough - which it won't be - the Treasury will give them an extra ring-fenced sum. Don't forget they're going to save money in the long term.'

'This is all tied-up with new technology, isn't it? Replacing human beings with machines.'

'That's coming, Marie, as you know. Micros are a serious threat to lots of jobs, not just in your area. But what this is all about is quite simple. It's about making us - working people - pay for the economic crisis without affecting the wealth of the top few.'

'So where do we go from here?'

'Take the newsletters, issue them to your members and spread the word. Sneak them onto general notice boards so even non-members can see what's going on. Union Side is holding a special meeting next week to discuss how to respond. I'll try and get our HQ official along, not that we need him. We've got backing from the Branch to take any action against the cuts, including strike action.'

'But it would be a good idea, Tony, to go back to the members before we take that step. *If* we take that step...'

'Of course, Bashir. We'll do that. After the Union Side meeting, we'll hold a Branch meeting to report back. We'll need solid support from the rank and file and I'm sure we'll get it because it's all about their livelihoods and their futures.'

'Management have to consult us, don't they?'

'They do, but if Bull has his way it'll be a *fait accompli*. Like it or lump it. There might be some hand-wringing by Board members, but they'll go along with it. They'll want their medals at the end of the day.'

'What if Labour get back in at the next election?'

Maloney shrugged.

'Wait and see. If it were a right wing Labout government, I'd have no faith in them whatsoever. They started the cuts in the seventies after promising the opposite. As it's likely to be a left wing government committed to what they call "democratic socialism", then in theory they'll scrap the cuts. But Thatcher's got another 18 months before she's got to call an election. The cuts need to be fought now by the rank and file.'

'I think we'll have trouble getting people out over this,' said Vince. 'It depends how bad the proposals look when we get them, but the pay strike is still fresh in people's minds and that turned out to be a waste of time.'

'Strike action is never a waste of time.'

'Don't get me wrong,' said Vince. 'I'll be out there if it comes to it, but other people might think twice. They've seen what's happening in the NHS. They're getting nowhere - and that's after months of action supported by their members with all the big unions behind them...'

'Nonsense. They may not win their claim, but the Tories have been forced to backtrack on privatisation. *The NHS is safe with us.* That's a significant climbdown by Thatcher. The point is - every struggle produces some kind of reward. And the working class is being educated all the time. They're learning they need to fight on two fronts: not only against the government but against their own so-called leaderships.'

'I think we need to move on,' said Simon. 'The action is - Reps to distribute the newsletters. TM and SH to arrange Branch meeting.'

'And keep arguing the case with members. Keep stressing Branch policy.'

'Okay, okay. Item 5 - Personal Cases.'

Maloney gave a half-laugh, half-sigh. He closed one brown file and opened other.

'Well, there's no getting away from you, is there Vince? You're Personal Case No. 1. The others are small beer. Not worth discussing here.'

'Yay,' said Vince holding up interlinked fists.

'Naughty Vince,' said Marie. 'What have you been doing?'

'Nothing,' said Vince. 'Nothing deliberate anyway. They're having a go at my sick record and my so-called lateness for work. But I have every faith in our leader to establish the truth.'

'That's easy, Vince,' said Maloney leafing through the tagged papers in front of him. 'The truth is you've had 68 days sick leave in the last 12 months. You've been late for work 23 times. To make matters worse, line management have actually done what they're supposed to do, which is almost unheard of in this place. As far as I can see, they've given you the correct warnings in the correct manner at the correct time.'

'I've been *sick*, Tony. I can't help it. Line management want to get rid of me because I'm a thorn in their backsides. That's why they've been careful to do everything right.'

'I'm sure they want to get rid of you, Vince. But we can't go into a disciplinary hearing and say that by following the correct and agreed

24

procedure, they're discriminating against you. We'll be laughed out of the room. I might get some mileage out of lack of sympathy, lack of support, but let's look at the details. You've had flu twice-'

'Just a minute,' said Simon. 'Aren't the details supposed to be confidential?'

Vince looked around the room.

'I don't care. We're all on the same side here, aren't we?'

'No, no - Simon's quite right. I won't say that having flu twice in one year as well as four other completely unrelated types of illness sounds to a cynic - not me of course - like someone's taking the piss.'

'But almost all of it, Tony, is certificated. I just can't help it. I've had a bad year.'

'You've certainly got a sympathetic doctor. Or a doctor who'll do anything for a quiet life. Look at this - three weeks off with back pain, which you also had the previous year - yet he's never referred you for a hospital check.'

'*She* said if it didn't clear up, *she* would refer me. *She's* been very sympathetic. If it wasn't for *her*-'

'Okay, I get the message. Though 70% of doctors *are* male and we still live in a patriarchal society.'

'You said it,' said Simon.

'The only thing you haven't done is exceed your uncertificated allowance. Only six days when you could have had ten.'

'Well I was holding a few days back in case of emergencies.'

'Your doctor's not a lonely old spinster by any chance?'

'She's not my type, Simon. Plus she's about fifty. And she's got photographs of her kids on the wall.'

'Vincent, when you say you held a few days back in case of emergencies, that sounds like...'

'Like what?'

Bashir raised his eyebrows but said nothing. There was a deep silence around the table.

'That I held them back in case I'm really ill? Is that what you're saying? Jesus! Guys! I can't believe I'm hearing this. Aren't we union brothers and sisters? Where's the solidarity around here?'

'Vincent, let's just cut the crap,' said Maloney. 'This is nothing to what the disciplinary board will throw at you. It doesn't matter whether every one of those 68 days is genuine sickness. As far as management is concerned, it makes you an inefficient worker. A liability. And in view of what we were talking about earlier, they'll be delighted to sack you. It'll save them a bit of redundancy money. Yes, I will defend you, but that sound you can hear is my fingernails scraping the barrel.'

'But-'

'Last year, your record was almost as bad, the year before - almost as bad again. And the same kind of illnesses. You've had six recorded oral warnings, three formal warnings. There's no way we can avoid a final warning. The only thing I can do is argue that line management haven't given you enough help or support and try to make the terms of the warning as generous as possible. Oh - and they'll almost certainly refer you to the Medical Advisory Service.'

Vince shrugged.

'Well, that's all right, Tony. I do appreciate your help. And it's not all bullshit. I do get ill sometimes and I do get depressed.'

'Oh, Vince. You'll have us all in tears,' said Lesley.

'What about the 23 days lateness?' said Simon.

'Well that's mainly to do with, you know, not feeling right in the mornings. Real difficulty getting out of bed.'

'But you live nearby, don't you?'

'Brunswick Square.'

'Three minutes walk away. And you're supposed to get here for...?'

'9.30,' said Maloney. 'He's on late cover.'

'You're late for late cover?'

'Well we're only talking about once per fortnight.'

'Wait a minute. *Wait* a minute.' Simon tapped on a calculator. '226 working days in a year...minus 68 when you were off sick...leaves 158 days when you came to work...divided by 23...means you were late every 6.8 - well, let's be generous and call it every 7 days.'

Vince shook his head sadly.

'Simon, you'll be a manager one day. I can feel it.'

'The lateness will be a final warning too,' said Maloney. 'Our only real hope is if the MAS doctor finds there really is something wrong with you. We could then argue for more generous terms in the final warnings, but of course you may be more concerned about the diagnosis.'

Vince fingered the silver cross around his neck.

'Whatever will be.'

'That cross won't do you a lot of good,' said Don.

'I'm not religious. I believe God is dead, but the Devil is still alive. This is my protection.'

'Tell you what,' said Simon. 'Why don't we move on?'

The rest of the agenda was routine. Reports from the Membership Secretary and Treasurer, from the Safety Committee and from other sites, then a weary trudge through AOB.

'And *finally*,' said Simon, raising his voice as people were pushing back chairs and gathering bags. 'Two things. Lesley - can you please circulate the minutes asap. Secondly, I'll be in the Black Swan tonight from 6pm to mourn my birthday. You're all welcome to join me.'

'I'll be there later, Simon, as you know,' said Maloney.

'I have an evening class, but will come along for half an hour,' said Bashir.

'I'd love to Simon, but...' said other people.

'I'll be coming,' said Vince. 'But did you say the Black Swan, not the Fountain?'

'Yep, Black Swan. Six pm. We're boycotting the Fountain. They added 5p to a pint of beer last week.'

'You haven't seen it today then?'

'What, the Black Swan? No, I haven't been that way.'

'They've been carrying out some external redecoration over the weekend.'

'That's nice to know.'

'And it now has a new name.'

'Okay, but it's still in the same place, isn't it?'

'It is, but it's now called The Falkland Arms.'

There was a brief and awkward silence.

'Interesting,' said Maloney.

'You're joking,' said Simon. 'Fucking hell...that's unbelievable. What am I going to do? We can't drink in a pub called the Falkland Arms.'

'Urgent phone calls are in order again.'

'Yes, but where are we going? The Tavern? That's a gloomy dump. Moon and Stars? The beer's piss...'

'Look, far be it from me to suggest a compromise,' said Maloney. 'But why don't we lift the boycott on the Fountain? We've made our point and unfortunately, it's the best pub in the area.'

'Tony, I can't believe it. You're talking sense...'

27

'Vincent, do not bite the hand that will save your skin. Or try to. The Fountain, Simon - yes?'

'I suppose so.'

And Maloney was gone, the door clumping shut behind him.

'I'll tell you what we could do,' said Vince conspiratorially. 'We could meet in the Black Swan, right? Sorry - the Falkland Arms. Sit around a table, *not* buy any beer, then when your friends turn up, stage a walk out. Chanting something, you know - *Maggie! Maggie! Maggie! Out! Out! Out!*'

'Vince, I need a drink, not a demo. Several drinks. Even more drinks than I was going to have. I'll ring round and we'll meet in the Fountain.'

It was after five when Simon got back to his desk in the Records Office and grabbed the phone. No-one else was there to distract him and within fifteen minutes he'd reached all his friends except Lizzie whose ward number was busy. He felt he could trust her to realise why they weren't in the so-called Falkland Arms and try the Fountain instead. Or he could ring the place from the payphone in the Fountain and ask them to call out her name. And if she wasn't there, he could offer his condolences for their stupid fucking-

The phone rang.

'Simon *Hayes*.'

'Hello, this is Reception. There's a young lady here to see you...'

That was better. He pulled the thick Branch Committee file from his bag, crammed it into one of the desk pedestal drawers and left the office. Past the lifts, he took the side stairs down two at a time until reaching Reception. Molly was sitting on the visitors' sofa next to a low glass table which bore a shiny rubber plant and a glossy copy of the Institute's Annual Report on a display stand. She didn't see Simon at first and then a warm smile spread over her face and settled in her eyes. She was a few inches shorter than him when she stood and he pressed his lips briefly to her crisp black hair, unwilling to go any further in front of the security guy. When they had gone through the brass-handled doors, down the marble steps and a few yards along the pavement, they stopped and kissed properly while footsteps and voices passed around them. It was dark already and lamp-posts were glowing one after another along the street.

'You remembered to put your clock back then?'

28

'Yes! A whole hour's extra sleep yesterday. And I didn't doze off in the bath this morning either.'

'Good. I worry about you falling asleep in the bath.'

'Aw'. They put their arms around each other and walked on. 'It's the warm water and bath foam. I'm still half asleep when I get in and then I feel my eyes start to close. Not for long though. I never have enough time to drown.'

'You need strong coffee in the mornings. I'll make you some with breakfast tomorrow. If I'm not too hungover...'

'Will you? How will you do that? Come round to my little flatlet?'

'Er, well I sort of thought-'

She patted him.

'I'm teasing. But we never decided on your place or mine.'

'Well I sort of thought it was my turn. I know we'll have to creep around, but...'

'Hmm, d'you think we'll be able to do that after an evening in the pub? I have squeezed a few overnight things in here' - she patted the straps of her shoulder bag - 'but I'm hoping you put my clothes in the wash? The clothes I left last week?'

'Course I did.'

'Did they snigger at you in the launderette?'

'No more than usual. I'm always washing women's clothing in there.'

She giggled.

'Aw, they probably think you're a...what's the word?'

'Lumberjack?'

'Cross-dresser!'

'Yes, well. That's more likely than lumberjack.'

By now, they were approaching the main road and, for a moment, Simon felt like forgetting the pub and his friends and just walking on with Molly into the autumn city evening to dine and drink in deepest Soho, perhaps, and sit under the neon-lit statue of Eros in Piccadilly Circus or on a lamplit park bench with her soft body against his and her lovely scented skin...

'What are you thinking?'

'Oh, nothing. How was yesterday?'

'It was okay... Mum cooked a roast and my sister and her husband came from Reading. That was nice. We looked through old photo albums - again. How's today been?'

He told her briefly about the car journey around North London.

'...and the next place couldn't do it because they were all out on a nursery demo or something and the person they'd left behind was just "holding the fort". The third place wouldn't do it because we hadn't applied in advance and filled out their forms. Finally, we went to a women's centre in Islington fearing for our lives, or at least our balls, and they let us do it.'

'Ooh! Did they give you a lecture on male chauvinism?'

'Well, actually, apart from letting us in and making some tea, they took very little notice of us.'

'They made tea for you? I didn't think feminists were allowed to do that.'

'Would you describe yourself as a feminist?'

'Well, yes, equal pay, equal rights, creche facilities, a woman's right to choose - I support all that. But I'm not a bra burner or a man-hater. Obviously...' She gave him a squeeze. 'Hey, the Black Swan's that way, isn't it?'

They had dodged and dived across the main road, still clinging to each other, and now Simon was trying to steer Molly westward.

'Oh, sorry. I forgot to mention. The Black Swan has apparently changed its name - you're not going to believe this - to the - wait for it - *Falkland Arms*.'

'You're joking. The Falkland Arms?! D'you have to salute when you walk in?'

'Exactly. So we've decided to end our boycott of the Fountain, having obviously brought the brewery to its knees. But actually' - he stopped and looked at his watch - 'we've got a few minutes. Why don't we just stroll back there and have a look? It was Vince who told us this and I wouldn't put it past him to be taking the piss.'

'Vince the biker guy?'

'Well, he wears the gear or some of it, but I doubt whether he's ever ridden a bike in his life. Not one with an engine, anyway.'

They turned around and walked past a row of shops, a restaurant, a small art gallery, a hairdresser and a mansion block of flats until the pub came into view on the corner. The exterior was still obscured by scaffolding and plastic sheeting, but a new sign board projected over the pavement and they gaped up at it. The words 'Falkland Arms' were engraved in gilt lettering above a giant sheep that stood over a strip of green land and a sailing ship afloat on white waves. Below this, the motto read *Desire the Right*.

'Fucking hell,' said Simon.

'I like the sheep.'

He nodded grimly.

'It's so big, it looks like it's eaten all the other sheep. And *Desire the Right* - that's a loaded message if ever I saw one.'

'Is it? Oh, the *right wing*. You read politics into everything.'

'Maloney's drummed that into me. Politics *do* affect everything. Let's just go in and have a quick look round in case anybody's here.'

Inside, the pub was unchanged and quite busy for a Monday evening. Simon did a quick circuit of the large single bar. Most of the seats and tables were occupied, but he saw no-one he knew. A pool game was in progress as usual in the corner, ersatz reggae was playing on the jukebox and a small colour TV behind the bar showed a game of cricket in progress far away in some sunny land. He rejoined Molly at the door.

'Good, nobody here.'

'Nobody here? The place is heaving. No-one seems bothered by the name change.'

'Most of these fuckers haven't even noticed. Come on, let's go to the Fountain. It's a sanctuary compared to this place. An abode of bliss.'

They put their arms around each other again and walked back along the pavement.

'I'd quite like to go round that pub - posing as a journalist, maybe - and ask people what they think about the name change.'

'Ask people what they think? That's a revolutionary idea.'

'It's not a revolutionary idea, my little bundle of joy. A revolutionary idea is to *lead* the people. Asking for their opinion is just petty-bourgeois.'

'Don't let Comrade Maloney hear you. He might think you're not serious.'

'He knows I'm not serious - not by his standards anyway.'

'You're serious by mine.'

'I am serious about the need for revolutionary change. I just can't commit myself to the extent that he does. Also, I think it's got to come genuinely from the people. You can't drag them behind you or drive them ahead of you like, well - sheep.'

31

Molly nodded as they stopped at another busy junction.

'I think you're right but you'll have to wait a long time before the people stir themselves.'

'We'll see.'

They crossed and carried on walking.

'We're like the beast with two backs,' said Simon. 'Inseparable even in motion. *Especially* in motion.'

'What's that then?'

'Well, actually, I cannot tell a lie, it's a metaphor for sexual intercourse. Comes from Shakespeare. When two people, or two beasts, are making love, they're like one beast with two backs.'

'So what's the one beast doing? Making love to itself?'

'Hmm, I never thought of it like that. It means two people sort of...oh, never mind. I was just thinking that from behind, we must look like one beast because we're so close to each other.'

'Can't get much closer, can we? Unless I jump up and wrap my legs round you.'

'That might be a bit much at the moment. Later maybe...'

They turned into a side street and the Fountain could be seen further down. A modest-looking place without an ad board on the pavement or hanging baskets bulging with flowers, but a few stainless steel chairs and tables against its front wall.

'So who's coming that I haven't met yet?'

'Er, well...Lizzie you haven't met. And Ronnie - I don't think you've met?'

'Any previous girlfriends?'

'Of course not.'

'This Lizzie seems to be a big friend...'

'She's great, but not that sort of friend.'

'I hope they're not going to be yap-yap-yapping about politics all the time.'

'Nah, they'll talk about anything. Music...politics, travel...politics, gossip...politics, gossip about politics, the politics of gossip...'

'Shush!'

'Most of them are like me really. Politically committed, but... freelance. Here we go.'

And they entered.

3. A Dip in the Fountain

'Hello, mate. Been away?'

'Yeah, sort of...'

'Usual?'

'And a Pils, please.'

'A Pils for the lady...'

The bar ran almost the length of the pub which was divided into two halves by a smoked glass screen with a gap that had once been a door. The front half where Simon and Molly stood had fixed seating along the walls, small round tables and stools, and a fruit machine. The back half was a mix of nooks, crannies and open space with a staircase leading to the upstairs room.

It was almost a fortnight since Simon and Maloney had expanded their discourse with the landlord beyond the usual pleasantries. *Oh, what! You're joking, mate? 73p a pint? Bloody hell!* This had provoked the inevitable reply. *It's the brewery, mate. Not me.* The landlord was a sandy-haired survivor who shrugged off any discontent, his own included, with man-of-the-world unconcern.

'Where shall we sit?' asked Molly as they waited.

'Let's grab that corner table. Those two look as if they're going soon.'

Molly went and sat next to a couple who were deep in discussion over empty glasses.

'There you go, mate.'

'Cheers, mate.'

He pocketed the change and carried the drinks over to Molly. The man and woman rose to go and Simon dropped his carrier bag onto their table and spread his scarf and Molly's coat across the stools around them.

'It's good that no-one else is here yet 'cos I can give you these.'

She pulled two gift-wrapped packages out of her bag and a card in a white envelope. Simon took them with silent delight. The card had a cascade of bright-coloured words on the front and a message inside written in the large elegant script that he was beginning to recognise. *Happy birthday Simon! With love from me to you (Yeah! Yeah! Yeah!) Molly xxx.* It was the first time she'd used the word 'love'. He stood it on the table between their glasses and opened the smaller of the two packages. *Graveyard Spin* emerged, the latest literary blockbuster by Nate Morden, set in several cities around the globe and spanning most of the twentieth century to date.

'Oh, wow!'

He read the first sentence. *Finding the place was not always easy for it was on the small side as cemeteries go*. Then flipped to the last page to check the number at the bottom.

'I'd no idea what to get you really, but you said you liked his last book.'

That had been extra-curricular reading at university a decade ago, but maybe he ought to get back into contemporary literature.

'That's great, thanks. I shall look forward to reading all 760 pages.'

The second package was obviously an LP. He recognised the cover while still pulling off the wrapping paper. *Low and Dry*, the latest album by SiN.

'Oh brilliant, thanks. You've saved me a trip to Virgin.'

'It's had good reviews. I want to listen to it too.'

'Yeah, it's supposed to be even better than *Honky Tonk Parade*.'

As he spoke, a besuited figure halted in front of the table.

'Bashir! You're first to arrive.'

'Well, Simon, I can only stay half an hour because of my evening class. But let me get you and your friend a drink.'

'We're okay, honestly Bash. We've only just got here. This is Molly, by the way.'

'I'm very pleased to meet you, Molly. Excuse me one moment...'

When he returned with a tomato juice, Bashir sat down opposite them, picked up the LP and scrutinised it at arm's length through his gold-rimmed spectacles.

'SiN? Is that the name of a group?'

'Yeah, it's short for Safety in Numbers.' Simon spoke as if to an ageing relative. Bashir nodded sagely.

'Oh, yes. I understand.' He tapped the side of his head. 'I am quite familiar with popular music, Simon. Vincent has spoken to me at great length about a group called Turmoil. They are very good, I believe.'

'They're heavy metal, Bashir,' said Molly. 'Very loud...'

'I gained that impression, Molly. I like Nat King Cole, personally. And the music of my birth country, of course.'

They talked for a while about musical tastes and Pakistan and Bashir's family. Then he looked around.

'But where are your friends, Simon? Did you get through to them?'

'I did. But they're not the sort of people who turn up on time. Actually, I sit corrected. Here's one of them now.'

A blond-haired figure was striding towards them from the door.

'Simon! Happy birthday! To you!'

'Not so loud!'

Ronnie threw his bag down on the floor and stood grinning before them, his blue eyes flitting from one face to the other. Simon pulled a crumpled pound note from his trouser pocket.

'Go and get yourself a drink and calm down.'

'Good man. I'll get the next round. We haven't met before, have we? Molly? I'm Ronnie.' He shook her hand and turned to Bashir. 'We *have* met, haven't we? On some march or other. I hope there's vodka in that...'

'No, this is pure tomato juice. I have to go to an evening class...'

'An evening class on Simon's birthday? Give it up, mate. You'll learn more here tonight than you ever will at evening class.'

'What's your class, Bashir?' asked Molly.

'It's a course on economics at Birkbeck.'

'Economics! That's right up our street!' said Ronnie. 'We can tell you everything you need to know about economics in five minutes, can't we Simon? Unless Maloney's coming? In that case, it'll take a bit longer. Maybe you should go to your evening class after all. I'll just go and see if the landlord's got any balloons.'

Bashir smiled, but looked puzzled.

'Why does your friend want me to stay unless Tony is coming?'

'He means that once Tony starts talking about the economic platform of Trotsky and the Left Opposition, you'll lose the will to live.'

'Oh, I see. It sounds like "business as usual" this evening then!'

'That's what I'm worried about,' said Molly. 'Does he never take time off?'

'Don't worry. We'll be drunk enough to shut him up by the time he gets here. Actually, let me put these away before any beer gets spilt.'

He picked up the book and LP and stuffed them into his carrier bag. A minute later, a pint of beer was set down unsteadily in front of him.

'There you go,' said Ronnie. 'The landlord doesn't have any balloons, but he's given you a free pint instead. And he'll organise a singsong later.'

'A free pint - that's nice. So where's the change?'

Ronnie sighed. He pulled up a stool and sat down.

'All right. I told the landlord it's your birthday and he said "very nice". He didn't seem receptive to anything else. I had to add nearly 50p of my own money to buy you that. Expensive in here, isn't it?'

'Tell me about it.'

'Now let me just explain Marxist economics to our friend Bashir...'

'I will have to go any minute, Ronnie.'

'It's very simple. In a capitalist society, the production of goods is designed to create profit, right? Profit which goes to the owners and shareholders of the company after deducting production costs, wages, taxes etc. Right?'

'Well that's what happens, yes.'

'We'll just talk among ourselves.'

'No, I want to listen,' said Molly. 'I might learn something.'

'Now that is done by ignoring the labour value of the workers, right? They produce not only the product but its *value* in the market. But that's the only area where the owners can make their profit, so what do they do? They pay the workers far less than the return they get on sales. Just enough for them to house and feed and clothe themselves and maybe have a bit of pocket money to distract themselves with. The rest of the profit - the surplus value as Marx called it - is kept by the owners.'

'Yes, but of course it could be argued that the business wouldn't exist in the first place and the workers wouldn't have jobs or be able to produce anything if the capitalist hadn't invested his money in setting it up, in buying all the machinery and raw materials and so on. So he is *entitled* to a bigger reward. It's just a question of degree.'

'Well of course that can be argued, Bashir. But just tell me this. How come only one man or a small number of men have got the wherewithal to start the business?'

Bashir looked at his watch.

'Ronnie, I'm sorry but I really do have to go.'

'Just let me finish...'

'You'll never finish,' said Simon.

36

'It's very interesting to hear your views, Ronnie. I think we are reaching the Marxist approach to economics soon and I will see what my lecturer has to say.'

'I can tell you exactly what he'll say unless he's a Marxist. Even then, I wouldn't trust him to make it clear.'

'Simon, I wish you a very happy birthday again and it's been very nice to meet you, Molly. And you Ronnie.'

'Cheers, Bashir.'

'Ah, these look like more of your friends. And your number one personal case!'

Bashir departed with a nod to the newcomers - Joe and his girlfriend Kath - and a word with Vince who was trailing behind them.

'Simon, you poor old birthday boy!' said Joe. 'We've come to help drown your sorrows.'

'That might take some time,' said Simon. He pulled more pound notes out of his pocket. 'You'd better fill up first.'

Joe got a round in with help from Vince who sat slightly apart when they settled around the two tables.

'So, let's get this straight.' Joe spoke slowly and solidly through a brown beard flecked with ginger curls. 'The Black Swan, a hostelry of historic renown as you once bored us at great length about-'

'Mentioned in Dickens,' said Ronnie.

'Mentioned in Dickens,' said Joe. 'Used to host the Singers Club with those filthy commies Ewan MacColl and Peggy Seeger, has now become a super-patriotic establishment known as the Falkland Arms. The only pub in London to do such a thing and we almost went there...'

'Actually, we had a quick look inside this evening and it's exactly the same as before. But...we can't patronise a pub that celebrates imperialist war-mongering.'

'Definitely not,' said Ronnie.

'So we're back in this dump which was once patronised by the great bohemians of the Thirties - as you once bored us at great length about.'

'Dylan Thomas,' said Ronnie. 'He's the only one I've heard of.'

'Well, it's a safe bet that Dylan Thomas drank here at one time or another,' said Simon.

'This is getting far too cultural.'

37

'All right, change the subject. How's it going at the Job Centre then?'

'How's it going on the front line, you mean? Well...the rules still keep changing and we still get lots of aggro from the punters. I had a chair thrown at me last week - no damage done but they're going to screw them to the floor now. The chairs, that is - not the punters. Still we do actually have some jobs on offer. It's far worse up north from what I hear.'

'It's always worse up north.'

'Well, hopefully Labour will get back in and do something about it. Invest, create jobs, get people back to work. Particularly up there. The Tories do not give a fuck.'

Ronnie snorted.

'Labour are just the acceptable face of capitalism. Even if the current left leadership stays in power, they won't do what needs to be done.'

'So who is going to? The SWP? You've declared a downturn. We're supposed to sit around examining our belly buttons until the next great crisis of capitalism.'

'We're reflecting the reality of what's happened. The working class has been divided, bought off - for the time being.'

'I left the SWP because of that and I don't regret it. We have to work with whoever we can and the action has moved to the Labour Party now. Yes, they were useless in the seventies, but the left - the real socialist left - has come to the fore.'

'Joe, we're never going to achieve real socialism, a real and permanent shift in power, through parliament. You know that in your heart of hearts.'

'Yes, we might have to depart from the parliamentary road at some point. But right now, Thatcher is trying to destroy the working class. The first step is to get her out. And we have a chance of not only doing that but getting a genuine left wing government.'

As the argument wore on, Simon sat back and drank some beer and thought about his tangled relationships with Ronnie, who'd stayed in the SWP and Joe who'd left. His own departure, a year or so after Joe, had not been over any particular issue. He'd seen through the 'Party' long before, but remained a member because of the friendships made and the structure it had given to his drifting life. In the end, he'd left simply because he was tired of it and didn't want to

38

be defined as an SWP member any longer. It felt - and he'd never said this to Ronnie - as if he had voluntarily put a dunce's cap on his head. He was an English Literature graduate used to reading elegant, exciting, rigorously-expressed texts about the common complexities of human existence. It insulted his intelligence to remain in an outfit dominated by a cadre of 'hacks' who enforced whatever simplistic half-truthful line had been conveniently decided behind closed doors. Besides - but then Molly broke through his thoughts...

'I knew it would be like this. I told you...'

He felt her warm breath in his ear.

'Well these are my friends - for better or worse.'

'Till death do you part?'

'Well, for now. Don't worry, they'll lighten up after another drink or two.'

'Vince looks pretty out of it.'

'He's a member of the Blank Generation.'

In fact, Vince was staring at the upper windows of the pub in which dislocated images of the bar were projected on the black backdrop outside.

'All right, Vince?' Simon called.

Vince looked across at him.

'Yeah, yeah. I am listening to the great debate. Just tired, that's all.'

'I'd give you one of my pints' - Simon nodded at the two glasses on the table in front of him - 'but I know you don't drink the real stuff.'

Vince sighed.

'Nah, lager's good enough for me. It peps me up. Somehow you can't cry into lager...maybe it's the bubbles.'

'Did you know,' said Simon to Molly 'that Vince has been on TV?'

'No, really?'

'Tell her, Vince.'

Vince stirred himself reluctantly. His leather jacket creaked.

'I belong to the Sealed Knot, Molly. You know - Cavaliers and Roundheads. I'm a Roundhead - a foot soldier in one of the Parliamentary regiments. We do re-enactments of Civil War battles. I get knocked about quite a bit sometimes which is why I don't always get to work on Monday mornings...'

'I had you down as a biker.'

'I've tried that, Molly, but I'm not safe on a bike. Anyway, I was in this Civil War TV series two or three years ago. I played the part of a blood-stained corpse.'

'Wow!'

'Sadly, he didn't get mentioned in the credits.'

'No, but I had my 1.5 seconds of fame as the camera panned over me. It was beautiful. Actually, they repeated it last year and my sister bought one of these new video recorders and recorded it. If you look very closely, you can sort of see me in one or two other shots as well.'

'Well that's more fame than I've ever had.'

'Vince used to have a name card on his desk at work that said *Oi You.*'

'*Oi You*? Oh I get it.'

'They made me change it. "Oi, you!" they said. "Change your name to Vince." That's when I became active in the union. To fight for the rights of the working man.'

'You belittle yourself, Vince - that's your problem. You extract the piss from yourself to try and prevent others from doing it. A sure sign of low self-esteem.'

'Hang on, I'll just put a few stools together and lie down.'

'No! Get up, stand up. Throw off your psychological chains.'

'Are you a man or a mouse? Squeak up,' said Molly.

Vince smiled.

'You make a good double act.'

'Actually, Simon' - said Molly, putting her hand on his arm - 'you seem to be saying almost that Vince doesn't need to be in a union to stand up for himself.'

'No, everyone who works for an employer should belong to a union, otherwise they're little better than serfs. But unions fight for the common good and for practical things like better pay, equal rights and so on. They're not really there to help people solve personal problems.'

A good union should be like a school,' said Joe who'd listened to the tail-end of this conversation.

'Well that would put me off joining!' said Molly.

'I don't mean you'd be sitting at desks. In fact, if it's done well, you'd hardly notice. There'd be ground rules to start with like the importance of solidarity, acceptance of majority decisions and so on.

Then the use of meetings and newsletters to educate people and counter what management and the government and the media are saying. Then you'd get the members involved in industrial action. Then - a bit like an Outward Bound course - get them to support other workers in struggle by going on marches and visiting picket lines. Keep going up a level in other words...'

'It's like consciousness raising,' said Kath, the first time she'd spoken.

'Exactly.'

'I see the union as a way of getting revenge,' said Vince quietly. But no-one paid any attention. Instead they debated back and forth until one of the bar staff appeared and took away most of the glasses.

'Kitty?'

'Pound each.'

A small heap of pound notes materialised on the table top. Ronnie gathered them together and got to his feet.

'I'd like to thank you all most sincerely for your contribution to Party funds.'

'Somebody go with him for Christ's sake,' said Joe. 'Otherwise he'll do a runner.'

'I'll go,' said Molly. And just as she rose to her feet, a new voice broke in on the gathering.

'Just in time I see.'

'Matt!' said Simon. 'Welcome. One pound admission.'

'Two pounds for a manager, surely?' said Joe.

'He's still on probation.'

Simon watched Matt talking to Ronnie at the bar and remembered a conversation with Molly the week before. *'I'd fancy Matt if I were gay,'* he'd said. *'Yeah, he's hot stuff, I suppose,'* said Molly. *'Nice and slim, jet black hair. A bit too baby-faced for me though...'*

Matt brought some drinks over and sat between Vince and Simon.

'Happy birthday. Is this the big one?'

'Next year.'

'I remember it well.'

'It was a good party. What's it like now to be that old?'

Matt shrugged.

'No different really. Nothing happens. You don't suddenly start drooping or sagging with age.'

'I'll try and remember that next year.'

'Try and remember what?' said Molly as she settled back beside him.

'That my thirtieth birthday will just be a day like any other instead of some grim milestone...'

'Oh, I thought we were going to go away somewhere? Can't it be a happy milestone?'

He put his arm around her and kissed her cheek, but the voices around him wouldn't stop.

'There'll be local area councils where everyone can have their say,' Ronnie was saying. 'The workers will choose their representatives, not some back-room committee. And they'll decide national policy. That's the ultimate in democracy.'

'You're talking about a revolutionary socialist government, I assume?' said Matt.

'Any kind of socialist government would be revolutionary because we've never had one before,' said Joe. 'Not even under Atlee. The thing is, there's no exact blueprint. We just have to go forward in good faith. But we've learnt enough lessons from the failure of the Bolshevik revolution and other so-called revolutions to know what to avoid next time around.'

'There's nothing wrong with the Bolshevik model.'

'You're dreaming,' said Matt. 'The masses have told you what they think of socialism by electing Thatcher and her cronies. The idea that they'll support some neo-Bolshevik party is ludicrous, even if capitalism does collapse.'

'Firstly, rejecting the Labour Party at the polls is not rejecting socialism. Secondly, when capitalism does collapse, it'll be obvious that socialism is the only way forward. The only way that the masses will be able to eat...'

'And there'll be a self-elected Central Committee with its tentacles out in your local assemblies, influencing them, making sure they toe the line.'

'Okay, it won't be perfect initially...'

'Initially?!'

'...because there'll be massive organisational problems to overcome and counter-revolutionary forces at work...'

'Ronnie, it'll be at its best initially, then all the screws will be tightened.'

'Matt, I hate to use Marxist-Leninist cliches, but you're retreating more and more into petty-bourgeois cynicism.'

'I wouldn't support anything that involves violence,' said Molly. 'It just leads to more and more violence.'

'Too right,' said Vince whose eyes were fixed on the upper windows again.

'Yes but it's a little bit unrealistic, Molly' - said Joe - 'to think that there won't be some need for physical force, if only in self-defence.'

'Of course, if people just want to shuffle along the way we do now with this travesty of a fair system...' said Ronnie.

'Living our little lives...' said Simon.

'...but the shit will hit the fan eventually because capitalism ain't built to last.'

'The blood will hit the fan,' murmered Vince.

At that moment, the stiff old pub door swung open with such force that it banged against the wall and the landlord looked around open-mouthed from the bar. A tall blonde woman called across to him without breaking her stride.

'Sorry, darling, I don't know my own strength.'

Lizzie Keaton was wearing what Simon called her coat of many colours, bought that summer in a Moroccan souk. She pulled a spare stool over to the main table and squeezed in forcing Joe and Ronnie apart.

'How was that for an entrance then?'

'Not bad,' said Simon. 'D'you want a drink?'

'In a minute. I've been turning the fucking Black Swan upside down looking for you. I see they've changed its name. Isn't it pathetic? From swan to sheep - that's what they want us all to be. Here, happy birthday Simon. I was going to give this to the first beggar I met if you weren't here.'

She pulled a neatly wrapped present out of the tasselled bag on her lap.

'Oh, Lizzie. You shouldn't have.'

'You're probably right. Anyway, I thought you were boycotting this place?'

'They were, but the need for beer won out,' said Joe.

'That must be the shortest boycott ever. Has Maloney agreed to that? Where is he anyway?'

'On his way. Oh...'

Simon had unwrapped Lizzie's present and found a plastic box containing a dozen squares of fudge.

'They're home made and one piece has an extra special ingredient.'

'Oh, God - how do I know which one?'

'You don't - that's the whole point.'

'It's pot luck!' shouted Ronnie.

'Yeah, genius,' said Lizzie. 'Why not tell the whole pub?'

'I can't share these unfortunately, otherwise one of you might eat the special piece.'

'Well, I wouldn't eat them now. I know someone who mixed dope with beer and was horribly sick. Take them home. Have them for breakfast with your corn flakes.'

'How did you get the hash into just one piece?' asked Matt leaning forward cautiously.

Lizzie smiled.

'Trade secret.'

'This is Molly by the way,' said Simon. 'I haven't introduced you.'

'Hello, Molly. Welcome to the madhouse. If I'd known you were coming, I'd have made two special pieces. Here, let me get you both a drink. I can't buy for everyone, I'm sorry.'

'There's a kitty,' said someone. But Lizzie had departed for the bar leaving the silence of disrupted conversation in her wake.

'She's fun,' Molly whispered in Simon's ear.

'Told you.'

'What were we talking about before Hurricane Lizzie?' asked Joe wryly.

'The fantasy of revolution,' said Matt.

'Oh there he goes,' said Ronnie. 'What about all the other revolutions that have happened? Were they fantasy? Everything's a fantasy until it actually happens.'

'This one's not going to happen. The masses may be exploited, but they're not downtrodden and they don't want a revolution. It's as simple as that.'

'Of course it's not going to happen - just yet,' said Joe. 'It's linked to the downfall of capitalism. Capitalism is inherently unstable - I know, I know - I hate phrases like that too. But it's true. It's not founded on anything solid other than greed and dog-eat-dog. It's all determined by market forces and it leads to speculation, bubble economies, big profits for the few...and every time it collapses, we -

the people - have to bail it out. One day, the people will say - fuck that.'

'They might say that, but I bet you they still won't rise up in revolution - whatever that means. Even when I was in the SWP and supposedly being educated, it was never clear how the people are actually going to seize power in a modern state.'

'It's difficult to predict exactly how it will happen,' said Ronnie. 'But a revolutionary vanguard will have to do the actual seizing of power and then mobilise the masses into defending it.'

'It won't be led or sustained by fringe groups,' said Joe. It can only be led by people working within the established labour movement who'll be able to communicate with people and persuade them that this is the only path that makes sense.'

'What are you talking about?' asked Lizzie after she put drinks on the table and sat down.

'The revolution. Matt thinks it's not going to happen,' said Ronnie.

'Of course it's going to happen. There's just no need to be so fucking *earnest* about it. Lighten up. You'll bore the masses to death if you ever get the chance to address them.'

'Amen to that,' said Matt and he raised his glass. 'Here's to the masses.'

Simon raised his glass too without saying anything. Joe looked at him steadily.

'I like you, Simon - you know that. But you are a bit of a fence-sitter at times, aren't you?'

'I'm on your side, Joe - you know that. But there are fences within fences.'

'Simon's a good boy, really,' said Lizzie. 'He'll stick with us when the revolution comes, won't you Simon?'

'Of course.'

'And what about you, Molly? What are your politics?'

'I don't know. I hate Thatcher and the Tories. I'm on the left, I suppose, and I support women's rights. But to be honest, I find politics quite boring.'

'It is quite boring a lot of the time, I agree. Especially arguments about the finer points of Leninism and Trotskyism. But that's mostly backward-looking men who make it boring.'

'An outrageous generalisation,' said Ronnie.

'Well you would say that, wouldn't you? But it does turn people off. Molly finds it boring, Kath's not said a word and that guy over there is falling asleep. Is he with us?'

Vince was going through the classic cycle of closing his eyes, drooping forward, then jerking awake for a few seconds.

'He's with us in body,' said Simon. And on an impulse perhaps of solidarity, he put his arm round the woman who found politics boring.

'Ah, that's sweet,' said Joe. 'Isn't it?' He put his arm briefly around Kath who nodded and smiled.

'And when do you see a woman with her arm around a man?' said Lizzie. 'Not very often. I've seen Sandy Reed with her arm round her boyfriend. And he's a biker. I used to put my arm around Stu. And that's it.'

'I can't get my arm around Simon when we're sitting down.'

'Of course you can - just give it a try. Simon, shrink!'

Molly stretched her arm around his shoulders and Simon sank down against her body. It felt as if he was doing something private in public.

'It's not very comfortable,' he said. 'And I feel...unequal. There's no other word for it. I see your point.'

Lizzie nodded.

'You see it all the time. A man drapes his arm around a woman's shoulders while she stands half-facing him, arms at her sides. It's a symbol of second-class status.'

'It depends who it is,' said Molly. 'If it's someone you're in a relationship with, then I don't see it matters that much.'

'You see it in all sorts of circumstances, whether they're in a relationship or not. There are so many male urges expressed in it. Wanting to control and subordinate the woman, wanting to protect her...supposedly, wanting to fuck her...'

Kath spoke at last.

'A lot of men feel if they work with you, like in the same office, that entitles them to do that.'

'Exactly. But what do you do when it happens?'

'Well, it's difficult. I usually just make an excuse and say I have to go and do something. But with Joe, it's different. It's a sign of closeness. I'm not going to brush him off because some feminists don't like the idea.'

'Absolutely not. But real feminists are not like religious nuts - you know, thou shall not touch except once a week in the dark. If you're partners or good friends, it's different. But physical contact including what you do in bed should be on equal terms with the woman free to lead and explore. That's all part of the idea of equal status.'

Simon watched Kath as she nodded. It was hard to tell if the faint blush in her cheeks was shyness or embarrassment. He pulled himself upright again.

'Actually, Maloney and I encountered a very helpful pair of feminists this morning.'

And he told them the story. As he did so, Maloney came into view at the far end of the bar. He had entered presumably through the side door and stopped to talk to someone. Simon tried to think of some other phrase than 'speak of the devil', but it did feel as if he'd summoned Maloney simply by uttering his name. He watched him pull a *Workers' Struggle* from his bag and exchange it for a coin, then with a nod to his customer move on around the clusters of talking heads, his keen eyes seeking them out.

'Here's the man himself.'

They looked round and Vince woke from his nap.

'I am not Him,' said Maloney.

'What?'

'You look as if you're all waiting for the Messiah.'

'Fat chance.'

'I am the voice of one crying in the wilderness.'

'Have you had a knock on the head, old chap?' asked Joe.

'No, but there are some things you never quite get out of your system. Let me buy you a drink, Simon. I can't afford a round, especially in this place.'

'I'm surprised you're back in here after only one week.'

'Lizzie, that was just a joke as far as I was concerned. Protesting about beer prices is petty-bourgeois nonsense. I'll leave that to fucking CAMRA and *consumer* groups. When prices go up, we just have to demand more pay.'

'Absolutely. At least keep the profit level under control.'

'There's a kitty.'

Maloney foraged in his pocket and threw in a pound note, then gathered up the money and went to the bar. Lizzie got up and followed him.

47

'So, Simon,' said Matt. 'What's it like to celebrate your birthday with a bunch of rabid politicos?'

Simon shrugged.

'I've done it this way for the last four years. But we are thinking of doing something different next year for the big one.' He looked at Molly. ' Going away somewhere...'

'That's forward planning, Simon. You should become a manager.'

'I wish people would stop saying that.'

More drinks began appearing on the table, then Maloney sat down and rummaged through his carrier bag.

'Unaccustomed as I am, etcetera...I have a little present for you.'

'He's going soft,' said Ronnie.

Maloney passed something across the table that was loosely wrapped in red paper decorated with a hammer and sickle.

'I hope you like the wrapping paper. It comes from an old poster I found in our Centre.'

Maloney pulled the paper away, then laughed - partly in relief. A real present from Maloney would have been worrying.

'Thanks, Tony. Just what I've always wanted. A grubby copy of Trotsky's autobiography from the floor of your car.'

'Note the bookmark.'

The bookmark was a five pound note.

'Money as well? What's going on?'

'He owes it me.'

'You gave me an idea, Simon. When I got to our Centre today, I looked through our so-called library and found an even better book.'

He pulled Trotsky's *History of the Russian Revolution* from his carrier bag and briefly showed it to them.

'I'm going to use this in our educational class instead of that, though that's good.'

'My God, it's twice as thick,' said Simon. 'I'll stick with this.' He flipped through the pages. 'I assume you're suggesting I should read it?'

'Of course you should read it.'

'It's an amazing coincidence that Trotsky was born on the same date as the Revolution,' said Ronnie.

'It's meaningless,' said Maloney. 'Trotsky says that he didn't even realise it until three years later.'

48

'What?' said Matt. 'You mean he didn't wake up thinking "Woo-hoo, it's my birthday!" I wonder what Vladimir Ilyich will give me?'

'Trotsky fainted from stress and hunger that night. He doesn't mention getting any sleep.'

'It's a good book, Simon,' said Lizzie. 'I've read it. In fact I should have given it to you instead of that silly fudge.'

'Fudge? Seems quite appropriate to me,' said Maloney.

'Ooh, vicious.'

'So are we going to build strike action against the cuts then? What's happening in the DE? The Caucus needs to know.'

Thus Maloney brought them back to the present and another tangled argument began over the froth and swill of beer. Matt tried talking to Vince for a while about music and concerts. Molly tried talking to Kath, but gave up after each exchange dried up. She nudged Simon.

'What's this caucus they're talking about?'

'The Left Caucus. It's an independent group within the union that some of us belong to. Maloney, Joe, me...and others. Independent of the SWP and the Broad Left.'

'Oh God, it gets worse. How many more groups are there? No, don't tell me. When are we going for a meal?'

'Soon. Are you hungry?'

'Yes. And I'd like a change of venue.'

'Okay, let's finish these drinks and then make a move.'

He put his arm around her again and they sat and listened.

'I don't understand how working people...influence of the media, Murdoch especially...buy your own house, become a shareholder ...forgetting its own history...Labour gave them the NHS, better education, better status...political consensus...the ruling class and its stooges...no more real power than it had before...their freedom is fake...all the workers have to do...'

Simon felt Molly stir impatiently against him. He straightened up.

'Comrades, we have an announcement to make.'

'You're getting married?'

'No, we're going for a meal.'

'I won't be joining you, Simon,' said Maloney. 'I have to get home.'

'Ah yes, your nice little terraced house awaits...'

'You have a *house*?' said Molly.

'It came with the mortgage.'

'You have a *mortgage*?'

'Why not? While we're living under this system, it makes sense to have a mortgage if you can get one instead of paying rent to a private landlord.'

'But you've just been railing at the workers for buying their own houses,' said Matt.

'They're letting themselves be sucked into the capitalist system. I'm not. I'm exploiting the exploiters. With a house, we can offer accommodation to party members, visitors from abroad, people coming down to London for conferences and demos and so on. It makes sense. After the revolution, home ownership will be replaced by guaranteed tenancies and I don't have a problem with that.'

'I'd have thought you'd want to live in a council flat surrounded by the workers,' said Molly.

'We live in a working class area of East London. I have a white collar job, Wanda's a teacher. We can afford a mortgage. There are waiting lists for council flats, you know - with more deserving cases than us.'

'I've lived on council estates all my life,' said Joe. 'Some of them are shit, but where we live now there's an active tenants association and a real sense of community.'

'I live in a squat on a street of squats,' said Ronnie. 'One big community. I know nearly a hundred people.'

'Lucky for them,' said Lizzie. 'I live in a commune which has its good points and bad points.'

'I pay rent to a private landlord, but I don't feel I'm being ripped off,' said Molly. 'He does look after the place.'

'I pay rent to a private landlord and he's a useless bastard. I only ever see him when he comes for the money.'

Everyone looked round at Vince, but no-one seemed to know what to say. Simon stood and manoeuvred round the table, patting Vince on his leather-clad shoulder.

'Right! You've heard it from the man. Private landlords are money-grabbing bastards. Now let's go if you're coming.'

Maloney and Lizzie stepped aside to talk, while everyone else gathered coats and bags and filtered out onto the pavement. For a few moments, they stood under a lamp post looking somewhat disorientated in the quiet side street.

'Chez Maloney,' said Simon to break the silence. 'Sounds weird.'

'I know,' said Joe. 'You don't think of hundred per cent revolutionaries having a home at all. More like sleeping on other people's sofas or in communes or something.'

'Or in squats,' said Ronnie.

Lizzie joined them and they walked up to the main road. After crossing to the other side, they proceeded through side streets on a zigzag course perfectly suited to their intoxicated condition before descending into a basement Greek restaurant, red lit and half empty. Here the waiters moved two tables together and they ordered the meze along with bottles of red and white wine and worked their way through flatbreads and dips, stuffed vine leaves and felafel, calamiri, spicy sausages and much else. And as the plates were cleared, they sang. Sealed and protected by alcohol and friendship, they roared their way through The Man Who Watered the Workers' Beer with, of course, an ironic stress on the word 'queer'.

I am the man, the very fat man
that waters the workers' beer.
I am the man, the very fat man
that waters the workers' beer.
And what do I care if it makes them ill,
If it makes them terribly queer?
I've a car, a yacht and an aeroplane
and I waters the workers' beer...

When coffee arrived, Simon delved into his bag and brought out the little container of fudge.

'Come on, one piece each. Wash it down with the coffee.'

'But someone might eat your special piece,' said Molly.

'I'll make some more,' said Lizzie.

The container went around the table.

'It makes a change from passing the joint,' said Matt.

'It might be a while before the special piece takes effect.'

'You're all so pissed, you probably won't even notice,' said Lizzie.

Simon offered a piece to the waiter who shook his head but smiled. You wake us all up,' he said. 'It's good.'

So they sang *Pie in the Sky*, *Blackleg Miner* and a medley of Beatle and Bowie songs. And Simon noticed how even Vince was singing

51

along over his second helping of baclava and even Kath was moving her lips when they sang the middle eight from *We Can Work It Out*. Somehow he felt that he'd got it just about right. This was true camaraderie. And the day wasn't over yet.

4. The Joy of Sex

Conjoined again, Simon and Molly walked and swayed along the Bedford Square pavement with a dim sense of the grand Georgian houses beside them which were dark and silent now as offices are at night. In the central garden, the trees were reaching outward and shedding their leaves, some of which had been swept or blown against the black railings. Everyone else had headed for Tottenham Court Road, but they had decided to 'get some air' and cut through Bloomsbury en route to Russell Square underground.

'What time's the last train?'

Simon looked at his watch.

'We've got about three quarters of an hour.'

'Uh huh. Do you know something?'

'You're beautiful.'

'Well, yes of course. But something else...'

'I'm beautiful. We're both beautiful. We are the beautiful people.'

'You're drunk. Something else...'

'*What*?'

'I think I ate the special piece of fudge. I'm starting to feel sort of - spacey...'

'Oh, really? You feel happy and relaxed do you? That's just the effect of being with me.'

'No, that's normal relaxed. This is different. There's definitely something going on.'

'Well don't panic. I've eaten Lizzie's fudge before. She doesn't overdo it.'

'I've never eaten dope before. Why don't you smoke it like everyone else?

The traffic was sparse and there were few other people about. Nevertheless he steered her carefully as they crossed Gower Street into Montague Place.

'I can't inhale cigarette smoke. I've just never been able to do it. When I've tried, it's just made me feel nauseous. It's one of those things I can't do like swimming.'

'That's weird. I don't smoke much, but when I do - well, inhaling just happens.'

'Not with me. I had a bad experience at university. The classic scene - sitting in a circle in this flat, about eight of us. Someone rolled a huge spliff, it got passed around, my turn - I really tried and almost immediately felt sick. I got to the loo just in time to throw up.'

She had taken her arm away and started to walk a bit faster, forcing him to keep up and keep his hand on her shoulder. Drifts of dead leaves crunched under their feet.

'What are these bloody great buildings?'

'That's Senate House and that's the backside of the British Museum.'

'They're like huge mausoleums.'

'It's the Portland Stone effect.'

'The what?'

'They're made with giant slabs of stone from the Isle of Portland to try and impress you.'

'Well I don't like them. They're *op*pressing me. Can we go and sit down somewhere?'

'Yeah, well - we'll be on the tube soon.'

'I just want to sit down for a few minutes and see what this dope's going to do to me. Or for me.'

'Well let's go in there. There are plenty of benches.'

He pointed ahead to the dark green gardens of Russell Square with their tall trees and thick bushes massed behind railings.They crossed the road and walked past the cabmen's shelter to the corner of the square where there was an entrance. Inside, a few people were strung out along the central path, following its course across the square. They turned onto one of the side paths where foliage provided cover and softened slightly the noise of traffic on Southampton Row. A man in a ragged overcoat was stretched out asleep on the first bench, his head on an old khaki knapsack, a carrier bag at his feet. They walked further along and found another bench set back in front of a huge rhododendron.

'Will this do?'

'Anywhere will do.'

They sat down, looked at each other and began kissing. Simon went through his usual routine. A teasingly brief kiss on the lips, then lingering kisses on the brow, the eyelids and cheeks, the lips briefly again, then the throat and sides of the neck, pressing his nostrils against the lightly perfumed skin. Then back to the lips with intent, softly pressing, opening enough to touch tongues and...

Molly pulled away.

'We were asked not to do this in that pub, remember?'

'Of course I do. It was only a fortnight ago. Embarrassing, though.'

'If I felt like I do now, I'd have told them to fuck off.'

He moved his hand up and felt one breast, then the other under her soft blouse and bra. After that, he let it rove down under the loose skirt and slide forward slowly along the thigh, then back again. Molly gasped and hissed.

'Keep going.'

He kept going and managed to get a finger under everything and rub it back and forth over the gentle ridges and damp folds of her vagina. They began kissing as well, breaking off now and then for Molly to moan. And then another sound pricked the bubble - the clearing of a very deep throat. Simon jerked around, then slowly slid his hand out from under Molly's skirt. A man in municipal uniform was standing on the path a few feet away, looking grim.

'Closing time.' He held up a bunch of keys on a large silver ring.

'Oh, right. Closing time. We'll er...'

'Go,' said Molly. She stood and smoothed down her skirt with the casual demeanour of a dope-eating libertine. They began to gather their bags.

'Is the entrance on the far side still open? We're going to the tube.'

'It is.'

'Okay, we'll go that way.'

The man turned silently and walked off.

'Are you thinking what I'm thinking?' Molly whispered.

Simon nodded and looked at his watch.

'We haven't got long though.'

They heard voices from further along the path. African and English accents, the park keeper and the park sleeper. For half a minute or so, the voices conducted an argument which grew fainter and then stopped.

'What if he comes back?' Molly whispered.

They listened intently, but could hear only traffic and a siren somewhere towards Euston.

'He's going the other way. More gates to lock...'

'How will we get out? Climb the railings?'

'We'll find a way.'

They put their bags down and sat on the bench again.

'God, I feel disconnected now,' said Molly.

'T'll soon get you going again.'

And within a minute Molly began to squirm under the movement of his finger.

'Get it right in. Find my clit!'

He delved into the flesh under her hood, but his finger kept slipping.

'Ow - you're catching me. Your fingernails are too long.'

He withdrew his hand and looked at the nails. She was right. And she'd mentioned it before but he'd done nothing about it.

'Well what d'you want me to do? Have you got any nail clippers?'

'Don't be ridiculous. Use your tongue!'

'What *here*?'

'Yes, here. Where else? *Please* - go down to me.'

'Jesus!'

'Please *please* - do it for me.'

Simon got on his knees. Molly pushed her knickers and tights down and pulled up her skirt. He interpolated his head between her thighs, planting some fleshly kisses along the way, and began to lick her vulva. A gasping commentary came from above as his tongue probed under the hood.

'No, not there. There! No, you've lost it again. *There*. Yes...no...'

Before long, his jaws and neck were aching.

'Hang on.'

He withdrew slightly to rest. Above him, Molly was silent. When he went back in, she stayed slumped on the bench.

'It's not going to work,' she said.

He came out again.

'Sorry, I haven't done this very often. And never on hard ground.'

'It's not your fault. I just wanted...it must be the dope. I feel dizzy now.'

She started to take deep breaths. He stood up and looked around. Something beyond the gardens caught his eye - a building glimpsed between trees.

'Oh, God - that's the old Faber and Faber building.'

'What?'

'Where Eliot used to work.'

'Who?'

'T. S. Eliot. The poet...'

Molly sighed.

'Yes, I've vaguely heard of him. Didn't Dylan mention him in one of his songs?'

'*Cats*! The new musical. That's based on his Book of Practical Cats.'

'Oh, *that*...'

'Old Possum...I wonder if his ghost still haunts the place. He might have been watching us.'

'Well, no wonder it didn't work.'

Simon looked at his watch.

'Jesus, we'd better go.'

'Actually, I feel better now,' said Molly as she sorted herself out. 'I don't know what came over me.'

Simon smiled.

'I'm going to take a wild guess it was the dope. It can have different effects on different people, so I've heard. It can reduce the sex drive or the opposite. You're obviously in the latter category.'

'The raving nympho category, you mean?'

She linked her arm through his and they walked towards the north side of the square. Molly seemed in no hurry and Simon held up his watch arm.

'Look. We've only got five minutes. Quick march - left right, left right. Oh, God - how're we going to get over those?'

The railings had come into view. They were tall and spiked.

'I'm sure they weren't like that when we came in.'

'S'all right. We can just climb up one of those big trees, crawl along the branch on our bellies and drop down onto the other side.'

'Okay. So the dope hasn't worn off yet.'

He went into the shrub border and looked for bent railings, but they appeared solidly upright in both directions.

'Fuck!'

It looked as if they'd have to get a taxi and he wasn't sure he had enough money.

'Look!'

Molly was calling from the path and pointing towards the main corner. He joined her and looked. The park keeper was staring back at them from the other side of the gates, but his hand held one gate slightly open. They ran towards him.

'Use all your charm, Moll.'

57

'I'll offer him a quick one. In the bushes.'

'That's my girl. Don't laugh - he might think we're taking the piss.'

The man pushed the gate further open and they squeezed through onto the pavement.

'Sorry, we got lost.'

'It's a wilderness in there.'

'Sorry to mess you about.'

The man grunted and gave a cautious smile.

'You are lucky. I got delayed, but I thought you might still be in there. I was looking across for you as I went round the other gates.'

'You're a gentleman,' said Simon, patting him on the shoulder. 'And you're welcome here.'

'I hope so, sir. I've been here since the war.'

'Fantastic. Sorry, we've got to dash. Last train...'

'My father worked in the docks.'

'Bye...wait!' Molly ran back and kissed him on the cheek.

They darted across Southampton Row and ran frantically down Bernard Street to the tube. In the small ticket hall, the gate was open and they rushed straight into the lift. Recovering their breath on the way down, they ran out of the lift at the bottom straight down the stairs to where the last train was standing at the platform, A few seconds after they'd slumped into their seats, the doors closed.

'I haven't got a ticket,' said Molly in his ear.

'Well there wasn't time, was there? Don't worry - I'll see you right at the other end.'

The train thundered through the tunnel. Conversation was difficult, but Simon sat with his arm around Molly kissing her hair from time to time, aware of but indifferent to the people around them. After King's Cross, few people got on. Caledonian Road was enveloped in desolate silence. Holloway Road and Arsenal hardly registered and if the journey had been any longer, they might both have drifted into sleep. But Finsbury Park came just in time and they shuffled off the train, following others to the escalator. At the surface, they headed for the Wells Street exit where the man at the barrier took Simon's return and glanced at Molly. Simon dug his hand into his pocket.

'How much from Russell Square?'

'Don't worry, mate.'

And they were waved through, simple as that.

'Why is everyone so nice to us this evening?'

'Cos it's your birthday.'

'Yeah, but they don't know that.'

'They just look at us and think *Aw, young love*.'

There was that word again. Twice in one evening, written and now spoken.

Simon lived in a three-storey Victorian house which backed on to a disused railway embankment. He was the only tenant and rented the ground floor front room while his landlady, Anne-Marie, lived on the upper two floors. He was allowed to use the ground floor kitchen and a small bathroom under the stairs into which a shower had been squeezed. Anne-Marie's son, Alex, lived upstairs too though he was away at university much of the time. She hadn't talked about her personal circumstances, but Simon assumed there was an ex-husband somewhere. A male 'friend' visited once or twice a week.

She had interrogated him quite sharply when he'd come to view the room back in April.

'You are single, yes? This is a room for a single person.'

'You have a good job, yes?'

'Why are you moving?'

He'd been living in a house of bedsits since splitting up with Diana the year before. He was moving because the room was too small and the transport connections poor. That's what he told Anne-Marie. He didn't mention the man in the next room who was attacked regularly at night by evil spirits and screamed to be left alone. Or the American peace crusader in the room below who sang anti-war songs at full volume.

'I will provide you with milk every day and you can help yourself to eggs...' She had a hen run in the back garden. 'The chickens? Well I was brought up on a farm in Normandy and that is - what do you call it? - a hangover.'

He knew that milk and eggs could constitute provision of 'a meal' and allow her to subvert tenancy rights and evict him whenever she wished, but the room was a good size and the location convenient. He took it and they had rubbed along well enough, although a little bit of tension could lurk under the surface. One day she told him how her parents had been active in the Resistance during the war, right under the eyes of German soldiers who visited their farm to buy milk and eggs.

59

'That is why I give them to my tenants now because the British were such good allies.'

On one occasion, the farm dog had barked at the Germans and one of the soldiers had kicked it.

'My father apologised to them and I felt ashamed that he hadn't been braver. Of course, they hadn't told me about their Resistance activities. I was only nine or ten.'

Her eyes were moist.

'When they told me after the war, I felt ashamed again that I'd doubted my daddy. Of course, I knew that the Nazis were bad men but I didn't know...the full extent of it then.'

Simon mentioned the National Front and how he had been on 'one or two' Anti-Nazi League marches.

'Poof! They are just silly men dressing up, causing trouble like football hooligans and - what do you call them? - the shaven-headed ones? Skinheads. They are just *thugs* - all of them. And they give the communists an excuse to provoke violence. You don't want to get mixed up in all that.'

He'd said no more. The real struggle was out there, not in Anne-Marie's kitchen.

Now the street was quiet and the house in darkness as he and Molly approached. He scanned the top floor windows where sometimes a faint light still glowed when he came home late. But not tonight.

He unlocked the door and walked softly along the hallway to where it curved round by the stairs. There was no light under the kitchen door either. He went back and signalled to Molly who was standing half-hidden by a laurel bush in the front garden.

'The coast is clear,' he whispered with mock furtiveness.

'Great. What about the house though?'

'It's *safe*.'

He steered her inside.

'Have you ever thought-'

He shushed her, unlocked his room door and ushered her inside.

'Have you ever thought' - he put his arms around her - 'that if she is listening, she'll wonder why you're creeping about?'

'Nah, she knows I'm a good lodger who's trying not to disturb her.'

They kissed, then took off their coats and hung them behind the door. He pulled her two presents out of his bag and stood her card on the mantlepiece.

'Cup of tea, dear? Make yourself at home.'

'I need the loo. Hang on, where's my toiletry bag.'

He escorted her to the little bathroom, then slipped quietly into the kitchen. He had to stifle a jaw-breaking yawn and then intercept the kettle before it began to whistle. Molly came in as he was pouring water onto the tea bags.

'Ooh, nice. I didn't get a look at this last time. I don't like the hanging lamps though or the curtains. Nice table. She's got a lot of herbs. Oh, look, onions on a string - very *français*. Does she cook nice meals for you?'

'She doesn't cook for me as such. In fact, I'd get worried if she did. But she offers me food that she's cooked from time to time. She made me some soup when I had a bad cold just before I met you. That was good...'

'I bet she likes mothering you.'

'Sort of. Look sorry, but this is making me edgy. What if she comes down and finds you? Let's creep back to my room. It's fun creeping.'

Molly crept back with him.

'This is like a silent comedy,' she whispered. 'Pity there isn't a table in the hall that I could bump into and knock over.'

'Yeah. With a vase on it.'

When he brought the tea back to the room, she had turned the main light off, the bedside lamp on and was half undressed. He sat down on the sofa and half-stifled another yawn. He felt weary and oppressed by the heavy burden of alcohol in his body. And anxious. He had managed to do the job last time, but what if...

'I'm not keeping you awake then?'

Molly had put on a blue cotton nightdress.

'You look absolutely gorgeous.'

She came over and sat on his lap.

'It's just that it's been a long day. Actually, I've been round in a big circle today. I met Maloney at the Finsbury Park bookshop - just on the other side from where we came out of the tube. I can't believe it was only this morning.'

'Well there's one more job to be done and then you can sleep.'

She rubbed her nose gently against his neck.

'You like that, don't you? I remember this little voice saying *nuzzle me*.'

Simon smiled and felt his cock stirring against the tight denim crotch of his jeans. They talked a while longer and drank the tea, then he went to the bathroom. When he returned, Molly was lying in the bed. He climbed over her and squeezed in between the wall and the solid softness of her body. They kissed and stroked each other and he lifted the edge of her nightdress, snaking his hand up under it to cup each breast. Then his calf muscle spasmed with cramp and he had to stretch and press it frantically at an angle against the wall while Molly cooed her sweet concern. When that was over, she started to stroke his cock using all the fingers of her hand.

'Okay?'

He bore it for a while, then said as kindly as he could...

'I can do that myself.'

'I'm sure you can.' She sank onto her back.

'Actually, sorry - I just need to get a drink of water.'

He climbed over her again, pulled on his jeans, put the door latch on and padded down the hallway. In the kitchen, he filled a pint glass from the tap and drank some of the water on his way back to the room. Molly had turned on her side facing the wall.

'Do you want some of this?'

'No thank you.'

He got back into bed lying on the edge. After a while, Molly said:

'Could you turn the light off if nothing's going to happen.'

He didn't want to do this. Instead he swooned into an unpleasant dream in which a man in a camel-hair coat was threatening to harm him. When he forced his eyes open, he could sense that Molly was still awake. He turned and stroked her back, kneaded her shoulders and pushed his lips under her hair to plant kisses on her nape. When he pulled away, she turned towards him.

'Look, whatever you want me to do for you, I'll do. Whatever you don't want me to do, I won't.'

He was moved and felt a dangerous moistening of the tear film.

'Oh, Molly! You're beautiful, you're lovely - the fault's all with me.'

She pulled her nightdress over her head and tossed it down on the bed.

'Just give me a cuddle. I need you to keep me warm now.'

He put his arms around her and with the pressure of her naked body and the mingled scent of perfume and skin, his cock began to harden and grow and he knew this was the moment. It was awkward in the narrow bed but he managed to get on top of her.

'Help me in,' he whispered.

She helped him in and he went to work, thrusting to the hilt, almost withdrawing, thrusting again. Arms straight in the press-up position, then down brushing against her breasts, then up again and so on a few more times. Then down on top of her, one arm around her neck, the other around her back, her arms clinging around his neck and shoulders. Then up slightly on his knees, the beast with two backs rocking, thrusting until finally not wanting to lose it he came with a long *Aaaahhh* and Molly smiled and said *Yes* as bliss closed his eyes, emptied his head and held his Adam's apple rigid in his throat. After which he lay on her body, happy. It seemed to have taken much longer than three minutes.

After another minute, Molly cleared her throat with two guttural notes, the second slightly higher than the first.

'Yes?' he said teasingly.

She cleared her throat again and looked at him meaningfully.

'Oh, I see. That was so amazing you're lost for words.'

She cleared her throat again and this time the seond note was loud and pronounced, almost a shriek.

'Shhh...you'll give yourself a sore throat. I get the message.'

He rolled off and then, with an arm around her shoulders and his back against the wall, began the delicate operation of bringing her off. After some general massage, he slipped his middle finger once more unto the breach and-

'Stop! Stop - wait. Please...pass my little bag. It's down there.'

He sprawled over her and found the toiletry bag on the shelf under the bedside table. She unzipped it and took out a small pair of scissors.

'Give me that finger.'

He wiped it on his thigh and presented it. Sitting up, she carefully cut the nail.

'They never do this in films.'

'Well, you should take better care of your nails. Give me your index finger as well. Look, there's dirt under here...Have some respect for my private parts.'

He laughed and found it hard to stop.

'That's hysterical. You're quite right but it's still hysterical.'

She gathered the trimmings and tipped them onto the bedside table.

'There. You can do the other fingers tomorrow.'

'Yes, Molly.'

She turned the bedside light off and he resumed his duty. It was easier to find and stay on the clitoris with his finger than it had been with his tongue earlier, but it still took a while. His arm began to ache.

'Yes, yes...no. Oh, please keep going...'

He concentrated on applying just the right amount of pressure on the spot and soon they were in the run-up as her body tensed and her cries grew louder. When she came, he carried on rubbing until with a giggling 'no no' she pushed his hand away.

'Thank you,' she said.

'No problem...I love you.'

'I love you. I'm sorry if I got a bit stroppy earlier.'

'C'est la vie.'

'I hope I wasn't too loud. I was trying to keep it down. I hope your landlady didn't hear.'

He shrugged.

'If I get thrown out, I get thrown out.'

They held on to each other for a while, then slowly pulled apart. Soon, Molly was breathing the slow rhythmic breaths of sleep, but Simon - despite his tiredness - lay awake for a while. It was the first time they had said those three words directly to each other and it gave him something to think about.

When he awoke, grey light was edging in around the drawn curtains. He had little room to move and his back, legs and head hurt when he tried. Molly was still asleep, although she stirred a little when he crawled to the end of the bed and slumped down on the carpet. He felt raw, heavy-boned and nauseous. Only the dawn chill and a full bladder made him move again. He pulled his jeans on and a sweatshirt and crouched before the gas fire to light it. Then he picked up their mugs and left the room. At the foot of the stairs, he paused and listened but there was no sound from above. In the bathroom, he did a long pee, a loose crap, examined his face and beard in the mirror and mussed his hair into shape. In the kitchen, he rinsed the mugs out and made some coffee. He had a shelf in one of the cupboards where his meagre supply of groceries sat. From it, he took four slices of bread and put them in the toaster. He'd left the kitchen door ajar and listened for any sound of movement from above, ready to abort one of the coffees if need be.

When he left the kitchen with two mugs in one hand, a plate of toast in the other and a banana in each trouser pocket, he heard a door open upstairs and hastened back to his room. Molly was sitting on the edge of an armchair close to the fire. He switched the main light on and winced.

'Fucking hell.'

'Exactly.'

They sat at the table and ate mostly in silence. Gradually the coffee and toast worked its magic and Simon felt his brain cells expanding.

'I'm thinking.'

'Oh, no,' said Molly. She seemed to be livening up too.

'I'm thinking I can't go on creeping about like this, pretending you're not here. It's ridiculous. I'm going to tell Anne-Marie about you and ask if you can stay the night. I'll say "from time to time" and we can see how it goes. What do you think? It's either that or I stay at your place whenever we - you know - want to?'

Molly had a room and kitchenette in a house without landlord or landlady on site. It was further out from town in the upper stretches of Walthamstow.

'And what do you think she'll say?'

Simon shrugged.

'I don't know. I think she'll be reluctant but - as long as I play down the frequency to begin with - I think she'll agree. After all, I'm a good tenant, I pay my rent on time. If she throws me out, she'll have to find someone else. Better the devil you know...'

'It is ridiculous,' said Molly. 'Not only do you have to smuggle me in, but you'll have to stand guard while I go to the bathroom, then smuggle me out. If she comes down, I could end up being late for work just waiting for her to go back up. And what if she peers through a window as we're leaving? It's best to be honest. She'll hear us sooner or later anyway - especially me!'

'I'll talk to her.'

'Actually, this is quite a nice room,' Molly said, looking round as she finished her coffee. 'It's got potential. And it's a double room really. The bathroom's a bit grotty, but we could offer to do it up for her. The kitchen seemed lovely when I looked at it last night. We'd need a bigger bed, but I could see myself...living here.'

'Really?'

'It's an easier journey to work.'

'Uh huh.'

'Not a bad area.'

'Yep.'

'Of course, she may not want a couple living here.'

She looked around the room again.

'But it's worth thinking about.'

Part Two

January 1983

5. I Hate Mondays

Breakfast at Molly's that morning was a hurried affair. Unusually, Simon had stayed over on Sunday night after they'd spent the evening with friends living nearby. In fact, they were Molly's friends rather than his and he'd drunk too much wine and felt thickheaded and out of it much of the time. On the way back through suburban streets, he'd seen some snowdrops in a garden and stepped over the low wall to pick a few for her. She wouldn't hold them. Back at her place, he put them in a glass of water on the kitchen window sill. It was just after midnight and they fell asleep soon after getting into bed.

Dressed now in the same clothes as yesterday, he sat on the outside toilet that Molly had cleaned and painted and taken over for herself. He shivered on the plastic seat and it took him a while to push the crap out. When he got back to the kitchen, Molly was sitting at the little table finishing her coffee. The milk that she'd poured on his cereal had dried up and he added some more. The toast had long since gone cold.

'What takes you so long?'

'I've told you. You know. I suffer from piles.'

'Yes, but...' She shook her head and looked at her watch.

'I'm going to have to go in ten minutes.'

'I'll be ready.'

She put her dishes by the sink and went into the bedroom. He ate standing up, looking out of the window. Dawn had barely broken but there was enough light to see a small lawn bordered by concrete paths and narrow beds with plants bare-stemmed or leaved in dull green. A trio of sparrows perched briefly on the back fence, then sped off elsewhere. It had rained during the night and looked as if it would soon start again. He stuffed half a slice of toast in his mouth, poured some lukewarm coffee from the pot into a blue-ringed mug and stacked his bowl and plate next to Molly's. The snowdrops were bearing up in their glass.

'Have I got time to do the washing-up?' he called.

'No, you should have done it already.'

He gulped down most of the coffee, threw the remains into the cracked butler's sink and ran the cold tap to clear it. Twenty seconds to brush his teeth, then into the main room just as she moved towards the door, coat on, bag over shoulder, keys in hand. Four months, he reflected as he put on his coat. Not only were they still living apart but she hadn't even offered him her spare set of keys. He had no spare keys to his place ('I'm always in if you forget them,' Anne-Marie had said). It seemed as if they were in a perpetual state of uncertainty, hanging about for each other, observing old routines. It wasn't his fault. Was it his fault?

He thrust his toiletry bag into the little black rucksack she had given him for Christmas and moved out into the hallway. Molly locked her door and they went out onto the street. He held out his hand and she took it.

'I hate Mondays,' she said. 'I don't just "not like" them, I hate them.'
'Yeah, it's difficult to get going again.'

They walked past 'the Green' with its skeletal trees, empty benches and shelter, starlings poking in the grass, litter flapping in the wind and crossed the main road to the bus stops on the broad pavement. Simon slipped into the newsagent and bought a *Guardian*, then rejoined Molly in the throng outside. When their bus arrived, they trooped upstairs and had to sit one behind the other for a while. Simon leafed through the front half of the newspaper and read about Thatcher's preference for a 1984 election, the planned siting of Cruise missiles on British soil, the gunning down of a judge by the Provisional IRA and the shooting of a film editor by the Metropolitan Police (*a tragic case of mistaken identity*). He leant forward and tapped Molly on the shoulder.

'We missed the launch of Breakfast TV.'

Molly shrugged. She had a 14" black and white set in her bedroom.
'Who's got the time?'

'I think it's a service for the three million unemployed.'

When they were sitting together, she borrowed the paper.

'I can read about the news or listen to it, but watching it on TV is just too depressing,' she said.

'Breakfast TV sounds more like a chat show.'

'Waste of time. I can't stand the newsreaders either, especially the female ones.'

'Reagan's popularity has fallen, that's good news.'

But she was reading an article headlined *Ben's informed me he's giving up sex.*

'What've you got on today?'

'The usual.'

'We've got a committee meeting to plan Wednesday's strike action.'

'Oh, yeah - I'd forgotten about that. You didn't mention it when we were talking about Maloney yesterday.'

'No.'

'He must have a lot on his mind, what with that and the affair with Lizzie. And his wife throwing him out.'

'He's always got a lot on his mind. And by the way, it's not common knowledge about his marital problems.'

'Well who am I going to tell? I don't know anyone who'd be remotely interested. I expect Lizzie will be joining him on the picket line, will she?'

'I expect so. There'll be no lovey-dovey stuff though.'

'I can't make it, I'm afraid.'

'I wasn't expecting you to. When are we going to meet up then?'

She folded the newspaper and gave it back to him. Her stop was coming up.

'Well actually, Wednesday evening is about the only one I have free this week.'

'Okay. Not sure what condition I'll be in though. I expect we'll be in the pub from half eleven to three.'

'Well that's my best offer...'

He stood up to let her out. They kissed briefly.

'Outside Leicester Square tube?'

'Yep. Six pm.'

He watched from the window as she stepped on to the pavement and walked off. She looked as lovely as ever and he felt a pang as the bus moved away. It was worrying.

Simon had two offices at the Institute. One was the Union Office in a faraway corner of the top floor. The other was the Records Office, halfway up the building, where in theory he worked. He went to the latter first to deposit his coat, establish his attendance and explain why he would be elsewhere for much of the day.

When he got there, Bob was sitting hunched in his chair at the far end of the room, working his way methodically through a card index and wearing the dark suit and owlish glasses which helped him pass for a manager. His domain was a dumping ground for various human misfits and liabilities unable to carry out a proper day's work. The

71

current batch included Conor, the sad shabby alcoholic who often went missing for days at a time. Geoffrey, a survivor of coronary bypass surgery who could allegedly lift nothing heavier than a postage stamp. And Mildred who wore the most suffocating perfume Simon had ever encountered and spoke of her many afflictions in a frail high-pitched voice.

'My word, you are early today, Mr Hayes,' said Bob ponderously checking his watch as Simon walked down the office.

'Spent the night at my girlfriend's. Came in with her on the bus.'

He perched on the chair beside Bob's desk.

'Oh, I see. She gets you up.'

'She certainly does, Bob, but that's before we go to sleep.'

'What? Oh...heh heh heh.' Bob's portly frame shook. 'Whoops.'

'Your tongue will get you in trouble, Bob. Oh, Jesus - you've got me at it now.'

'What?'

Bob's brow furrowed as his brain searched for the joke.

'Never mind. I've got meetings today, I'm afraid. Meetings followed by meetings.'

'Meetings about meetings?'

'That too. It's the cuts, Bob. We've got a strike coming up on Wednesday. Don't you know?'

'What is my union doing?'

'Supporting it, locally and nationally. They're a bit half-hearted about it as usual, but you should be out.'

'Well I shall have to see. It would be difficult for me to go on strike because of all this...' He waved his hand vaguely at the desks littered with index cards, paper and files. Simon went through the motions of making a case.

'It's all about jobs, Bob. Your job, Bob, could be at risk. And if your job goes, that reduces promotion opportunities for us. We all risk losing jobs. This government - and the bosses they represent - are out to screw us. Slash and burn, privatise and profit. That's the name of the game.' He nodded at the desks before them. 'This lot will be computerised in a few years. Ordinary people will be thrown on the scrapheap or end up doing the shit jobs that even robots won't be able to do.'

Conor listened to this in blinking stupefaction. Geoffrey didn't raise his eyes from the card index in front of him. Mildred stood up briskly and huffily, pulled her cardigan tight around her shoulders and picked up her handbag.

'I'm going for an early tea break, Bob, if you don't mind.'

Bob blinked.

'Of course, my dear. Don't be too long.' But Mildred was already half way to the door.

Bob sighed.

'That's all very well,' he said to Simon. 'But it seems to me that the Tories are just continuing the job that Labour started.'

'Well, yes - up to a point. The old Labour Party has a lot to answer for.'

'So where does that leave us?'

'Up Shit Creek, but...' Simon felt a surge of inspiration - '*with a paddle. A metaphorical paddle, of course* - meaning we're not helpless. We can protest. Walk out. Fight back. Do not just roll over and do as we're told.'

'Hmmm...'

'Never say die. Never say "the struggle nought availeth". And actually, Labour have at last got a bit of backbone under Foot.'

'Hmm...but he's not going to defeat Thatcher, Simon. The tide has turned in her favour. People think she's put the "Great" back in Great Britain and all that nonsense.'

'We shall see.'

'We shall indeed.'

'Even if she does scrape back in somehow, there'll be a big movement against her. A solid wall of resistance.'

'Citizen Smith!' said Geoffrey loudly, but without looking up.

'Oh, no,' said Bob. 'Our Simon is far more eloquent than that.'

Simon got up and walked back down the office. He ignored the wretched Geoffrey, but stopped beside the wretched Conor and smelt the whisky and decay.

'How are you doing?'

Conor peered up at him from beneath white tangled eyebrows. He spoke softly.

'Not so great, Simon. I have to keep very still because every time I move I feel sick.'

'Have you been to see the Welfare Officer?'

'I've got an appointment with Sarah this afternoon, but what she can do for me I don't know.'

73

'Well you've got to do something.'

'I feel better than I did. All I could manage after the New Year was two spoonfuls of powdered milk in a glass of water. For days on end...'

'For fuck's sake, Conor - that's not eating!'

'Oh, I've been eating the last few days, Simon. A bit. That's why I feel sick...'

'I'll have a word with Sarah too.'

'You're a good fellow, Simon. And Bob too.' He spoke louder. 'He shelters me. He's like that Schindler fellow they've been talking about that saved Jews from the Nazis.'

'Jesus, Conor. I wouldn't go that far. Not even Maloney would go that far. Well, not on a good day...'

'Did he say Schindler?' asked Bob. 'The factory owner chap? You can't compare me to him.'

'No you can't,' said Simon. 'But I was talking about comparing our management to the Nazis.'

'That's true,' said Conor. 'I meant Bob has got a big heart. Our management are just watching their backs, doing their jobs. But you know - where have you heard that before?'

'Hmm...' said Simon. 'Anyway we're on strike on Wednesday. I trust you'll be joining us?'

'If I'm still here, Simon, I'll be out.'

And he tapped the desk with one finger.

'Okay, that's great. if you're still here, you won't be *here*.'

'Either way, he'll be out,' said Geoffrey, half-turning in his chair but without looking at anyone.

'Very true,' said Simon. 'But if he's not here, we'll have a bloody good wake for him.'

And with this reassurance, he patted Conor's thin tweed shoulder and walked back to his desk.

A few phone calls later, he took the lift up two floors, then climbed a flight of stairs to the attic or penthouse floor as they called it. Here a narrow corridor ran between obscure offices and store rooms leading at the end to the Union Office - a small room with two desks facing each other, a row of cabinets against the back wall and a skylight window through which Simon had often watched the passing clouds. It was meant to serve all three unions in the building, but he and

74

Maloney had more or less taken it over and the others conducted their business elsewhere.

Maloney was there now, talking on the phone. His hair was perhaps slightly more unkempt than usual, his uniform of black cord jacket, black pullover and plum-coloured shirt was marginally more dishevelled, but apart from a holdall on the floor there was nothing to suggest any change of circumstances. Simon sat down at the opposite desk and waited. After half a minute, he mimed *come back later?* Maloney shook his head.

'Yep. Yep. No idea. Yep. Okay, I will. Yep. Listen, I've got to go. Yep. Someone's here. Okay. I'll ring you this evening.'

He put the phone down.

'How's it going?'

'How's it going?" Maloney ran his hand through his hair without disturbing it. 'I'm thirty three years old and I have no fixed abode. That's how it's going.'

'Staying with comrades?'

'I've been staying with one comrade. I don't want it generally known within the organisation that I'm homeless. But his lodger's back today, so I'm trying to get hold of my brother.'

'That was Lizzie you were talking to, I assume?'

Maloney nodded.

'Can't you stay with her? Oh, no - she's still living in the feminist commune, isn't she?'

'She says I *could* stay with her - men aren't banned from the house. But she doesn't think I'd be very happy.' He shrugged. 'I'll stay there if I have to but really I want to get back with Wanda. Moving in with Lizzie isn't going to help.'

'You could stay at mine. I've got a small uncomfortable sofa you could sleep on. But my landlady tends to be more on the prowl now that Molly stays.'

'I thought she'd agreed to that?'

'She did, but reluctantly. If it's more than once a fortnight, she gets in a strop.'

'Okay...well, tempting though your offer is, I'm not going to sneak around dodging landladies.'

'Absolutely. I just thought I'd offer.'

'Anyway, let's not get too petty-bourgeois about this, Simon. It's actually quite interesting being thrown out on the street and seeing close-up how other people live. It's good to have your normal domestic life disrupted every now and then. It's a trap after all - settling down.'

'Absolutely. So how does being married and being a property owner go with wanting to overthrow the whole system?'

'Oh not that again, Simon. Overthrowing capitalism doesn't mean destroying everything. You know that, or you should do. It means seizing control from the rich ruling class and changing the economic basis of society. In the meantime, having a settled home base means you can focus on the revolutionary struggle.'

'But you've just said-'

'That it's good to have that disrupted sometimes? Sure. Well, not good but educational. Anyway...'

He hesitated and drummed his fingers on the desk.

'I haven't told you that Wanda's pregnant, have I?'

'Whaaat? No - you haven't. Jesus Christ. Does Lizzie know?'

'Of course she knows.'

'Well how does she feel about it?'

Maloney shrugged.

'Conflicted? Confused? I don't know.'

'You don't know? You haven't discussed it?

'We've discussed it but not as a soap opera or some big emotional drama. We're grown-ups in a physical and intellectual relationship.' He paused. 'Lizzie's good company and I will admit I'm very fond of her, but...it's not enough to make me want to uproot everything. Especially when I have a child coming along.'

'When's the baby due?'

'Oh, not for another three months. Plenty of time to sort it all out. Lizzie's very pragmatic. She'll be okay.'

'That's definite then - you've decided?'

'When that baby arrives, I want to be there. Fathers can be present at the birth now, you know.'

'What if Wanda won't have you back?'

'She will.'

He looked at his watch and stood up.

'Come on, let's go and have some tea. I'm seeing Vince to discuss his final warning. You can sit in. You're more empathetic than I am.'

And Simon rose to follow Maloney with the odd feeling of having been promoted to an adult.

76

Vince was already there when they reached the Staff Restaurant, a hunched figure in black seated stiffly in a corner of the room. Simon gave him a mock salute as he and Maloney stood in the queue and thought how from a distance Vince could pass for a jazz cellar existentialist rather than a resolutely non-intellectual heavy metal freak. The image was dispelled as you got nearer and sensed a blankness behind the horn-rimmed glasses and the generic South East accent.

'How's it going, Tone?'

Maloney dropped Vince's case file on the table before they sat down. It gave a flat inert thud.

'I haven't weighed it, but it's got to be one of the heaviest personal files I've ever had to carry around. Almost as thick as the Eddie Adeyemi file in 1979 or the file that grew out of the Sandra Downes debacle last year.'

'The year before actually,' said Simon.

'Debacle? They're on the Croydon pub circuit. A bit too lightweight for me.'

'Very funny, Vincent. You may have noticed I'm not rolling on the floor with laughter.'

'I don't blame you, Tony. Look at it. That floor hasn't been swept for days.

There was a silence. Vince sighed.

'Oh for gawd's sake, lighten up guys. It's all over now, isn't it? I really appreciate what you've done for me, you know that.'

'You're on a final warning, Vince,' said Simon. 'A real final warning. It will be all over for you if you don't stay within these limits.'

He tapped the letter which was at the top of the file Maloney had opened.

'Well not quite,' said Maloney with some impatience. 'If he doesn't stay within these limits, the whole thing can still drag on. We can argue with management over any infringements, we can appeal for a further extension, we can get headquartes in again, we can threaten them with going to a tribunal if they sack him - Vince knows all that. But I'll be pretty pissed off because it's not why I'm doing this job. It's a monumental pain in the arse. A massive distraction from the real struggle.'

77

Vince nodded with a sad smile of acceptance.

'I've never hidden the reasons why I do this job, have I?' Maloney went on. 'I've never hidden my politics. I do this job to defend workers who are *really* being screwed by management. I do this job to help workers stand on their feet and defend themselves and their rights. Workers create the wealth in this society and provide the public services. I want to see them take control, not be herded about and exploited. But they won't fight to save someone who doesn't pull his weight in the workplace, who's not there half the time they are, who won't help himself. And you know what? *I don't fucking blame them.*'

Vince was not smiling now.

'I have been ill,' he said. 'I've been physically ill and mentally depressed. All right, I accept I could have made a greater effort to come in sometimes. And I've been too flippant about it all. But that's because I find it hard to face up to...*things.*'

'No-one's saying you haven't been ill, Vince,' said Simon. 'Just that you've been taking too much advantage...and in obvious ways. Not coming in on Mondays, for example, after your Sealed Knot exertions. That's the problem with taking days off when you're not really sick. They accumulate and then when you're really sick, they take you over the top.'

'I mean for fuck's sake, Vince,' said Maloney. 'All you have to do if you're feeling a bit bruised or a bit *down* is come in for two hours. *Two hours.* That counts as a day's attendance. Moan and groan while you work, then say you're feeling bad and you need to go home.'

'Management have to take action if your sick leave reaches this level, Vince,' said Simon. 'It's their job. And there's always someone higher up breathing down their necks.'

Maloney cut back in.

'As for the lateness, I don't mind defending someone who's persistently late. It's a challenge, a test of my skills - especially when that person only lives a five minute stroll away. But I don't want to have to do it over and over again. I'd feel as if I were being punished.'

'Like being chained to someone else's vomit,' said Simon.

'What?'

'Nothing.'

78

'You know what this is like?' said Vince. 'Good cop, bad cop. You'll both end up as managers - I can sense it. That's what they do here with people who're a thorn in their side. Promote them.'

'You don't say,' said Simon. 'Well I've never heard that before.'

Maloney closed the file and tapped it on the table to straighten the paperwork inside.

'So you think I'm going to take promotion one day, do you?' His face had hardened even more. 'Let me tell you something. If I decided to give up on politics, if I decided that the idea of revolution is just a mirage, if I decided to settle down in this society and try to *better myself* and earn more money, d'you know what I'd do? I'd leave this place just like that.' He snapped his fingers. 'I'd go back to college and retrain. Too late for medicine - maybe law or social work. Something like that. The last thing I'd want to do is manage a bunch of wankers in a useless fucking parasitical institution like this. Is that clear?'

He stood up.

'We'll see you at two o'clock.'

Vince looked confused.

'Committee meeting to plan the strike. Meeting Room K.'

'Oh yeah. Right. I'll be there...'

'And don't overdo the teas breaks either.'

'This is facility time.'

Simon stood up too. He didn't want to be left with Vince.

'He didn't mean it. About the Institute.'

Vince's face was blank again.

'That's a great comfort,' he said.

Only five people were present at the start of the meeting that afternoon down in the warm secluded basement. Maloney, Simon, Bashir, Don Gable and Andy Appleton who was on a rare visit from Pine Street, the Institute's other main site.

'Where's Vince? Anyone seen Vince?' asked Maloney.

No-one had.

'Are we quorate?' asked Don Gable.

'We don't need to be quorate,' said Maloney. 'We're not making any decisions. This is an informal meeting to plan Wednesday's action.'

'Is Lesley coming?'

'I've had apologies from Lesley. But we don't need a minute taker - just someone to take basic notes. Can you do that, Simon?'

'I can do that, Tony.'

Maloney picked up a pile of A5 leaflets.

'These are just reminder leaflets calling for 100% support for the strike and maximum attendance on the picket line. I've already given some to Lesley, Vince and Marie. Could the rest of you get them out this afternoon.'

He gave out wodges of the leaflet.

'I've got official placards in the office which we'll be storing at Gordon Square as usual. Lesley will be there with the keys at 6.45 on Wednesday, as will Simon and myself, and we'll bring the placards round here. We need pickets in place from 7.00 am at both entrances. A minimum of six people to begin with - four at the front, two at the back. We can build up the numbers as more people arrive.'

'I come in from Dorking, Tony, as you know,' said Bashir. 'But I am setting two alarm clocks, my own and my son's Mickey Mouse clock which is very loud and which I will have to remove from his bedroom after he has fallen asleep. I should be here a few minutes before 7 o'clock.'

'Good man.'

'I'll be here before 7.00 - no trouble,' said Don.

'Good man. We've got the official leaflets to hand out on the day and Simon's going to bash out something pithier this afternoon to go with them. We could use some help tomorrow stapling the two together. Actually, Vince is meant to be staying late today and surreptitiously photocopying your leaflet, Simon. I hope I haven't pissed him off too much this morning.'

'This morning?' said Bashir. 'What happened this morning?'

'An in-confidence discussion about the need for him to get his act together after the final warning.'

'Oh yes, indeed. I hope they don't hold the strike day against him.'

'They can't count it. We'll wipe the floor with them if they try that. Anyway...as you know, the Society is supporting the strike. They usually get about 50% support from managers, of whom about 2% turn up on the picket line. Imogen will definitely be there, not sure about Chidebe. The Professionals are not supporting the strike. A National Committee decision. Although the cuts will hit research hard, they're not prepared to down tools. Or whatever they use. I think the local branch probably would have come out, so expect a lot of hand-wringing and embarrassment as they come in.'

'They have agreed not to do any of our jobs,' said Simon.

'Big of them, eh?' said Maloney. 'The revolution starts here.'

'I don't think they know how to,' said Bashir.

'Well they're not going to lower themselves to do our jobs,' said Don. 'In any case, no mail will get through.'

At that moment, the door swung open and Vince stood in the frame.

'Sorry I'm late, guys. My line management are getting heavy about facility time. They've allowed me half an hour.'

He stumbled over someone's bag and subsided into the nearest chair.

'Are they coming out on Wednesday?'

'Course not. They're going to try and keep the service running. I think the majority of photoprinters will be out though.'

'Good. They're about the closest we've got to industrial workers in this place.'

'It's difficult though, Tony. Like you've been saying, I have to keep my head down a bit given the trouble I'm in. I can't just go around looking like I'm stirring up the troops and not doing my job.'

'Just do what you're allowed to do. Distribute the leaflets-'

'Done that.'

'Talk to the members during tea breaks, make sure the material on the union notice board is up to date and so on.'

'We don't expect you to martyr yourself,' said Simon.

'*But* - I would like two things from you. One is to print out the branch leaflets when Simon's written the text...'

'That should be okay. Statham who's the real bastard is going at four thirty for a dental appointment. Veena who's the supervisor will turn a blind eye if she even notices...'

'Good. The other thing is to get here for seven am on Wednesday.'

Vince blew out air and slumped in his seat.

'I'll try, Tony. I'll try.'

'You're three minutes away. Bashir is coming in from Dorking. Two alarm clocks...'

'I've got two alarm clocks. What I need is an ejector bed.'

'We'll get coffees. There may even be sausage rolls...'

Vince fingered his cross again.

81

'There'll also be darkness and cold. I don't think I've ever seen seven am before.'

'I'll take that as a "Yes" then. Andy - what about Pine Street?'

Andy had been silent for most of the meeting but now shifted in his seat and came to life. In his late thirties, lean with prominent cheek bones, he wore a suit, shirt and tie as if still wedded to the idea that a clerk should look respectable. He cleared his throat and spoke carefully, hesitantly.

'Well I think we'll have about 75% out as usual' - he turned his narrow cufflinked wrist both ways to indicate *more or less* - 'and probably' - with a lift of the shoulders - 'a little less than 50% of the Society members. I think we had about 40% last time. I'm able to get in for seven o'clock as you know.'

He cleared his throat again.

'If you could get some placards on the van tomorrow, then I think Marcus the security guard will look after them for us and pass them out on the day. He's done that before. I'll get these leaflets out and hopefully all will be well.'

He concluded with what was probably meant to be a beaming smile.

'Okay, thanks Andy,' said Maloney who hadn't listened to a word.

'Hang on, hang on,' said Simon. 'What about the pickets?'

'Oh, we're never short of picketeers - is that the word?' Andy was warming up. 'The Indian ladies in particular are very conscientious about picket duty. It's almost a social thing for them. One or two bring fold-up chairs and knitting.'

'Wow, I didn't know that,' said Vince. 'Can I join *your* picket line?'

There was a gentle ripple of amusement around the table.

'Look,' said Maloney. 'I know people are still a bit battle-weary after last year, but this is an important *fight*. Not a social occasion. There'll be job losses if these cuts go through. We need to fight on our feet, not on our backsides. We need to be *active* on the picket lines, handing out leaflets, opposing would-be scabs, trying to turn back vehicles, exhorting people from other unions to put pressure on their leaderships and so on. We need to look as if we mean business.'

'I'm sure that's how people will respond on the day,' said Simon. 'Andy, can you at least ask your Indian ladies to picket properly until ten o'clock when everybody who's going in will have gone in.'

82

'Oh, absolutely. I didn't mean that they sit down as soon as they get there. Only later when most people will have entered the building. But that's what I meant to check. When are we picketing to?'

'We picket until the second post has been turned away. That's usually around eleven thirty.'

'When the pubs will be open,' said Vince.

'Don, how's your crowd?'

'Solid, Tony. Even Gloria who I know has had some financial problems - she'll be coming out. I don't think we'll see many of them on the picket line, though. Cynthia, maybe...'

'But we'll see you at seven, Don?'

'You certainly will, Simon. I've never been late for a picket line yet.'

'Excellent. So let's be clear,' said Maloney. 'Everyone around this table will be in on Monday by seven am - yes?'

There was a general murmuring of assent.

'That gives us six here with Lesley. Andy - you normally start with four, don't you?'

'Yes I should have at least three others at seven am.'

'OK, tomorrow, here in particular, we need to go around checking who else is turning up for the picket lines. And putting pressure on if necessary. Okay?'

There was a general nodding of heads.

That evening, Simon and Maloney hurried through the crowded streets of Central London to the Blind Horse - a cavernous pub deep in Soho with skull and skeleton transfers gleaming in its blacked-out windows. Inside, a model of a laughing jackass stood on the bar while a jukebox blasted out metal to a motley crowd of bohemians, market traders and sex addicts.

'Vince would love it here,' shouted Simon.

They bought drinks and began to thread their way into the interior, shielding their pint glasses against jostling bodies. At the rear, the crowd thinned out and the Left Caucus Committee came into view seated around a corner table and looking even more conspiratorial than usual as they leaned in towards each other to hear and be heard. Simon scanned the faces. Joe, Sandy Reed, full-time officer Paul Piper from Society HQ, veteran activist Albert Mullins, vague intellectual Tim Parrish and Mick McLeod from the Revolutionary Communist Current, dubbed 'the red hand gang' by Maloney.

83

'You're late,' said Sandy, her voice grinding through the hubbub.

'Sorry but who the fuck chose this place?' said Maloney as he and Simon slid into the seats reserved for them. McLeod tapped his chest and scowled defiantly.

'I like it,' he said.

'It's good for me too,' said Piper. 'No-one who knows me would ever come in here.'

'Gentlemen, we need to get started,' said Mullins. 'Sandy has been nominated and seconded as Chairperson.'

'Excellent.'

Sandy launched in.

'Comrades, I've no desire to hang around for very long in this place, being one of the few women here, so I'll be brisk.'

'Good start,' nodded Simon.

'Item One. Strength of support for Wednesday?'

They went round the table.

'Strong in the DE,' said Joe. 'I'd say 80-90%.'

'Good at the Institute,' said Maloney. 'Maybe 70-80%.'

'About the same in my place,' said Mullins. 'I get a feeling though from talking to other activists that the support is there, but not quite as strong as last year for the pay strikes. But people are starting to fear for their jobs...'

'I'd say we're going to get a majority out, but not enough to really frighten the fuckers,' said McLeod. 'That applies to my workplace and in general.'

'I *tend* to agree,' said Tim Parrish. 'And looking beyond this week, I'm not sure there's enough *anger* at the moment to *sustain* a long campaign against the cuts.'

'More anger would be good,' said Maloney. 'But what we really need is more *political* education of the rank and file - which of course won't come from the union leaderships. They don't want a serious fight over cuts and job losses, they just want to do deals. Members have got to be made to realise this before we can really get anywhere.'

'That's very important,' said Piper. 'In the meantime, we've got to be aware that even in your union, the mandate for militant action is not as strong as it was. As for the other unions, the Society is half-hearted about striking as usual and the Professionals just don't want to know. They prefer to go on talking. But things can change...'

'We've got to light the spark,' said McLeod. 'Once the spark is lit, things can move very fast as in 1917. *Iskra* - the spark!'

'Okay, okay,' said Sandy. 'At the moment, we don't have enough activists in the other unions to make much of a difference. All we can do is lead by example and if we're successful, the message should start to spread. In my-'

McLeod interrupted.

'That's all very vague. What's the definition of success?'

'Well, obviously, forcing the government to back down. If that's not going to happen, then we have the opportunity to provide a clear analysis of the failure and propose a remedy - an alternative to build on.'

'What's the situation in your department, Sandy?' asked Mullins.

'There's a bit less fight than last year, but we'll still get about 70% out. Look, overall I think we're agreed. There'll be a majority on strike, but there's still uncertainty at rank and file level, except maybe in the old left wing strongholds. So what are our next steps after Wednesday?'

'We carry on campaigning for No Cuts and further action,' said Joe. 'The NECs of both unions will look for concessions and compromise, but we must oppose that. The Broad Left will carry on calling for No Cuts but will be ready to do a deal - *the best deal we could get in the circumstances*, etc. The SWP will obviously campaign for No Cuts but won't ally themselves with us.'

'Correct,' said Maloney. 'But as Sandy said, that gives us a chance to make our own mark.'

'Exactly,' said McLeod. 'Who wants to end up fighting alongside the SWP anyway? Hacks and half-wits...'

'Concrete actions?'

'A leaflet after the strike? A public meeting? Attend any Broad Left and SWP meetings? Argue the case?'

'Okay, let's start with our own public meeting. Can we get a good public speaker?'

'Got to be someone from the NHS.'

'What they achieved and what they didn't. And why they didn't.'

'Lizzie? She's good when she gets going...'

'Lizzie might be willing. Actually, she knows a COHSE shop steward who's in their equivalent of the Left Caucus.'

'Can she contact him?'

'I think he's a she.'

'Sandy, I'm surprised at you,' said Mullins teasingly.

'It was a reasonable assumption.'

'Lizzie will get hold of her. I'll get hold of Lizzie.'

'Okay. Look, sorry but I'm going to have to go soon. This place is giving me a migraine. When do we meet again?'

'Well we need to respond fast to Wednesday's action. I'd say Wednesday afternoon.'

'Okay. Where? And let me just say - anywhere but here. There's a fight breaking out now from the sound of it.'

The music had stopped. A threatening cacophony of loud male voices, pounding footsteps and falling furniture came from the main bar area.

'East London for a change.'

'East London is too out of the way.'

'Let's just make it the Fountain,' said Maloney. 'Everyone should be able to get there. Two o'clock. I'll see if I can get the upstairs room.'

'We're not talking about a public meeting though.'

'I know but it'll be packed downstairs. All the regulars, plus strikers.'

'Okay. But please don't be pissed by the time the rest of us get there, comrades from the Institute.'

'As if,' said Simon.

'Okay, that's it.

Maloney was on his feet already with bag in hand and seemingly in an even greater rush than Sandy.

'Hang on!'

Simon grabbed his own bag, but knew he wasn't meant to catch up. He watched Maloney hurry away, skirting the crowd of spectators gathered around the fight. He saw a familiar figure slip off a bar stool and meet up with Maloney just before the door. Then the crowd parted to let a member of the bar staff escort a swaying youth with bloodied face towards the toilet. Simon stopped to watch and became aware of McLeod standing beside him.

'Well at least he hasn't got blood on the flag,' said Simon referring to the Union Jack embossed on the youth's sweatshirt.

'Flag!' McLeod spat the word out. 'The butcher's apron, that's what we call it. Drenched in blood. The blood shed by British imperialism. Rivers of it-'

86

'Yeah, see you...'

Simon pulled the door open and stepped out just in time to see Maloney and Lizzie bent forward in close conversation disappear around the corner. He stood somewhat at a loss in the narrow sidestreet and wondered if anyone was staying for a drink. McLeod would be - that was the problem. There was a pile of stinking rubbish bags outside the back door of a cafe, a puddle widening from a blocked drain, an alarm ringing somewhere, a siren howling over by Oxford Street. It was the start of the apocalypse, it was a normal evening. He sighed and set off for the tube.

6. The Great Day

The alarm clock woke Simon at five am, shattering a dream in which he was living back home with his parents. He struggled upright, pushed away the heavy blankets and swung his legs out to sit on the edge of the bed. The great day had arrived. Faint light from a street lamp filtered through the thin curtains and after a few moments of revery about the strike and about Molly who would still be asleep, he switched on the bedside light. It was not painfully cold but he pulled on the jersey that he wore over his t-shirt on winter mornings and crossed the room to light the gas fire. After that he yawned, prised some sticky stuff out of his eyes and looked at himself in the mirror. As usual, his hair stuck up and out in various directions.

A small flask of coffee made the night before stood on the table. He unscrewed the lid and poured some out. It was still hot but could be sipped and then gulped down. Feeling livelier, he took a towel from the back of a chair and went out into the hallway. Street light through the front door glass panes lit his way round the corner to the little bathroom where he peed and washed his hands and face. He also combed water through his hair and with fingertips arranged it in the usual manner. Moving on to the kitchen and squinting at first in the harsh electric light, he ate a bowl of cereal and made some toast while Jeanne - one of Anne-Marie's cats - purred and rubbed her black fur against his pyjama leg.

'I hope you're going to bring me good luck today,' he said softly. But Jeanne stalked back to her basket in the corner. Anne-Marie was the only person who could talk to her.

He took the toast to his room and ate it while standing before the mirror again, using more fingertip action to keep his drying hair on track. He dressed while finishing the coffee and then had to pad back to the bathroom for a comprehensive crap. After that, he felt ready to face the day. Just after six am, in black anorak, bescarfed and with rucksack full of leaflets, Simon locked the door of his room, pulled the front door quietly shut behind him and walked through the sepulchral streets of Stroud Green to the tube. The platform was sparsely populated and he shared a carriage with manual workers absorbed in tabloid trash and elderly black ladies holding bags on their knees.

At Russell Square tube, he went up in the lift and out into the dark again. On Woburn Place, the traffic was building up and exhaust fumes drifted through the chill air. He turned left into Tavistock Square, crossed the road and glanced to his right between bare trees. The bronze figure of Gandhi could be seen squatting on a plinth in the centre of the gardens. He crossed a junction and at Gordon Square turned right along the pavement past famous Bloomsbury homes to a house near the end where the Institute's accommodation service was hidden away. As he approached, Maloney and Lizzie came round the corner ahead and walked towards him side by side. He glanced at his watch. By some miracle, it was exactly six forty-five.

'Comrades!'

'Hi Simon, how are you?'

'Fine. I'm just amazed that we've got here on time.'

'Well we've had enough practice,' said Maloney.

'Are you here in support?'

'I am,' said Lizzie. 'Bringing my experience of front line struggle. Is Molly coming?'

'Nah, she has to go to work. I'm seeing her this evening.'

Maloney was looking down over the house railings into the area.

'Lesley will be in the basement, I expect. Let's go down.'

He tried the little gate and it opened. They went down the steps and Maloney pressed a small white button beside the basement door. There was no audible ring or buzz, but a light came on within and soon Lesley was pulling the door open.

'Come in for a minute,' she said.

They went into the lobby area which had whitewashed walls and a flagstone floor. A pile of strike placards was propped against a black metal door. Lesley led them forward through another door and then into a galley kitchen off the corridor. A large cloth bag stood on the work surface and she went through its contents.

'I've made two flasks of tea which will have to do until someone goes to the cafe. I've put sugar cubes in that bag for anyone who's not sweet enough. The flasks are mine - I want them back. The plastic cups are left over from last time. And there's a packet of biscuits out of the goodness of my heart.'

'Lesley, you're a true sister.'

'A medal with red ribbon will be presented later.'

90

'Thank you Simon, but the only reward I want is to get rid of this fucking government.'

Simon was impressed. He'd never heard Lesley swear before.

'This is Lizzie, by the way,' said Maloney.

The two women shook hands.

'Are you new to the Institute?'

'I'm a nurse, actually - at the Whittington. I was very active in the nurses' strike last year.'

'Oh, we came out on strike for that as well.'

'22nd September,' said Maloney.

'It was a great day,' said Lizzie. '150,000 people marched through Central London. We had loads of support from other unions like yours. But the union leaderships took fright and backed off. We ended up with an extra half per cent pay, a so-called Independent Review Body and a load of bullshit from Saint Margaret of Assisi. The NHS is safe in their hands. They're already talking about contracting out parts of it.'

'It was a partial victory,' said Maloney. 'Anyway we'd better go.'

'Okay, let me just make sure everything's in order here.'

Lesley pulled out the kettle plug, closed a cupboard door, then picked up the cloth bag and herded them back into the lobby again. Maloney looked at the black metal door with interest as they picked up the strike placards.

'Where does this lead to?'

'It's a store room that goes under the pavement. All the houses along here have them apparently.'

'Wow,' said Simon. 'Are you sure it doesn't lead to a secret tunnel?'

'It's very well concealed if there is one.'

'Or maybe to a bomb-proof shelter? Or the old British Museum tube station?'

'No, sorry. I think it was probably a large pantry. This would have been the kitchen and scullery area where the maids and servants worked. The Downstairs as opposed to the Upstairs.'

'What's in there now?' asked Maloney.

'All sorts. Spare furniture, light tubes, electric fires, trolleys - you name it. In fact there's even a few racks of wine bottles that we send over to the main building for Board dinners and the like.'

'Really? Why don't we liberate a bottle. Or two.'

'No way. Arthur would notice even one bottle. He orders the wine in the first place, he chooses the bottles that go over there and he knows exactly what's in stock.'

'Who's he - your boss?' asked Lizzie.

Lesley nodded.

'He's the Chief Accommodation Officer. Actually he's on the branch committee of the managers' union. In fact he was Branch Secretary once upon a time.'

'So we'll meet him on the picket line then?'

'I doubt it. He's on holiday.'

'He saw the strike coming,' said Simon.

'He booked it months ago. He's in Spain with his - well, I'll say no more.'

'A man of fluid principles in my experience,' said Maloney. 'Come on, we don't want to be late for our own picket.'

They shuffled out into the basement area.

'I'm going to lock this door, then go upstairs, set the alarm and exit via the front door,' said Lesley. 'No-one is getting in here today.'

'Excellent.'

Bashir and Don Gable were waiting for them outside the Institute. Regular guys in overcoats and scarves, they were transformed into union agitators the moment they took hold of the placards. Behind them, a dozen steps led up to the main doors of the Institute which had just been unlocked by a shadowy figure within.

'Who was that?'

'Gromwell, I think.'

'Bastard.'

'Are we standing on the steps, Tony, or not?'

'We're standing just in front of the steps.'

'But leaving a gap - yes?'

'Leaving a gap, but not a very encouraging gap. We need to impose ourselves on people approaching the building.'

'Okay.'

'Shit. I know what I've forgotten,' said Maloney as he spread out the placards. 'String! I want to tie some of these to the railings, that lamp post, that tree. Establish our presence. Nobody's going to cross this picket line without knowing it.'

'Well I'll get some,' said Lizzie. 'A newsagent would sell it, wouldn't they? Or a stationer?'

'There's a place near Russell Square tube. But let's wait till more people arrive. Simon and Don - you need to get round the back, pronto. I'll send reinforcements as soon as I can.'

'Okay, guv. Come on Don, my son.'

'Your son? I'm old enough to be your father.'

'Grandfather, even.'

'They picked up some placards and began their walk around the block to the Institute's unsightly backside.

'Were you here extra early then, Don?'

'I could have been, but I got a lift in with a mate of mine who's a cabbie. He lives on the same estate as me and we stopped off at the cabman's shelter in Russell Square for a cuppa.'

'Oh right.'

'So I got here about quarter to and Bashir turned up five minutes later. All the way from Dorking - remarkable.'

'Yeah, he's done well, you've done well.'

'Well I only live in Lambeth.'

'Look, it's starting to get ever so slightly lighter.'

Don looked at his watch and up at the sky.

'Yes, we're passing from nautical twilight to civil twilight.'

'Twilight? I thought that was only in the evening?'

'Nah, we get it in the morning too. I was in the Merchant Navy many years ago and learnt all about it. At the end of the night, we have astronomical twilight, then nautical twilight, then civil twilight. At the end of the day, it's the reverse. It takes quite a while to get from darkness to light.'

'You're a fount of knowledge, Don.'

They turned the corner and walked along to the vehicle entrance, a narrow cul-de-sac between a block of flats and a featureless office building. It served only the Institute and could therefore be blockaded. A few yards into it stood a small glass-fronted kiosk from which the barrier was operated. Don spread out the placards and positioned himself in the centre of the roadway with the confidence of a picket line veteran. Simon went to have a few words with the security guard, a dapper individual who looked out warily from the kiosk.

'Hello, mate. Strike action today.'

93

'Yes, sir. I've been informed.'

'We'll be stopping the Royal Mail and anything else that tries to come in. You should have a quiet day.'

'Right, sir.'

'Unless you want to join us, of course?'

The guard looked at Simon with a touch of colour in his chalky cheeks.

'It's not too late. I can sign you up to the union and then you'll be protected.'

'I can't do that, sir. I have a wife and children to support.'

'Well so do a lot of the people who're striking. They're not doing it for fun. Their jobs are at risk and then they won't be able to support their families at all.'

There was a rigid silence.

'Well, if you change your mind, let me know. Or let Don there know. You know Don, don't you?'

'Yes, sir.'

Simon walked back to the entrance.

'It could only happen in Bloomsbury.

'What's that?'

'A far left strike leader is addressed as "Sir".'

Don chuckled.

'Make the most of it, Simon.'

'I hate it.'

It was quiet for the first hour. Simon skimmed through Don's *Daily Mirror* and found a short piece about the strike ("Public Servants Take On Maggie") on page 6. Around seven thirty, they were joined by two more strikers and it began to feel like a proper picket line. They turned away a couple of vans, though another driver went through with the usual "jobsworth" excuse. They hassled a middle manager whose cheeks flushed pink as he strode between them.

'Bit early for you, isn't it?'

'You're not supposed to enter the building this way!'

'Your union's supporting this strike!'

'Happy to put people out of jobs, are you?'

At eight o'clock, the Royal Mail van arrived and after a brief exchange through a lowered window, the driver pulled away to applause.

'Red is the colour! Let's have a chant!'

94

'No ifs! No buts! No more public spending cuts!'
They repeated this several times. It felt rather foolish in the quiet side street. One or two passers-by looked around and a pair of pigeons shifted away. Then a driver honked his horn and Simon roused them to another chorus.

'Come on! If we're going to picket, let's picket!'
'No ifs! No buts! No more public spending cuts!'
They repeated this several times, banging their placard sticks on the ground until telepathy or self-consciousness told them to stop. Simon tried to improvise another chant.

'If me no ifs!. But me no buts! You know what you can do with your...spending cuts! Hmm...maybe not.'

He had substituted the word 'spending' for 'fucking' out of respect for Daffy, one of the other picketers who he knew to be some kind of Christian socialist and an habitual wincer at the use of coarse language. She nodded her head.

'Maybe not, Simon. How about...Maggie Thatcher, job snatcher. No...Maggie Thatcher, hear us say...please don't take our jobs away.'

'Please?' said Simon. '*Please*? You think we should beg?'

'Maggie Thatcher, milk snatcher, throw her up and catch her - they used to say,' said Don.

'Throw her up and drop her - more like.'

'I don't think I could bring myself to touch her,' said Daffy with a shudder.

'Okay, let's go with - Maggie Thatcher, hear us say, don't take our jobs away.'

They chanted it a couple of times, then stopped.

'Maybe not,' said Simon. 'And you were still saying *please*.'

'Sorry,' said Daffy. 'I just can't help it.'

At eight twenty, Lesley appeared with two more people for the picket line. She left a flask and some plastic cups before returning to the 'front line'. By eight forty five, they'd turned away a courier, a food supplier for the canteen ('there's no-one in to eat anything') and a photocopier engineer. A few minutes later, a sharp-suited blonde guy came out through the back door of the building and strode confidently down the access road towards them.

'Hi,' he said with a knowing smile. 'I'm Adam from PR. How's it going?'

'Great,' said Lee, a lanky young Liverpudlian who worked with Don in the Post Room. 'Why don't you join us?'

'Oh, my union's not involved in the strike. Listen, I appreciate what you're doing, but we've got a *really* important delivery coming around ten o'clock.'

'Oh, that's good 'cos we'll still be here.'

'Right. But I'd appreciate it if you could just let this one through because it's really important for the Institute.'

'Is it coming in an ambulance?' asked Simon.

'Sorry?'

'Or a fire engine? Because those are the only vehicles we'll let through.'

'It's coming in a taxi. Six boxes. The security guard has got the details.'

'Sorry then, but no. This is not a game and we don't take special requests. We're on strike.'

'But this is ridiculous,' said Adam. 'I'm making a perfectly reasonable request. This is documentation that we need to have today for our Board and ultimately for the government.'

'Perfect,' said Simon. 'If it's for the government, there's no way we'll let it through. We're fighting against government cuts that will affect people's livelihoods and throw people out of jobs.'

Lee nudged his elbow and Simon turned around to see Maloney walking towards them.

'What's going on?'

Simon nodded at the PR man.

'This is Adam from Public Relations. He's not very happy.'

'The Chief Executive won't be very happy. The government cuts are not the Institute's fault and we're losing precious time.'

'He wants us to let a delivery through so they can provide information to the government.'

'You're joking,' said Maloney. 'This is a strike *against* the government. It's *meant* to disrupt your activities - and theirs. That's the whole point of it. Besides, you've had enough notice.'

'This is outrageous.'

'No it isn't. We're operating within the law and fully entitled to do what we're doing. Look...' Maloney raised the camera he was holding. 'I came to take a photograph. You can be in it if you like.'

Adam the PR man strode away.

96

'Prick. Where did they get him from?'

'I've never seen him before. He can't have been here for long.'

'Well that's obvious. He's wet behind the ears. All he's got to do is tell whoever's delivering whatever-it-is to come back at lunchtime.'

'Or just tell us to piss off and drive straight through.'

'Young Lee, I expect better of you than that.'

'They shall not pass,' said Simon.

'I expect you to at least lie down in the road.'

'I'd better look my best then,' said Lee as Maloney lined up the six of them in front of the barrier. 'This could be my last photograph...'

He raised his fist as did Simon. The others clutched their placards. And the low winter sun found a gap between buildings as Maloney pressed the button.

'Right, Simon - I need to show my face at Pine Street. You need to come round to the front and take over there. Don - I'm leaving you in charge here. Don't not do anything I would have done.'

And leaving Don to think about that, Maloney and Simon set off around the block again.

'We've got about 20 people at the front including a few Society members.'

'Has Vince turned up?'

'Yeah, about half an hour ago. I gave him a mild bollocking but he wasn't very happy about it. Seems to think he's made a heroic effort getting here for eight thirty.'

'He's not that useful as a picket anyway.'

'He fills a gap and he can look quite offputting. Lizzie and Lesley - or should I say Liz and Les? - have gone to get some bacon rolls by the way. I asked them to get you one.'

'Thanks. I'm salivating already.'

'See, I do think about you. Sometimes...'

'I know. It's worrying.'

The scene outside the Institute had changed considerably since seven am. As Maloney had said, about twenty people were spread across the pavement in front of the building. Some were talking in twos and threes, others stood firmly before the steps gripping placards with the *No Ifs, No Buts* message. More placards were tied to the railings for several feet on either side of the steps. It looked so impressive that Simon began to feel nervous at being in charge. He greeted a few people and raised his fist to salute Matt who stood

97

with a small group of Society pickets. Imogen, their bustling Branch Secretary, came over to speak to him. Would she mind if he started giving orders?

'How's it going?'

'Very well, Simon. It's a good turnout as you can see. We've stopped a few people who would have gone in otherwise.'

'Excellent. And the placards look good.'

Matt had joined them too.

'Hah!' he said. 'You missed the fun. Kenworthy told us to take the placards off the railings. *Defacing the Institute* he said. Gromwell came out to protect him.'

'So you took no notice?'

'Well, we started to take them down because technically the railings are part of the Institute building,' said Imogen. 'But as soon as they'd gone inside, we stopped. Or rather, we decided to leave it for a while. I think one or two became re-attached somehow...'

'Kenworthy's the biggest creep going,' said Simon. 'He was active in our union as a spotty young clerk. He was even a Conference delegate sometime around 1953.'

'He's still one of our members,' said Imogen.

'I bet that's where Bull gets his information from. Anyway, what about the people? The masses?' Simon gestured at one or two passers-by. 'Have they said anything?'

'Some have wished us luck, some have scowled, most have been non-committal really. A few cars honked their horns. Oh and one man wound his window down and shouted *Your tea's getting cold.*'

'Quite funny really,' said Matt.

'Photograph!' shouted Maloney. He stood on the kerb waving an arm and the pickets massed dutifully in front of the steps.

'Vince!' he called.

Simon looked round. Vince was standing to one side, a placard held loosely in one hand as if he was looking after it for someone else. He shook his head morosely but firmly.

'I'm worried about Vince,' said Marie.

Maloney concentrated on the photo.

'Altogether now - no squeeze, no freeze.'

Most of the people there had been through this before and chanted out the mouth-stretching phrase.

'Now one with me in it. Who'll?...Simon, can you take it?'

98

Simon went forward and took the camera.

'Button on the right!' called Maloney as he inserted himself in the midst of the strikers. 'Hang on! Here's Lizzie and Lesley. Put the bacon rolls somewhere out of sight.'

They put two boxes on the pavement next to Simon and joined the throng. Simon looked through the viewfinder and pressed the button.

'One more for good luck!' he cried unsure whether it had worked the first time.

'Wait a minute,' called Marie. 'Vince! Come on, join in. Just for me.'

Vince stirred hesitantly.

'Bacon rolls, Vince!' shouted Maloney. 'Hmm...smell them. Bacon rolls!'

Vince plodded forward red-faced and muttering under his breath to stand at the back of the group, barely visible in the viewfinder.

'Good boy,' said Marie.

Simon pressed the button again but they still weren't finished.

'Here's Chidebe,' someone said. 'He'll want to be in it.'

Simon looked to his left and saw Chidebe's familiar bulk moving along the pavement towards them. He appeared tense. Underneath his overcoat, he wore a suit, shirt and tie and under his arm carried an envelope briefcase. The idea flashed through Simon's mind that maybe Chidebe was dressed so formally to make a point like the clerk who turned up on Whitehall picket lines in a pinstripe suit with bowler hat and brolly. But really he knew what was going to happen.

'Hello Chidebe. Are you joining us?' called Imogen in her singsong voice. 'You're just in time for a photograph.'

'No, no. I can't.' He shook his head forcefully without looking at her.

'But we've talked about it, Chidebe,' she said coaxingly, dropping her voice, moving towards him. 'Surely-'

'No, no. I have to go in.'

Two or three pickets were also turning towards him, but Chidebe brushed between them and began to climb the steps.

'Quick, give me the camera,' said Maloney. 'Imogen - call his name again!'

Imogen's call was almost a wail and Chidebe turned around. When he saw Maloney pointing the camera at him, his face filled with disgust. He was at the top of the steps by now and he turned back, pushed his way through the doors and disappeared into the building.

'Got him,' said Maloney. 'Chief scab so far.'

Imogen was clearly struggling to control her emotions.

'Tony, it does no good to react like that. It just makes matters worse.'

'He is what he is. A union officer who's crossed his own workplace picket line. That's the ultimate example of scabbing.'

'I know him far better than you, Tony. I've had long conversations with him over the last couple of weeks. He's torn... He has a deep-rooted belief in justice and fairness but he doesn't really believe in strike action. He came out last year, but he wasn't happy. I think he believes it diminishes him as a person of honour-'

'Ridiculous. Every worker is entitled to withdraw his labour and the decision to strike was taken in a democratic manner. He's being dishonourable in going against it.'

'And he's got a wife and small children and relatives in Nigeria to support.'

'Lots of strikers have got family responsibilities. They're losing money because of their beliefs and he just walks in...'

'You don't understand how sad this is, Tony. I really thought I'd got through to him. I thought he'd at least respect my personal plea. It makes things very difficult.'

Maloney shrugged.

'Not really. Just tell him that for obvious reasons he can't continue as a Branch Officer. If he's really so honourable, he'll resign anyway. If he doesn't, call a Branch meeting and move a motion of no confidence.'

Imogen bristled.

'Of course, I'll do that. Don't teach me how to suck eggs. In the meantime, please don't go around showing everyone that photograph and humiliating him.'

Maloney paused.

'I'll give you the photograph when I've had them developed. You can decide what to do with it.'

'I'll tear it up. The image in my head is quite enough.'

Some of the pickets began to vent their own feelings about Chidebe. Maloney left Imogen to talk to them and took Simon to one side.

'I've got to go. You're in charge, but don't get carried away. It'll more or less run itself from now on.'

'What's Imogen's role?'

'Second-in-command. We have far more pickets than they do. I'll be back by half ten.'

He went over to Lizzie who was taking the bacon roll box around. After a few words, he took a roll and strode away along the pavement. Simon watched as he stepped straight onto a zebra crossing and brought two cars to an abrupt halt.

'He'll try walking on water next,' said Lizzie who'd also been watching him. 'Here, I've saved you a roll.'

'Thanks. How's it going?'

'What - the strike?'

'No - you and Tony.'

Lizzie grimaced. They moved away a little from the picket line.

'Well...nowhere really. You probably know the story. Everybody else seems to. She suspected he was having an affair. He decided to be honest and told her he was. She told him to leave, then just days later found out she's pregnant. Now he wants to go back to her, assuming she'll have him which she probably will, rather than be a single parent...and that's about it. Very petty-bourgeois...as Tony would say.'

Simon thought back to his conversation with Maloney earlier in the week.

'He wants to go back for the birth of his baby, but that's not for another three months.'

'Well he can't just go back when the baby's due and say "Here I am" - can he? Wanda will tell him to fuck off again if she's got any spirit. He needs to go back soon and try to make it work.'

'I got the impression that it's the idea of having a family that attracts him, rather than the idea of going back to Wanda.'

'I don't think he knows what he wants to do. I also don't know what contribution he's going to make to a family when he's virtually a full time revolutionary.'

'So what do *you* want him to do?'

'Oh, go back. Show some responsibility, I suppose. The glow's worn off a little for me anyway since I've got to know him. I'm still attracted to him but I need to move on. I'm not going to be his bit on the side and I don't want to get blamed for breaking up a family before it's even started.'

'Hmm...tough.'

'Not really. It's just that I still love the bastard, that's all-'

'But you just said-'

'I know, I know. But I'll get over it. How's it going with Molly, anyway?'

Simon shrugged.

'Okay...I don't think she's as keen on me as she was. But it's still going...'

'Are you as keen on her?'

He nodded.

'Well I hope it works out, Simon. I sometimes think I should have found someone by now. But then I think - well...you either have to take someone who's not quite what you're looking for, or forget it. Just live day by day. A woman should be sufficient unto herself.'

'Right on, sister. You're Lizzie Keaton. We expect you to be bold and strong.'

'Well I'll do my best, Simon. But I'm not accountable to you and your comrades. If I want to change my mind and settle down with Mr Almost Right, I'll do that.'

'Yep. It's your funeral.'

Lizzie smiled.

'Oh, Simon. Tony was right - you're such a cynic. Listen, I'm going to introduce myself to Imogen. See you later.'

Simon finished his bacon roll and wandered amongst the troops, stopping for a few words here, a few words there. It was just after 9.30 and most of the staff arriving now were members of the Alliance of Professional Public Servants if they belonged to any union. Here was one who, as Maloney had predicted, greeted the pickets with a pained look of regret that he couldn't stand alongside them. Here was another who patted a picket's shoulder and commended him before going up the steps. Here was an APPS committee member who stopped to talk confidentially with Imogen and laughed at something Lizzie said. Every minute or so, someone else came along and Simon observed the facial expressions: irritation, grim-faced determination, patronising cheeriness, superiority, businesslike breeziness, sheepish guilt...all provoked by the picket line.

102

At 9.45 or thereabouts, Gromwell appeared at the top of the steps, his shoes clicking on the marble. An ex-military man, his uniform now was a sleek iron-grey suit. Without descending to the rabble, he issued the instruction once again: the placards must be removed from the railings. No-one moved. Someone belched loudly. Simon had the strong impression it was Vince.

'Who is in charge of this picket line?' Gromwell bellowed. It was not really a question but a demand. Simon strolled forward as casually as he could, given the tension in his guts.

'Why?'

His voice sounded dry and weak. Gromwell replied as if addressing a village idiot who'd volunteered to be cannon fodder.

'Are you in charge of this picket line?'

But another voice answered from Simon's side, a quieter voice which still cut through the sounds of the street.

'We both are, Herbert,' said Imogen. 'What is your problem?'

Herbert! This was one of the advantages of being a manager. You had the right and confidence to address fellow managers by their first names and bring them down to earth. Such an appropriate name too. Gromwell blinked.

'It's not *my* problem, Miss Garrett. It is the *Institute's* problem.'

He indicated the building behind him with a wave of the hand in case they hadn't seen it before. His voice had softened slightly.

'It's not *Miss* Garrett, Herbert. It's *Ms*. And in any case, you normally address me as Imogen.'

'*Ms* Garrett. *Imogen*,' said Gromwell, pronouncing both names as formally as he could. 'I'm surprised, I have to say, that someone of your position cannot see the problem. The placards are likely to damage the railings, but more importantly they can damage the reputation of the Institute.'

'Oh, Herbert - don't be silly,' said Imogen. 'The placards are not going to damage the railings. We've been very careful in how we've attached them. And you can't seriously be suggesting that a few placards are going to damage the good name of the Institute?'

'The cuts will do far more damage,' said Simon who felt stronger now.

'Exactly,' said Imogen.

'Ms Garrett. Imogen. I'm not going to stand here arguing with you. I have my instructions. And if you refuse to instruct your staff - I'm

103

sorry, I mean your *pickets* - to remove the placards, I will have to get my security staff to do so.'

'I wouldn't do that if I were you, Herbert,' said Imogen. 'Any such action will be met with passive resistance by the pickets. Do you understand what passive resistance is? It means we will stand *peacefully* in the way and prevent your staff from reaching the placards unless of course they choose to manhandle us. Have you trained them in how to deal with passive resistance? I should add that we have a camera...'

'Imogen,' said Gromwell. 'Could I have a quiet word with you?'

He made a hand-signal as if expecting her to mount the steps towards him. Imogen stayed where she was.

'Herbert - I am on strike. Anything you wish to say to me must be said to all of us.'

She looked around at the pickets and there was clapping and cheering in response. Those who held placards lifted them in the air and someone shouted "One for all and all for one!" This time, Simon knew it was Vince.

'Then I have no option but to report your words to Mr Bull.'

And turning on his heel, Gromwell walked back into the building.

'Thanks, Imogen,' said Simon.

Imogen blew air out of her lungs, stirring the black curls that hung over her forehead.

'I'm not sure what we should do next though.'

The pavement was abuzz with debate and some of the pickets came up to praise her. When things had settled a little, she turned back to Simon.

'I made up that stuff about passive resistance. I saw *Gandhi* the film last month - I suppose that's what made me think of it. But I don't know if people would want to do that. If they were denying our right to picket, that would be different.'

'Oh, I'm sure enough people would be up for it, but we haven't got the camera. Tony took it with him.'

'Well they don't know that.'

'No, but that's the only real leverage we've got. The threat of us taking photographs of them pushing people around.'

'Hmm. A little voice has started up inside me though, saying perhaps I went too far. Herbert is so irritating when he gets on his high horse. I'll go and talk to my members.'

Simon did the same and got a mixed response.

'I am an admirer of Gandhi, even though he opposed partition,' said Bashir. 'Passive resistance can be a very powerful thing. But in this case, Simon, what is it for? What will it achieve? Management are in the right, really. It's their property.'

'I noticed his statue this morning on my way in,' said Simon. 'As if it were a premonition almost. You know - in Tavistock Square?'

'I know. I sit there sometimes in my lunch break.'

'It's not meant to be some highly-principled thing in our case. Just a bit of provocation.'

Bashir looked unimpressed.

'I admire the way Imogen stood up to Gromwell, but I was surprised when she came out with that. I'll tell you what Gandhi would have said. He would have said: let them have their railings!'

Lesley was in favour, Marie against. The pattern repeated itself as Simon went round talking to others. A glance across at Imogen's little group of Society members told him they were not enthused. Reluctantly, he walked over to Vince who was pacing the pavement away from everyone else, his eyes cast gloomily downward. He stopped and sighed at Simon's question.

'Normally, I'd be willing. And I've got the experience, I suppose. You get pushed around a lot in the Sealed Knot. It's just, you know, in my present disciplinary situation...'

'They're not going to discipline anyone over this. There'd be massive opposition. They'll just move us out of the way.'

'Perhaps I could just loiter in the vicinity and get accidentally caught up in it. Then I could sue them for assault...'

Simon turned away, then turned back.

'Are you all right, Vince?'

Vince was about to start pacing again.

'Yeah, yeah. Right as rain...'

Maloney returned and was briefed by Simon and Imogen. His face showed little reaction and there was no time for further discussion.

'Let's see how it goes,' he muttered as Bull appeared at the top of the steps.

Stocky but short, clad in a dark blue pinstripe suit, the Director of Administration stood silently at first, looking down at the messy gathering before him. Perhaps it was the high cheekbones and the pinched nose, but his face seemed to express contempt even when technically expressionless. He spoke with exaggerated formal courtesy.

'Imogen. Tony. Do you think I could have a word?'

He stood there alone, but the figure of Gromwell hovered behind the glass doors.

'Sure, Mr Bull, but we can't cross the picket line.'

Maloney gestured to the invisible line in front of him where pickets had left a gap at the foot of the steps. Imogen moved to stand on one side of him, Simon stood on the other.

'I see,' said Bull. The closely-shaven cheeks twitched, the nostrils flared slightly. But his descent of the steps was done with dignity and left his expression of superiority intact. He stopped at eye level with Maloney. Some of the pickets formed a semi-circle around their leaders.

'No-one denies your legal right to picket the Institute in pursuance of your campaign,' Bull began. His brown eyes were fixed mainly on Maloney with occasional side glances at the others. 'However, by attaching your placards to our front railings, they have in essence become part of the building fabric. Furthermore, your action may well be interpreted by the public and the media as suggesting that the Institute supports this campaign.'

'Nonsense,' said Maloney.

'Which of course, it does not. I would therefore like the placards removed. Without delay.'

'The placards are doing no harm whatsoever, either to the railings or to the Institute. No-one is stupid enough - not even the media - to think that the Institute would have put them there itself.'

'Exactly,' said Imogen. Bull gave a cursory snort.

'The inference, as you well know, is not that the Institute itself put them there. That would indeed be absurd. The inference is that by ignoring this trespass, the Institute tacitly supports the strike. If you are refusing to remove the placards, then I will arrange for security staff to remove them - passive resistance or no passive resistance.'

A faint blush rose on Imogen's cheeks.

'Well that will just about get everyone's backs up, Mr Bull,' she said. Not even Imogen used his forename.

106

'I also consider it quite reasonable to consider disciplinary action against the pair of you, and Mr Hayes here, for taking action that is detrimental to the interests and reputation of the Institute.'

'Naturally, that will escalate the situation,' said Maloney. 'Which is fine by me.'

'As I'm sure you know, Tony, I carry out my duty to the end. I have never yet been dissuaded by the threats of a trade union official.'

'*We* are carrying out *our* duty, as elected trade union officers on behalf of our members, to try and publicise our action as widely as possible. The suggestion that our placards will damage the Institute's reputation is just...' Maloney groped for an acceptable word - '...*hooey*. A flimsy excuse to try and divide and weaken us. It won't work.'

A glimmer of amusement appeared in Bull's eyes.

'Very well. We shall see.'

He turned and mounted the steps. Some of the pickets started cheering and from their outer fringe came the cry: *No ifs! No buts! No public spending cuts!* Vince again. The chant began to spread, but once Bull had gone inside the building, Maloney shushed them.

'Hang on! Whoah! Listen... We've taken this about as far as it can go. We've pissed them off and made our presence felt. Now let's start untying the placards before security come out.'

'What?'

'There's no point in giving them an excuse to take disciplinary action. We're walking into a trap. Headquarters won't support us. They'll sell us out. Take the placards down and hold on to them. When security come marching out, we can set up a chant and bang the handles on the ground. Mock them...'

'Good idea,' said Imogen with discernible relief in her voice.

'When they go back in, we can ever so gently *lean* the placards against the railings. Same effect...come on.'

Maloney and Imogen led the way and enough pickets joined in to make quick work of untying the nine or ten placards along the railings. Simon helped hand them out. Lizzie stood watching them with the camera in her hands.

'Here, you'd better have this back before I get some stupid idea about being a photographer.'

Maloney took it.

'I hope you captured the Great Confrontation?'

'Well I got you all in the frame.'
'I hope it shows my complete contempt for Bull?'
'We can draw horns on him when we get the print,' said Simon.
Lizzie smiled.
'You might not need to,' she said.

7. Pub Talk

Lesley bought the first round in the Fountain.

'I don't think I've ever been in a pub this early before,' she said.

The landlord nodded at the clock on the wall.

'It could be said that you're 45 minutes late, because that's when the sun passes the yardarm. In this part of the world at least. That's why pubs open at 11.00 am, see?'

Simon, who was standing with Lesley at the bar, thought this was the longest speech he'd heard the landlord make. Three consecutive sentences, one containing a subordinate clause. He was tempted to tell him about astronomical, nautical and civil twilight, but thought better of it.

'Oh, right,' he said.

They took the drinks to a table shared with Maloney and Lizzie. Imogen and two other managers sat at the next table with Matt on a stool in between.

'Facing both ways you face neither way,' said Simon. 'Ancient Chinese proverb.'

'I face the middle way,' said Matt. 'Cheers!'

Lesley glanced across at some of the other pickets who were sitting at a corner table.

'I thought Vince might come, but I lost track of him.'

'He just sloped off, I think,' said Simon. 'He was miserable all morning.'

'He did perk up a bit when we sang *Little White Bull*.'

'We must be the only pickets in the country to have sung that,' said Simon. 'In fact, the only pickets in the entire history of the labour movement.'

'I'm not happy about the way Bull left those two security guards on the pavement,' said Maloney. 'As if they were policing us...'

'Well, they were,' said Matt. 'Unfortunately, Bull isn't stupid. He must have guessed that the placards might reappear...'

'It was interference. In fact, it would have been intimidation if there'd been fewer pickets.'

'Don said only three drivers went through at the back during the whole morning,' said Simon.

'You had an effect,' said Lizzie. 'No-one in that building could have been in any doubt there was a strike going on.'

109

'Sure, but will it win anybody over? I doubt it,' said Matt. The tide's turning unfortunately - in Thatcher's favour.'

'Your needle's stuck,' said Maloney.

'Yeah, let's just give up,' said Lizzie. Let's just get drunk and go home and watch television. Let's just put our headphones on and listen to the latest sounds from the rock factory.'

Matt laughed.

'Well we've always done that, anyway.'

'She's not going to win another election,' said Maloney. 'I don't care what the opinion polls say. People are not stupid enough to vote her back in.'

'I hope the polls are wrong too, but that seems to be the way it's going.'

'Gloom monger!' said Simon. 'Cynic!'

'I have to agree with you, Matt,' said Lesley. 'I'm ready to carry on fighting, but I have a horrible feeling she'll get back in. The economy does seem to be improving. She'll be telling us we've never had it so good soon.'

'And we're *Great* Britain again after the Falklands victory.'

'That's wearing off,' said Maloney. 'As for the economy, it could go anywhere. It'll be even more unstable now they're going for a full-blown free market system.'

'All it has to do is stay on the up until after the next election.'

'Which could be anytime between now and May next year,' said Simon. 'Tony's right - anything could happen in that time.'

'She'll call an election well before then.'

'Are all the people she's thrown out of a job going to vote for her?' said Lizzie. 'The three million unemployed - are they going to say "Thanks, Maggie, here's our vote?" I don't think so. If she gets back in, it'll only be because the fucking SDP will split the vote.'

'The SDP are right wing labour, so they'll take some support away,' said Matt. 'But Labour will lose support because of other things. Michael Foot to begin with. He's got all the right policies, but he's not very persuasive because he's not remotely working class or "man of the people" or whatever you want to call it. Then there's the economy, the patriotism factor and specific Tory policies like the right to buy your house. How many working class votes will switch to Thatcher because of that?'

'Not many,' said Maloney. 'People may admire some of the things that Thatcher has done, but it won't last. Deep down, they don't like her or trust her. Churchill was seen as having won the war - a world war, not a minor skirmish like the Falklands - but the electorate still kicked him out in '45. Lizzie's right - a lot of people have been shat on by the Tories.'

'I think it will be close,' said Lesley. 'But I think they'll scrape back in. Thatcher's conning people and that won't last, but it's working at the moment. Anyway, where's the cuts campaign going to go now?'

'Up a familiar creek,' said Simon.

'Compromise Creek,' said Maloney. 'It depends how many came out today across the country, but eventually the cuts will be scaled down a bit and the union bureaucrats will claim some sort of victory. They're not fighting to win, to defeat the bosses. They're fighting to get the best deal.'

'That's capitalism,' said Lizzie. 'Wheeling and dealing. And the union leaders join in.'

'Unfortunately, the masses don't care,' said Matt. 'The best deal is all they want. They don't want a general strike, they don't want a revolution.'

'That's because they're misled.'

'The Tories will soften their approach for a while and the masses will vote them back in. Maggie's restored our military pride and the economy's on the mend.'

'I hope you're playing devil's advocate.'

Matt shrugged.

'I don't want it to happen, but at what point do we face reality?'

'It's not *going* to happen,' said Maloney. 'And I say that when part of me almost wants a Labour defeat because basically they're propping up a rotten system, even with Foot's so-called radical leadership. If the Tories get back in, they'll turn on the working class and the unions and the welfare state like never before. And the more that goes on, the more likely the working class is to revolt properly.'

'I admire your optimism,' said Matt. 'I just don't trust it.'

'You just don't trust the working class any more. That's your problem.'

'Guys, let's not fall out over it,' said Lesley. 'We've done our bit for now. Relax.'

111

'Lesley, the revolution awaits,' said Simon. 'The revolution is desperately needed. We can never relax until it's won.'

'I'll relax for a while with my fellow managers,' said Matt. And he swivelled round on his stool to face Imogen's table.

Maloney tapped his fingers on the tabletop and hummed. Lizzie sipped from her glass and looked away. Lesley looked at each of them in turn. Simon raised his eyebrows. Apart from politics, what could they talk about?

'Is it something I said?' said Lesley.

Maloney smiled.

'No, no.' He tapped his fingers again. 'Excuse me a minute. I just have to go and make a phone call.'

He got up and threaded his way out of sight to the other end of the pub.

'Is Tony all right? He did seem a bit distracted at times this morning.'

'Yeah, I think so,' said Simon. 'Probably just a lot going on.'

'What did you think about our little strike then, Lizzie?'

Lizzie was gazing after Maloney and had to think about this.

'It was interesting...to see white collar workers on a picket line. A bit odd though. There was some drama with the union guy who crossed the picket line but...other than that, it all seemed like a bit of a game really.'

Lesley nodded.

'We've been out so often in the last few years that it is getting like that. But what we do here doesn't make much difference at the end of the day. The real pressure on the government comes from elsewhere.'

Lizzie's gaze was straying again.

'Yes,' she said vaguely. 'It's just that...I was...very involved in the health workers' campaign, you know...and it was...very different. We did have some fun on the picket line but...I'm sorry, I just need to ...Simon, could you keep an eye on my bag for a moment?'

And she too set off for the other end of the bar. Lesley leaned confidentially towards Simon.

'I don't mean to be nosy, but is something going on there?'

'We-e-ll...sort of. Nothing too earth-shattering. Just a little bit of flirtation. Also, they're very close politically. Lizzie isn't actually a member of Workers' Struggle but they do work together on certain issues. But don't tell anyone else what I've said, will you? About there possibly being a little bit of, erm...'

'Hanky panky?'

'Well I wouldn't put it quite as firmly as that...'

'Don't worry, I'm not a gossip. I'm surprised though. I thought Tony was too dedicated to the revolution to have time for...oh, what am I saying. All men have time for that, don't they? I bet Lenin and Trotsky did.'

'I don't think they did, actually. They were exceptions to the rule.'

'Really? They saved their energy for leading the revolution, I suppose?'

Simon thought back to his recent reading of *My Life*.

'They were both happily married, as far as I'm aware. Which sounds quite bourgeois but their wives were active comrades in the struggle, not little women.'

'Good for them. My husband doesn't believe in strikes. He voted Tory last time, but we still get on. He's thinking of voting SDP in the next election, but I've told him he might as well vote Tory again. How's your girlfriend, by the way? The lovely young lady you brought to the Christmas do?'

'Oh, she's fine. Couldn't make it today, but I'm seeing her this evening.'

'That's good.' Lesley looked at her watch. 'Actually, I'm seeing the hairdresser this afternoon so I'd better think about going. Give my- oh!'

Lizzie had reappeared, her face expressionless.

'I've got to go,' she said quietly, picking up her bag. 'Nice to have met you, Lesley.' She managed a smile. 'Keep up the good work, whether it's official or otherwise. Simon - I'll see you soon.'

She leaned over to kiss his cheek and he smelt a faint perfume as her long fair hair brushed against his skin.

'You must come round sometime, yes?'

After patting Matt on the shoulder and saying goodbye, she was gone.

'Well, looks like something's gone wrong there, doesn't it?'

'I think they're just going to be good friends.'

After Lesley had left, Matt bought a round and sat down opposite Simon.

'Is it all over then?'

'Not sure really. Lizzie didn't look very happy.'

'I didn't think it would last much longer.'

'Yeah, but when I spoke to him on Monday, he didn't seem in any hurry. The baby's not due for another three months, he said.'

'The baby?'

'You didn't know about the baby? Well yeah, Wanda's up the duff. Maloney's left a bun in her oven...and so on. Don't know if they were trying for that.'

'Fucking hell.'

'Indeed.'

'Indeed *what?*'

Maloney was hovering over them again.

'You've been a long time...'

He sat down.

'Is this mine?'

'No, it's a top-up for me and Simon. We thought you'd buggered off.'

'What - and left my bag here? I've been making phone calls, several. I've had to dictate some detail about the strike for our paper. They want a photo as well.'

'About us? We're not exactly on the front line...'

'They've got other stuff. It's going to be a round-up. Anyway, what were you talking about? I heard *fucking hell* and *indeed*.'

'We were talking about you, of course. What else do we talk about when you're not here?'

'I don't know. Enlighten me...'

'About you and Lizzie and Wanda and the baby,' said Simon, his face reddening slightly.

'Oh, I see. You just gossip when I'm not here. Well the baby's not due for another three months as I told you the other day.'

'You've been keeping it quiet...'

'There are two reasons for that, Matthew. One, I'm a revolutionary. Politics is pretty much all I think about from the moment I wake to the moment I go to sleep. The practical problems of life get dealt with when they have to be dealt with. Two, I would find it tedious and embarrassing if people kept coming up to me and congratulating me. I'm not going to be dragged down to some petty-bourgeois plane of existence where birth, marriage and death are the only things that happen.'

'Wow,' said Simon.

Matt kept to the point.

'So what's happening with you and Lizzie then? She didn't look too happy when she left.'

'She wants to talk. I want to talk. We have unfinished business to deal with. But I can't do that at the moment. I'm still trying to sort out somewhere to sleep tonight. And tomorrow night.'

'I thought you were going to stay with your brother?'

'He's away until Friday and no-one else seems to have keys to his place. There is a set of keys at my house, but I'm reluctant to go back there at the moment.'

'Why not? Why don't you just go back to Wanda?'

'Because strategically, Simon, it's better to let the dust settle for a while. And what's happened to your feminism? "Going back to Wanda" is not entirely my decision, is it?'

Simon smacked his own hand.

'Besides, he wants to carry on seeing Lizzie for a while,' said Matt.

'I am actually very fond of Lizzie. Maybe more than that. Anyway, I don't want to just *dump* her.'

'But maybe dragging it out like this is making it worse for her...'

'Simon, I'm a revolutionary socialist. Have you ever noticed an Agony Aunt column in our paper? There isn't time for agonising over personal relationships. We just have to take that as it comes and try to deal with it as men and women, not fucking star-crossed adolescents. Lizzie knows that. The political struggle is more important.'

'Okay. I'll leave you to it. Not another word.'

We were just trying to be comradely,' said Matt. 'Anyway you're welcome to stay with us if you're really stuck. Anna won't mind.'

'Thanks. I might just take you up on that. I actually slept at our Centre last night.'

'At your Centre?'

'We have a guard rota. Two comrades sleep there every night. It wasn't my turn but I swapped with someone else.'

'What are you guarding against?'

'Anything. Fire, obviously. Fascist attacks, police raids, ordinary burglaries...'

'Fascist attacks? How do they know it's your building?'

'Well the Special Branch know. I'm sure their dirty tricks brigade will have passed it on. The State has an interest in seeing the two "extremes" wipe each other out.'

'Wow. D'you have to stay awake all night or can you sleep?'

'Of course we can sleep, Simon. I'd be like a fucking zombie if I'd been awake all night.'

'So how are you guarding the building if you're asleep?'

'We have a burglar alarm, you dingbat. It wakes us up.'

'And what if it's fascists breaking in?'

'There's a phone in the room we sleep in. We have a single point of contact. That comrade phones others and they respond.'

'Has it happened?'

'There've been two attempts. They didn't get in.'

'But what if they did? And what if they cut the phone line?'

'Simon, you're suffering from a severe case of...what's the word? *Vicarious*. A severe case of vicarious excitement.'

'I know, it's great. Supposing they get in, you pick up the phone and the line is dead?'

'Or even if it's not, your comrades can't get there straight away,' said Matt.

'And there are fascists stomping around in steel-capped boots...'

'We sleep in an upstairs room. We lock the door obviously. We assess the situation. There's an escape route if necessary. I'm not going into the detail, but it's all been planned.'

'Do you call the police?'

'Of course not. They're agents of the state.'

'But what if someone gets hurt?'

'If someone gets hurt badly in a way that we can't deal with, then we'd call an ambulance. It would probably end up with the police being called and we'd just have to deal with that, but we wouldn't press charges or make any statements. If there was a fire, then obviously we'd call the fire brigade - though we have trained ourselves in the use of fire extinguishers.'

'Smoke alarms?'

'Installed last year. That's our biggest fear, actually - arson.'

'Wow, you're really quite organised, aren't you?'

'That's what I keep trying to drill into you, Simon. We're a serious organisation. Revolution is a serious business.'

'I'm impressed,'

'I actually went to the fire extinguisher training for staff last year. Given by that nice Mr Gromwell.'

They laughed.

'He couldn't quite believe it when I turned up, but he had to let me take part.'

'He probably thought you were going to sabotage it. I'd be tempted to aim one at him. Give him a squirt...'

'Yeah, they'd be delighted to sack us.'

'*Tempted*, I said. Obviously I wouldn't do it. Unless I'd already given my notice in...'

'That's different,' said Maloney. 'I'm going to sneak into Bull's office on my last day and crap on his desk. And stick one of those little plastic Union Jacks in it.'

'God, that's disgusting,' said Matt. 'I was just thinking about getting some lunch.'

'My stomach is desperate for food.'

Maloney kept the seats while Matt and Simon went to the bar. They bought cheese and tomato rolls, crisps and another round of beer.

'Your friend there has booked the upstairs room for two o'clock,' said the landlord. 'Is that still going ahead?'

'Oh, yeah. There'll be other people here soon.'

'Okay. Well tell him as it's only for an hour and it's bringing extra custom in, I'll waive the charge.'

'Cheers, mate. That's very decent.'

The extra custom started to arrive soon afterwards. Everyone who had been at the Monday pre-strike meeting turned up again. The sale of beers, rolls, pies and crisps rose higher. They took over the next table as Matt and the other managers left.

'Is this a secret cabal?' Imogen asked Matt as she gathered her belongings.

'This is the engine of the revolution.'

'You're starting by taking over this pub?'

'Actually, we'll be holding a public meeting soon which you'll be welcome to attend.'

'Alas, my diary is very full over the next few weeks, but thanks anyway.'

McLeod was sitting at the table and watched her depart with ill-disguised scorn.

117

'Do you normally hobnob with management?'

'Imogen's okay. You should have seen her in action on our picket line.'

'The only management activists we talk to are either CP members or left Labour - none of whom can be trusted.'

'They can be trusted up to a point, which may be a useful point.'

'True. But we keep our distance socially.'

'I shouldn't think that worries them.'

'It's a political principle.'

'I didn't think you had much time for a social life in any case.'

'We haven't, but sometimes you end up in those sort of situations.'

Simon couldn't help laughing.

'It must be hell for you.'

McLeod looked at him, brown eyes glinting in a face of stone.

'You're a typical ex-SWP smart-arse, aren't you? Come the revolution, you'll be nowhere in sight.'

'That's no way to speak to a comrade, comrade,' said Joe who'd overheard.

'It's the truth.'

Simon said nothing. After a while, he went to the bar and got pints for himself, Maloney and Joe. The conversation when he returned had moved on to nuclear war.

'So what are you going to do if the four minute warning goes off?'

The question was aimed at Joe. He was ready for it.

'I'm going to go up to the top of our block, preferably with a bottle of whisky, and just...*watch*.'

'The revolutionary movement hasn't done enough to campaign for nuclear disarmament,' said Sandy Reed.

'It's a waste of time and energy,' said McLeod. 'You can't undo something like that. After the revolution, nuclear weapons can be brought under workers' control and pointed at America...'

Simon stared at him.

'Mad Dog McLeod!' he said quietly. 'And I thought you had no sense of humour.'

McLeod ignored this and carried on arguing with the others. Simon sank back in his seat and sipped some beer. He couldn't be bothered to participate any more. He couldn't be bothered even to listen. He felt heavy-headed and tired. He missed Molly...and Lizzie. He looked at Sandy and watched her lips moving. She had a patient face, but was so earnest, so orthodox, so correct. You had to use humour and imagination in the war of words. Fresh words skilfully placed and the weapon of gentle ridicule. Was that petty bourgeois? It was wasted in any case on someone like McLeod.

At two o'clock, they clomped up the back stairs to the 'function room' as the landlord called it. Varnished floorboards, tables and chairs all higgledy-piggledy, framed advertisements and cockeyed pictures on the walls, windows that looked down on the side street and the alley. They spent a couple of minutes putting tables together, arranging chairs, visiting the toilets. Then began with the usual question.

'Who's chairing?'

'Nominate Sandy.'

'Seconded.'

'No,' said Sandy. 'Not again.'

'No?'

'Look around, comrades. I'm the only woman here. If I chair, I can't contribute as I want to. I'm just facilitating something for a bunch of men.'

'Quite right,' said Simon.

'Nominate Simon,' said McLeod.

Simon ignored this and so did the others. Paul Piper was pressed into service instead and took over the ropes in his usual orderly manner.

'As I see it, there are only three items for the agenda. Factual Reports, Analysis and Where Do We Go From Here? Could someone take brief notes please.'

Tim Parrish agreed to do that.

'Okay. Item 1 - Reports. Bear in mind that we have one hour only for the entire agenda.'

They went round the table, each giving an account of the action in their workplaces and adding any information they'd got from elsewhere. With much hurrying from the Chair, this took about twenty minutes. Maloney spoke on behalf of the Institute while Simon drained his glass.

'Okay,' said Piper. 'The main impression I get from all that...is that in London, the response was neither overwhelming nor disastrous. Somewhere in between. I rang a few regional contacts as well on my

119

way here and the opinion is that support has held up in the usual areas - the big cities, the North East, Scotland and so on. Right, let's move on to Analysis. Who wants to lead off?'

'I will,' said Joe. 'Okay. They won't say this to the media but I'm sure the real verdict the union leaders will reach on today's action will be "only a moderate success". And maybe it could have been better. However, there is obvious rank and file anger at the proposed cuts. There is real concern about job security, increased workloads and so on. But the cuts are not yet as big or immediate an issue as pay was. And also the unions are split in terms of how the battle should be fought.'

'And that won't change,' said Piper.

'Probably not. In any case, all the union leaderships want - whether they support industrial action or not - is a deal. That's the height of their ambition, based on the idea of "fairness" with no challenge to the way in which society is structured. And they assume, probably correctly, that a deal can be reached because the Tories are thinking about the next election, even if it's another year away. And although they want to destroy us in the long term, the Tories don't want a prolonged fight at the moment. They don't want anything that might lead to another so-called "winter of discontent" because they're not certain that will benefit them as it did before. That, in essence, is what led to a settlement in the health workers campaign. However, there's more public sympathy for nurses than there is for us, so we'll get even less of a concession...'

Joe paused and looked around.

'Okay,' said Piper. 'Quick comments anyone?'

'Agreed as far as it goes,' said Maloney.

'I agree on the whole,' said Sandy. 'But to follow on from that last point, one thing that's different in the public sector union movement - as the nurses action showed - is the number of women workers involved. That marks us out from the traditional militant unions - the miners, the dockers, the railwaymen and so on. If we can put that at the forefront of our campaigning, if we're seen to be more than just a load of bolshie men, then I think we'll get more public support.'

'Good point,' said Joe.

'Marxists don't talk about "the public",' said McLeod. 'It's a phantasm, a will-o'-the-wisp created by the ruling class. *The public think this, the public won't like that.* How can there be a "public" separate from the class system? If there is, then it's a lumpen mass of bourgeois and petty-bourgeois stooges brainwashed by the media. We shouldn't give a flying fuck about public sympathy.'

'We have to at the moment,' said Joe. 'Whether it's a media-created thing or not. It exists. It's an influential force...'

'And I said public *support*, not sympathy,' said Sandy sharply. McLeod carried on regardless.

'Also, the implication that we need to link up with the higher-grade unions is wrong. Our aim as revolutionary socialists - assuming that's what most of us are - is to get the proletariat to revolt and seize the means of production. So who are the workers in our sector? They're those in the lower grades - our grades - who do the real work without which the hierarchical pyramid would collapse. We shouldn't be worrying therefore about the other unions, if you can call them that. We need to concentrate on building a truly militant fighting force of our own.'

'That's just ultra-left nonsense,' said Maloney. 'There isn't that simple level of class structure any more. A lot of people who are workers don't think of themselves as working class. We need to build a united front consisting of anyone who supports our basic aims. The more resistance spreads to the higher unions, the more worried and weakened the government will be.'

'The work that my members do is often the main purpose of the departments they work for,' said Piper. 'The same can be said of the Professionals. So-called "specialists" are as much the real workers as those in the lower grades.'

'And they're paid more and treated differently,' said McLeod. 'Change is never going to start with them. That's my basic point. And any united front that includes "your members" is going to be weakened because there's only so far they'll ever go. That's my other basic point.'

He pushed his chair back and stood.

'I'm going to get another drink.'

'How long will the landlord let us stay up here, Simon?'

'Till ten past, if not longer. But Mick can go and buy a drink. In fact, you could get a round in Mick...'

But the door was already swinging shut.

'I have a feeling that might not happen,' said Piper.

'I'd be rather glad of another drink,' said Tim Parrish laying down his pen.

'Me too,' said Simon.

'Actually, I'd like another drink as well,' said Joe.

Ten minutes later, after most of the comrades had visited the bar and returned with glasses full, Piper took a sip of his tonic and lemon and restarted the meeting. The previous argument was ignored.

'Okay. Where do we go from here? Who wants to begin?'

Maloney raised his hand and began.

'In a nutshell, we stick to our position of No Cuts Whatsoever and fight for it. We know what the Tories are trying to do. Divide and rule, paying particular attention to the working class. Better off workers get the right to buy their own houses and "move up in the world" while poorer workers fester in the dole queues. We have to make that clear to everyone. Also that any deal reached with the government will still mean cuts, will still mean job losses at a time of mass unemployment. The Broad Left will carry on campaigning on a No Cuts position as it's the official union policy, but in the end they'll do a deal and present it as some sort of victory. The right wing will try and have it both ways: oppose the official policy, oppose any proposed deal. We'll stand out therefore as the only grouping which truly supports the official policy. Apart from the SWP and they've lost all credibility. We'll be the only group offering an independent socialist alternative. And that in my view will enable us to build our support.'

He paused and there was a general nodding of heads and murmuring of assent around the table.

'That's all obvious,' said McLeod.

'Good. In terms of immediate action, we need to get a newsletter out reporting on today's action and arguing for our position. No Cuts, No Deal. Another day of strike action followed by selective strikes where it will hurt the most and a general work to rule. I suggest a properly printed newsletter with a few photos - a Special Issue. We then need to call a public meeting for the week after - as discussed on Monday. Finally, for now, a picket of the next NEC meeting which I think will take place next week. Next Thursday. That's when I think they'll start moving towards a deal.'

'Who's going to produce this newsletter?' asked Piper.

'I propose myself, Simon, Joe and Sandy.'

'Who's going to picket the NEC?' said McLeod. 'Just us?'

'I think the first thing is to go back to our branches and canvass some of our members, see if they'd attend. I'll confirm the date and ring round tomorrow. We could also suggest it to the SWP. They won't respond officially, but some of their members may come along. And bring people from their own union branches.'

'I think we should occupy HQ if it looks like they're going for a deal,' said McLeod.

'Hmm...'

There was a silence around the table.

'I think that might be a bad idea,' said Piper.

'You would think that, wouldn't you?'

'How long would this occupation go on for?' asked Mullins.

'I don't know. Depends on how HQ react. Whether they call the Bill. What the people involved would feel...'

'How would the membership feel? said Sandy. 'That's the key question. How would they react to the occupation of their HQ by a small bunch of activists?'

'That's a loaded question.'

'Wouldn't it be what you Trots call *adventurism*?' said Joe.

'Hmm...what did Lenin say?' Maloney asked himself, tapping his fingernails on the table. '*Politics without the masses are adventurist politics*. I think that was in 1914. He considered Trotsky adventurist at the time. I think it depends on how many people turn up for the picket. If it's just us, then occupation probably would be wrong.'

For once, even McLeod seemed uncertain.

'Well...that might determine the nature and length of the action. It could just be that we enter the building and demand to address the NEC. Anything's better than picketing them at the start and then just going away. They'll take no fucking notice of that.'

At that moment the door opened and a young woman stepped into the room.

'Les says can you hurry up and finish please. It's nearly ten past.'

'Sure,' said Piper in his silkiest voice. 'We'll be two more minutes.'

'I'll take some of these. Can you bring the rest with you.'

She moved around the table gathering empty glasses.

'Let me hold the door for you.'

Piper returned to the table.

123

'Okay, where were we?' He gripped the open pages of his notebook.

'The occupation...' said McLeod.

'Well...let me just sum up first. Tony, you'll let us all know tomorrow the date and time of the NEC meeting. Everyone will then let their members know - call branch meetings or send round a notice. Is anyone going to contact the SWP?'

'I would say *no*,' said Mullins. 'I think it's a better idea to try and get branch members along there rather than just the same old faces.'

'Agreed,' said Maloney. 'If we get the newsletter out to the branches, the SWP may turn up anyway. That's up to them.'

'The sub-committee need to have the Newsletter ready as soon as possible, preferably by Monday. Could the same group organise the public meeting too?'

'Makes sense,' said Maloney. 'I nominate Joe to lead the sub-committee.'

'Bastard.'

'Seconded,' said Simon faintly. He was starting to feel sick.

'And I think we'll have to have a pre-meeting before the public meeting. Can the sub-committee think about that too?'

'We'll think about everything,' said Joe merrily.

'I don't think we can plan anything else until we hear what the union leaderships are going to to. Tim - could you circulate a proper note please via the IDS.'

'The occupation,' said McLeod grimly.

But the meeting room door opened again and this time the landlord stood in the frame. Without giving them a glance, he pushed the door back against the wall.

'Time! Gentlemen! Please!'

'Sure, we've just finished.'

'I am *not* a gentleman.'

'Me neither. Where's my bag?'

'We may want to book the room again,' said Maloney. Can I let you know by Friday?'

The landlord shrugged.

'Yeah, that's all right. As long as it doesn't clash with my regulars. The pigeon fanciers, the Bloomsbury Group...'

'The Bloomsbury Group? said Simon, so faintly that nobody heard. He was beginning to feel very sick.

'What do you do at these meetings anyway?'

'It's just union business, mate.'

'Okay. As long as you're not plotting to overthrow the government or anything like that.'

'Certainly.'

'As if...'

'*Somebody* needs to...'

The landlord brought up the rear as they went down the stairs one by one. Simon gripped the handrail. Downstairs, he put his beer glass on the bar and felt the sickness rising. Fresh air, the street...he must reach the street. The pub was empty apart from two bar staff and a woman who was wiping down tables. She had a vacuum cleaner plugged in to a wall socket and Simon managed to trip over the cable as he moved towards the door. He faltered but kept his balance.

8. An Evening With Molly

They gathered outside on the side street, then headed towards the main road. Even within his glazed bubble, distracted by nausea, Simon saw how the group arranged itself as it straggled along the pavement. Maloney and Joe side-by-side in close conversation - Maloney striding, Joe straining to keep up. Behind them, Paul Piper and Sandy Reed walking efficiently, talking earnestly with Piper gesturing in contained manner to illustrate his points and Sandy, thin lips closed critically when listening, looking directly at Piper when she responded. McLeod marching alone, independent of everything and everybody around him. Mullins and Parrish, together for company, scuttling like a pair of crabs, occasionally tossing a sentence to each other. And he, of course, by himself. When he lost his edge, when brain and tongue grew fur, he was a dull dog, an irrelevance, an aside - he knew that. Just as he knew he was going to be sick.

Twenty yards before the main road, it swept up from his gut. He managed to find a space between two parked cars as the vomit launched itself. After the big rush, there were two minor rushes, two or three dry spasms with acid etching the back of his throat, then he straightened up. He'd been aware of passers-by, but no-one had stopped or said anything. There was little traffic in the side street. He looked towards the corner. Piper and Sandy were departing, McLeod had gone, the others stood huddled together talking. No-one seemed to be aware, but as he started to walk towards them, Mullins looked round, then detached himself from the group and came to meet him.

'Are you all right, Simon?'

'Just been sick. In the gutter.'

'I can see. You need to wipe your mouth. There's a few bits in your beard as well.'

'Oh, shit.'

'No, vomit.'

Simon pulled out his handkerchief and wiped it around his mouth.

'That better?'

'One last piece there...perfect. No-one would ever know.'

'Thanks, Albert.'

He folded the handkerchief carefully and put it back in his pocket.'

'What's up, Simon?' asked Joe when they reached the others.

'Just thrown up. In the gutter.'

'Well that's what gutters are for, mate.'

'Too much alcohol. Not enough food.'

'You need some tea, Simon,' said Maloney. 'Settle your stomach.'

'You listen to your Uncle Tony,' said Joe. 'Where's that cafe you took us to last time?'

'Closed. On holiday.'

'We can go to the cafe in Russell Square,' said Maloney. 'That way you can stay in the fresh air. Well, the open air.'

'I've got to go, gentlemen,' said Mullins. Tim Parrish had to go too.

'And then there were three,' said Joe.

The cafe in Russell Square gardens was a shack with a large awning that stretched forward over a dozen or so tables. Only two other people were there. Simon sat down while Maloney and Joe went to order. It was just about warm enough. He zipped up his anorak and remembered the last time he was here with Molly when their relationship was still close. Only three months ago. Going down to her for the first time and then that weird idea about how the ghost of Old Possum might be watching. A ghost from the Church of EngLit where he'd worshipped before being nabbed by politics. He could feel the nausea returning and took several deep breaths. A cup of tea was set down before him and Joe brought a plate of cake for sharing.

'How are you feeling?'

'I think it's coming back again.'

'Drink some tea.'

He tried but it was too hot. A minute later behind some nearby bushes, he went through the motions of throwing up again with a series of spasms that ejected mostly liquid. When it had stopped, he tottered back to the table and wiped his mouth with a napkin. The tea was cool enough to take a few sips.

'That'll sort you out.'

'There was hardly anything there.'

'We've left you a piece of cake to fill the void. It's very bland.'

'Virtually tasteless. Just what you need.'

He nibbled it cautiously.

'Hmmm. Let me eat cake. I think I'm on the road to recovery.'

'Excellent. In that case, back to business. Tomorrow evening, Simon. 6pm. The Fountain. Sandy said she could make it. Your presence is required.'

'One hour only. Bring notebook and pen.'

'We'll give you the gist of the main newsletter piece. Sandy's going to bring something on women workers. You hone it all...'

'*Hone it, boy!*'

'With your superb literary skills.'

'But not too literary...'

'By Monday morning?' asked Simon between mouthfuls of cake.

'First thing. I'll meet you somewhere, take it to our Centre, edit it if necessary, get it typeset, laid out, photos added and hopefully printed by the afternoon.'

'I'm getting a feeling of *déjà vu* about this.'

'Don't worry. I'll sort everything out in advance. If we can't do it for some reason, Lizzie has contacts who will...'

'Lizzie? The same Lizzie who walked out of the pub today. Is she still talking to you?'

Joe looked at Maloney with raised eyebrows.

'You *are* on the mend, aren't you Simon?' said Maloney. 'Of course she's still talking to me. We're grown-ups fighting for a common cause. We don't let the personal intrude on the political.'

'This newsletter is not going to be plastered with ads for Workers' Struggle, is it?' said Joe.

'It may have one small discreet ad on the last page.'

'And you'll confirm definitely tomorrow that WS can do it?'

'Definitely. I'll get Lizzie to come along as well to be on the safe side. Also, she can give us some input from the nurses' strike. Lessons learnt...'

'Okay. I think we're done.'

'Can we leave you, Simon? Am I right that you're feeling better?'

Simon nodded. He gestured at the empty plate and cup.

'I might bring it all back up though.'

'You'll survive.'

'I'm meeting Molly at six.'

'Give her our fraternal greetings.'

Joe stood.

'Come on, Anthony. To the tube. You can tell me about the personal intruding on the political.'

After they'd gone, Simon stayed where he was and let jumbled thoughts of the morning's events, the newsletter and Molly float through his head. He bought another cup of tea and took some painkillers. The purging of his insides had gone some way to sobering him up. The afternoon was more or less dark by now and all the lampposts were lit around the square and along the garden pathways. The black railings and boundary trees were both prison-like and protective as the traffic rumbled and growled on every side. He got up at last and walked with a steady lope south-west out of the square down Montague Street, past the huge pillared temple of the British Museum and into secluded Bainbridge St behind Congress House where the regularity of his breathing and footfall helped smooth away the last traces of nausea.

He felt tired though and wondered about walking down to the Westminster Reference Library and taking a nap at one of their desks. What time would they close? He looked at his watch. It was 4.23 already. He crossed the clamorous junction of Tottenham Court Road and Oxford Street and set off down Charing Cross Road, but was soon distracted by bookshops - one after the other. A quick look in each shop turned into a long absorption in the printed pages of various books and magazines that lay in wait on tables, display stands and shelves. Time rolled on in the background and it was only when he entered Collets to check out the left wing press that he realised he had only five minutes left. Four minutes later, he emerged and walked down to Leicester Square tube. He felt not just tired now, but weary, bare-wired and tense. Molly was standing outside the narrow station entrance near the newspaper seller. Her face had a fixed look of impatience, her foot tapped down on the pavement as she looked around. She saw him as he crossed the street.

'How's that for timing?' he said, tapping his watch. She looked unimpressed.

'I've been here ten minutes. What have you been doing?'

She pulled away from a light kiss on the cheek.

'God, your breath is appalling.'

'Well, we were in the pub till half past three. Then I went for a cup of tea with Tony and Joe, then browsed in a few bookshops.'

'You look pale.'

He thought it best not to mention throwing up into the gutter.

130

'I'm very tired. I've been up since 5 am. That feels like a long time ago.'

'Well I want to eat at the very least. I suppose we can see the film another time.'

'Jimmy's?'

'Could do, though it's a bit of a walk.'

'How about Covent Garden? That Italian place we've been to before.'

He thought his stomach could handle pasta better than spicy Greek food and gut-rotting retsina and the mingled smells which permeated the basement at Jimmy's.

'Okay. But I need a drink first after the day I've had. Are you up to it?'

'Yeah, sure. Hair of the dog.'

'Hair of the dog is normally something you have the day after, Simon. Here?'

She nodded at the Porcupine right beside them. Simon pulled a face.

'It has bad memories.'

'Lamb and Flag? The Harp?'

In the end, they went to the Salisbury. The theatre crowd hadn't gathered yet and they found a table for two. Simon went to the bar and bought a Pils for Molly and a tomato juice for himself. He wasn't quite ready for hair of the dog after all.

'Strange place,' said Molly as they sat down. She looked around the tiled, pillared, engraved glass interior. 'I like big Victorian pubs normally, but this is a bit - I don't know - over the top.'

'I came here three or four years ago with a gay guy who used to work at the Institute. He took me in the back room. It was all mirrored and full of men eyeing each other up.'

'And did anything come of it?'

'You're joking. I'd already told him I wasn't gay. He just wanted someone to go to the opera with.'

'He didn't try anything then?'

'Of course not. He was a very civilised cultured sort of guy.'

'I thought they were the worst.'

'Molly...you're not-'

'I was joking...as you said.'

He sipped the tomato juice.

131

'So you've had a difficult day then?'

'I don't want to talk about it. The sooner I find a new job the better. How was your strike? I forgot about that...'

'It was fine. You've reminded me - I bought a *Standard* but forgot to look for their report.'

He pulled the paper from his bag.

'Won't be a minute. Hmm...as I thought. Short piece - unions claim mass support, government says majority worked as normal. Some delays but all essential services provided.'

'They always say that, don't they.'

'They always publish the union's version first, then the government's version as if it's a correction.'

'But some people might only read what the unions say, so they'll believe that.'

'Possibly.'

He told her about the picket line and all the business with the placards and the railings.

'Sounds like fun. Maybe I should have taken the day off after all. I wouldn't have got there for seven am though.'

'Lizzie did - with Maloney.'

'Oh, right. How's that going then - now he's a free agent?'

'Hard to tell. He's been staying with one of his Workers' Struggle comrades since Wanda threw him out. I'm not sure if Lizzie's been staying with him, but then he had to move from there...It's all quite chaotic really. He doesn't want to stay at Lizzie's because it's a feminist house and he thinks they'll - well I don't know what he thinks. Wanda's pregnant, by the way.'

'Blimey.'

'Due in three months. So now he wants to go back to her, but not before he's sown a few more wild oats with Lizzie. That's my assessment anyway.'

'Three months? How long has he known about it then? Wanda must have known for three months before that...'

'Good point. I hadn't thought about that...'

'Well I hope he doesn't sow anything more than wild oats with Lizzie.'

'She won't let that happen.'

'Nothing pisses me off more than men who go around making one woman after another pregnant and don't stay with any of them.'

132

'I don't think Maloney's quite like that.' He hesitated then plunged on. 'I get the feeling he hasn't had much sexual experience apart from with his wife. Not that he's ever talked about it. It's just a feeling you get about someone sometimes. And then, when he gets the chance to have a little bit on the side, he can't resist it...'

Molly patted his hand.

'So you and he have more in common than just politics? Apart from the fact that you don't have a wife or a little bit on the side...'

He didn't understand what she meant at first.

'How do *you* know I'm not having a little bit on the side?'

It was meant as a joke, but Molly withdrew her hand and her voice changed.

'Do you really want me to tell you? How I know that you're not having an affair with another woman?'

He shrugged.

'If you want. I'm too tired to argue.'

'I don't think there's any need to spell it out.'

Maybe that's why I'm not very good in bed with you, he thought. *Because I'm fucking someone else.* But it would have been a ridiculous thing to say. Instead, he sipped more tomato juice and glanced at the front page story in the *Standard*. Two police officers had now been charged with shooting the Victim of Mistaken Identity. To try and fill the silence, he pushed the paper towards her.

'Have you seen this? They've been charged.'

He watched her deep brown eyes moving down the page.

'Yeah, well - they had to, didn't they.'

'Gun crazy coppers. Shoot first, ask questions later.'

Molly sat back. She wasn't really interested. Meanwhile, the pub was getting busier and louder.

'I want to eat,' she said. 'This place isn't doing much for me.'

They left their table and set off for the Trattoria. Neither said much as they walked through the narrow Covent Garden streets. Molly looked at shop windows. Simon was entangled in his thoughts, but began to feel hunger again in the chilly evening air. Perhaps things would improve in the restaurant. And indeed, when they got there and settled into the solid wooden seats with rustic decor around them and short candles glowing in table glasses, the mood did seem to change. After they had looked through the menu and ordered, Molly put her hand on his for a moment.

133

'I didn't mean to be nasty. Let's just have a nice meal.'

'Amen.'

They shared some bruschetta for starters. After that, Simon had a lasagne which he thought would be best for his stomach. He managed a bottle of beer as well. The conversation went well at first but started to peter out as they worked their way through the main course. Every now and then, one of them would think of something to say, the other would reply and then it would tail off...

And Simon saw himself sitting in the Viva again as he had done recently while Maloney tried over and over to start the engine. A brief spark of power, then nothing but the death rattle. On a quiet road somewhere in East London, a side street, a dark cul-de-sac without street lighting, a pull of the choke, a sharp twist of the key, a brief chug and cut! Who was holding the torch? Someone outside looming on a country road, a frantic wrist twist over again and nothing at all but the death rattle, a very lively death rattle and an angry white face at the window, anxiety rising and Molly's voice sounding in the background...

He jerked upright up from a position less than six inches above his plate.

'Sorry, did I nod off?'

Molly sighed, then her face settled into contempt.

'Why don't I talk to this candle?' She tapped the side of its glass with her fingernail. 'Hello little candle. You're still holding a flame for me, aren't you? You're not going to burn out, are you?'

Simon put his fork down, slapped one cheek, then both.

'Sorry, it's just I've been up since 5 am.'

'I know. Do you know how? Because you told me two hours ago.'

'Okay.'

She leaned forward and spoke in a low voice.

'You got up at 5 am. You stood on a picket line. Then you went to the pub for four hours and drank yourself silly with your mates. At what point did you think about the fact that you'd be meeting me this evening and going out with me?'

'Molly!' He heard his voice quavering and made an effort to bring it under control. 'Molly, I just...you don't know how much I care for you...'

She shook her head and dropped a scrunched-up napkin onto her plate.

'I'm sorry - it's just...I've been in this vicious circle for so long,' he said. 'Meetings and marches and politics and getting drunk in the pub. It's hard to break out of it.'

Molly looked around and signalled to one of the waiters.

'Could we have the bill please?'

The man gave a slightly disconcerted look, then turned to Simon.

'Yes, of course. Nothing else, sir?'

'No that's fine, thanks.'

He departed and there was a silence.

'Are we going to the cinema, then?' Simon asked.

'I'm going to the cinema. I think you should go home.'

The waiter brought two small plates. One had a rose on it which he set down in front of Molly. The other had the bill which he set down in front of Simon. Simon couldn't help laughing as the man left them.

'Jesus Christ. Some things never change, do they?'

Molly stood up and took her coat from the stand.

'Look, I'll be fine now,' said Simon. 'Just let me pay this bill and I'll be right with you.'

She took her bag from the back of the chair.

'Go and get some sleep, Simon. That's what you need.'

'I need to be with you.'

She took out her purse and laid a five pound note on top of the bill.

'That's my contribution.'

He picked it up and held it out to her.

'No, I'll pay.'

'No, equal rights - remember?'

She picked up the rose and threaded it through a button hole in her coat.

'I might as well get something out of this.'

He sighed and sagged in his chair as she walked off, then sat up in case anyone was watching. He added another five pound note to the plate, then looked around The waiter was at another table. The restaurant had got busier but no-one seemed to be looking at him or to have noticed anything untoward. The waiter when he came looked at the empty chair.

'She had to go - the lady?'

'Yes.'

135

'Ah, the women, eh?' The waiter shook his head and pressed his lips together as if to hold back the sympathy that was welling inside him. Then he picked up the money.

'Thank you very much, sir.'

When he came out of the restaurant, Simon turned in the direction of Covent Garden tube which would take him to Finsbury Park and home. He trudged along the pavement down a one-way street of closed shops, moving in and out of the thin stream of other people, none of whom could be as alone or troubled as he was, until he reached the cobbled plaza of the old market. A flower stall was still open under one of the arches and a sudden mad idea came blazing out of the darkness and formed into three simple words which wobbled in the air before him, then stabilised.

DON'T GIVE UP!

He went over to the stall and grappled mentally with the variety of flowers, the extravagant colours, the astounding prices. But here were red roses packed into a slender cellophane funnel for only one pound. He picked up a bunch and inhaled. There was a very faint scent or was he imagining even that? No matter. Red roses were the thing. *My love is like...* She'd had a small pale pink rose from the waiter. She could have six full-blooded red ones from him. He handed a pound note to the flower lady and turned around to cut through King Street. After a while, he held the cellophane funnel down at his side. What was he doing - a revolutionary of some sort walking through the streets holding roses?

He passed the Salisbury again, crossed Charing Cross Road and went down one of the side streets into Leicester Square. A glance at his watch told him the programme would have begun, but there were still a few stragglers in the cinema foyer. He bought a ticket and walked down the narrow corridor to the auditorium door. An usher checked his ticket and a second usher started to lead him by torchlight into the big dark space where actors' voices bounced off the walls. Clearly this was not *Sophie's Choice* but the trailer for a film 'coming soon'.

He stopped and whispered to the usher.

"I'm looking for someone who's already here.'

The usher batted his eyelids slightly.

136

'Female, shorter than me, black hair, black coat with gold braiding, pink flower...'

He tapped his coat where a buttonhole would have been. The usher gave a mystified sort of smile, but began to scan the rows of seats with his torch. The place looked about three quarters full. Simon walked down the steps behind the usher, looking desperately at the mass of heads all facing the screen. She had to be here. He had to find her. If he had to sit alone and wait till the end of the film, this whole business with the roses would be a sad, silly anticlimax. Then suddenly, miraculously, he saw a pale face staring at him from the middle of a row.

'There!' he said to the usher who shone his beam as Simon threaded laboriously along the row towards Molly, holding the roses before him. She lifted her bag from the vacant seat beside her and he sank down into it, heart thumping. It was the first time he had really caught his breath since leaving the market. When he looked at Molly, she was struggling to suppress laughter. Then she held out her hand and he placed the funnel across her palm. She inspected the flowerheads, then leant towards him.

'Well you still know how to surprise,' she said.

'It was the least I could do.'

He sat back. It was dawn in the countryside, sunbeams were fanning out over a hill and the sound of sweet reverent violins slowly overcame the birdsong. In a farm kitchen, a woman was spreading an amazing new brand of butter on perfectly toasted bread.

'I don't know, Simon.'

'What don't you know?'

'What I want to do.'

'Let's talk about what *we* want to do.'

'We should talk.'

'I love you.'

'I know you do.'

She gave his hand a squeeze, then moved her hand to the roses. When he looked at her again, she kept her gaze on the screen where a ploughman perched on a stile was chomping cheerfully through a thick hunk of bread and cheese.

'Goldencup Butter. It butters you up!' he said between mouthfuls.

'We can work it out,' Simon said.

137

Molly gave a weak smile without turning her head.

Simon was drawn into the film when it began, responsive to its story and characters, but still felt the tension of his own petty-bourgeois drama. He glanced at Molly from time to time and reached out to stroke her arm during the 'choice' scene when he saw her tears. But she didn't respond and it brought them no closer. They sat apart like two dumb beasts until the lights went up at the end and conversation broke out all around them.

'Are you okay?' he said.

'Yes I'm fine. What a great film though.'

'Who's Kevin Kline? Have you heard of him before?'

'Never.'

They shuffled out of the cinema amidst the chattering crowd and stood on the corner of Leicester Square.

'Thank you for the roses.'

She had slipped them into her shoulder bag with the dark red heads poking out.

'You're welcome.' The words sounded awkwardly formal. 'I'm sorry I wasn't much good earlier.'

Molly looked as if she could say something, but didn't. Simon glanced at his watch.

'D'you want a last drink? They'll be closing in half an hour.'

She shook her head.

'I'm tired. I want my bed.'

They started to walk towards the corner and the tube.

'You can come back to my place if you want.'

'I have no overnight things, Simon. Anyway, you know I don't like coming back to yours.'

His consciousness streamed. They would get the Piccadilly Line together, but at Kings Cross she would change for the Victoria Line. What would happen? They had rarely been out together without going back to his or hers afterwards. It was par for the course. True, it had been Molly's place more and more, but she had a double bed and there was no need to keep so quiet. Anne-Marie had gone along with his 'from time to time' proposal, but in a prickly manner and he felt on edge and Molly felt unwelcome whenever she came to stay. And that single bed - so intimate for the first half hour, then so uncomfortable. Matt had described how he and Anna had shared a single bed for six months at the start of their relationship and learnt

138

to turn over in their sleep at the same time. Is this love, still? What should he do? Assume they were going back to her place and see how they reacted? Ask outright: *am I coming back to yours, then?* Wait until the last minute and decide on the spur? They passed through the tube entrance.

'You're right. We do need to talk,' he said as they stood on the escalator.

'Yes, but not now.'

Down they went so smoothly, each advert on the wall slowly revealing its message before gliding away from them.

'So am I coming back to yours, then?'

'Not a good idea really, is it? I'm tired, you're tired...'

He nodded and sighed.

'I suppose...'

'You can come over to my place at the weekend if you like and we'll talk.'

'Sounds good.'

He put his arm around her as they sat in the tube carriage, but couldn't think of much to say and the noise was deafening in the tunnel, though in the past he would have leaned close and whispered in her ear. At Holborn, she gave him a peck on the cheek before standing and a wave from the platform. Little things, he thought. There must be hope. Yet it felt like more than just an ordinary goodbye.

Part Three
April 1983

9. Brothers and Sisters

'Where the *fuck* is he?'

Simon looked at his watch. A loudspeaker announcement began. *The train about to depart from Platform 14...*

'Come on, let's go.'

He picked up his holdall and stood poised to move.

'I can see him,' said Lee. He was standing on tiptoe and Simon followed his gaze. Sure enough, there was the curly helmet of brown hair, the silver specs, the intent face bobbing and weaving in and out of sight on the crowded concourse. Lee waved his arms over his head.

'Which platform?' gasped Maloney as he reached them.

'This one. That's why we're standing here.'

'Sorry, but unlike you I've got a domestic life.'

'You'll be late for your own revolution.'

Lee was ahead, his long legs easily outpacing them as they raced down the slope and onto the platform. *The younger generation,* thought Simon. *We're being superseded. Already.* A guard watching with flag in hand turned to the carriage door behind him and held it open for them. After they'd scrambled through, he slammed it shut. As they began the long march down the train, the guard blew his piercing whistle and the floor seemed to glide backwards under their feet. They walked down aisle after aisle, through lobby after lobby, door after door, into the restaurant car with counter grille still down, through another carriage where they started to see a few familiar faces, then finally into the carriage where reserved seats awaited them.

'Jesus fucking Christ, what a hike,' said Maloney as he dropped his bag onto the table.

'Language, said Simon. 'It's Sunday. The Sabbath day...'

'For some.'

'It's the Lord's Day in my family,' said Lee.

'So it is,' said Maloney, his face clouding for a moment as if an old unwelcome memory had flitted across his mind. 'Anyway, they can turn the other cheek, the meek and mild.'

He pulled two thick files out of his holdall, then crammed it into the luggage rack. They settled into their seats. Conversation was sparse for a while as they leafed through the Sunday papers.

143

'This rag gets worse and worse,' said Simon.

'Know thy enemy,' said Maloney. 'That's the point of reading the Times and Telegraph. What's Roland fucking Tubb got to say this week?'

'Another load of shite in praise of Thatcher.'

'Who's Roland Tubb?' asked Lee.

'One of the three stooges of the Tory press - Benjamin Peak, Roland Tubb and Alexander Warden. In thirty years time, no-one'll remember a word they wrote.'

Just before Milton Keynes, a strained voice announced the opening of the buffet counter.

'Okay, *gentlemen*,' said Maloney. 'Who's going to get the coffees?'

'Er, you?'

Maloney shook his head.

'I've got to draft a conference speech.'

Simon looked at Lee.

'I knew you'd look at me. I'm just the errand boy, aren't I?'

'You have the privilege of being a Conference Observer,' said Maloney. 'That involves certain support duties.'

'Give us some money then. I'm poorly paid, don't forget.'

'Simon will pay,' said Maloney. 'He hasn't got a family to feed.'

'A family!' said Simon. 'You've got one baby who isn't even eating yet.'

Nevertheless, he thrust a hand in his pocket and placed a couple of pound coins on the table.

'Oh yeah, congratulations,' said Lee. 'When did this baby actually arrive.'

'Monday before last,' said Maloney, drum rolling on the table with his fingers. 'Two weeks early but doing fine.' He leant out into the aisle. 'Actually, I'll get them. I've just seen two people I need to talk to heading that way. I'll give out some leaflets as well.'

He took the coins, grabbed his carrier bag and rushed away. They were pulling out of Rugby by the time he re-appeared and set down a tray of plastic cups.

'Sorry about the delay. Long queue and lots of discussion needed. These should still be warm.'

The brown fluid was warm. Maloney drank his at speed, then leaned forward.

'Right, pay attention. The programme for today. The Left Caucus meeting, as you know, is this evening at the Grapes. I've no idea where the Grapes is, but we'll find it.'

'We'll just follow the crowd,' said Simon.

'I'm speaking on "Where Do We Go After the Cuts Campaign Cave-In?" Sally on "The Continuing Fight For Womens' Rights", Joe on "The Left Caucus - Who We Are and What We Stand For." The problem *is* - by deciding to get in before everyone else and hold the meeting tonight, we've left ourselves very little time to publicise it. Therefore we've got to hit the pubs in Blackpool as soon as we arrive - the likely pubs where delegates will be convening.'

'How do we know where the likely pubs are?'

'I have a list' - he produced it from an inside pocket - 'well, actually a map provided by a local comrade. Well, relatively local. He's been to Blackpool a few times.' He showed them a network of spidery lines inked on a page torn from an exercise book. 'Actually, he's a teetotaller, so there aren't many pubs shown on it. But there's North Station where we'll be coming in, Talbot Road, Abingdon Street, Corporation Street, Church Street...the Rose and Crown, the Tower Lounge, the Victory, Yates's Wine Lodge - there's bound to be people in there.'

'You're asking us to go into pubs and not drink, just hand out leaflets?'

'That's what the Sally Army do,' said Lee.

'It's only for an hour if the train's on time. You'll be spending the rest of the week drinking.'

'How're we going to know who're delegates and who aren't?'

'Oh, for fuck's sake, just ask around. They'll be in groups, they'll be wearing badges, they'll look different from the locals, they'll have different accents...'

'They'll have carrier bags full of leaflets,' said Lee.

'And what about our holdalls? Are we supposed to lug them around with us?'

'No. We'll stash them in lockers at the station and go back for them afterwards. Then we'll go to the boarding house and check in. It's only a few minutes walk across town.' He traced the journey with a finger on the spidery map. 'Then at four o'clock, we meet Joe, Sandy and some of the others in the Winter Gardens foyer and swap info. Then at five pm approximately and based on the discussion with Joe,

Sandy and so on, we split into twos and go round the town one more time giving out leaflets. Then at six pm, let's see...'

'You're beginning to sound like Dean Moriarty,' said Simon, thinking back to his first literary hero.

'Who?'

'Never mind.'

And so Conference 1983 began for the three of them with a sober pub crawl. Lots of hands took the leaflets, held them for perusal, put them down on bars or tables or stuffed them into pockets or bags. It was taken for granted that such hand-cranked screeds might be interesting and could indicate what lay ahead just as much as the Motions Booklet or any other official publication. And in various pubs, they met - in varying degrees of intoxication - some of the cadres of the far left, the Broad Left and the right wing Sunlight Group. A merry band of the latter were encountered in Yates's where there was sawdust on the floor and champagne on tap.

'The Left Caucus, eh? You'll be a left carcass if we have anything to do with it.'

'Are you even further out than the far left or d'you come between them and the Broad Left?'

'They're the Thin Left.'

'We're the Deep Left,' said Simon which produced a laugh. But he was duly admonished by Maloney as they walked back to the station to retrieve their luggage.

'You can't resist the witticisms, can you? That label could stick now.'

Simon brooded.

'I think it's too sophisticated for them. They'll go for Left Carcass.'

'Are there any delegates here who don't belong to a political group?' asked Lee.

'If there are,' said Maloney, 'they'll be like innocents abroad, babes in the wood.'

'That's a bit like how I feel.'

From North Station, they trekked across town to the boarding house on Albert Road. It was small and homely with fern green wallpaper, paintings of local views and ornamental knick-knacks filling every space. The couple who ran it - Pat and Gail - were

146

friendly even to hirsute trade unionists and had a picture postcard sense of humour.

'Sea View?' said Simon as he signed in at the reception desk.

'Well you're in the front bedroom just overhead,' said Pat pointing a pen at the ceiling. 'If you lean far enough out of the window with a telescope, you'll be able to see it.'

'You might be able to,' said Gail to Lee. 'You're nice and tall.'

They trudged up the narrow red-carpeted staircase to the first floor. Simon and Lee were sharing a twin bedroom with wash basin, wardrobe and single armchair. It was bay fronted and with a bit of effort Simon managed to open one of the windows and lean out. He had no chance of seeing the sea, even with a telescope. Lee leaned out too.

'Maybe with a periscope,' he said. 'Or from the roof.'

'Well at least there's a fire station just up the road,' said Simon.

'You think we might start a fire?'

'Somebody did last year at Eastbourne. By accident. We had to call out the brigade.'

He closed the window and looked around the room.

'It'll do.'

'It's clean - as my mam would say.'

After unpacking, Simon ventured along the corridor to find the bathroom. There was a separate WC next to it and he sat on the porcelain throne. A brown donkey bedecked with a bell-laden bridle stared at him from a poster on the back of the door. He wiped his arse, washed his hands in the small basin and went back. Lee was standing in the open doorway of Maloney's room next to theirs.

'Nice and compact,' Simon said peering inside.

Maloney looked up at him from the single bed which ran almost the length of the room. A heavy-looking wardrobe loomed ominously against the opposite wall. A holdall sagged emptily on the floor and a pile of files had toppled over alongside it. A plain cover tome by Lenin lay on the bedside table.

'Well I'm hardly going to be spending much time here, am I?'

They left Sea View and did the five minute walk to Church Street. Outside the Winter Gardens, they ran into Ronnie with some of his SWP mates and exchanged a few leaflets. The SWPers were heading for the amusement arcades and Lee, who'd met Ronnie before, went with them. Inside the Winter Gardens, Simon and Maloney walked through the long foyer with its tiled surrounds and vaulted glass canopy and found the core of the Caucus - Joe with Kathy on his knee, Sandy and Tim Parrish - squeezed together on a red leather bench next to an elderly couple who were clearly not there for Conference Week.

'That doesn't look very comfortable,' said Simon.

'Nah, it's not for the likes of us,' said Joe. 'Not for the workers. Let's go and find a greasy spoon somewhere.'

'I've been here before,' said Maloney as they moved off down the foyer. 'There's nothing that's really working class about it apart from the visiting workers. It's a glittering dead-end where they're fed the illusion that life in chains is worth living.'

'Oh, Gawd. Spare us the Marxist analysis.'

'A paradise of kitsch and tat,' said Simon who'd never been there before.

'It gets worse. I'm going to drown myself. I'm going to take all my clothes off and walk into the sea.'

Kathy giggled.

'I'm coming with you,' she said.

They found a cafe easily enough in Cedar Square and sat around a formica-topped table with mugs of tea. Dark clouds were massing overhead and raindrops started to patter against the plate glass window.

'The rest of the leaflets,' said Maloney, holding up his carrier bag. 'Couple of hundred, I would think.'

'We did the pub circuit earlier,' said Joe. 'Only had one drink.'

'Tim and I gave a few out in the pubs too,' said Sandy. 'But we kept getting into arguments.'

'Well they don't open again until seven which is too late,' said Maloney. 'I suggest we just wander around town for an hour giving them out, then find somewhere to eat.'

'We could try the amusement arcades,' said Tim.

'You just want to play the machines,' said Simon. 'Have fun...'

'My point is that's the sort of place where people will go. If only to get out of the rain.'

'Their hands will be busy though,' said Joe solemnly. 'And they'll be *concentrating*. I'm not sure they'll be at their most receptive...'

'They might be when they've run out of money,' said Maloney. 'Just say *Meeting tonight mate* and leave one on top of the machine.'

148

They headed off downtown and cruised the streets, sheltering in doorways from the heavier bouts of rain. A few local couples strolled and window-shopped, some early season holidaymakers roamed in waterproofed groups and everyone else was a Conference delegate. Eventually, they reached the North Pier and went round its noisy arcade offloading leaflets using the Maloney Method. Along the promenade, they zigzagged across tramlines and took a look at the sea, dodging the spray when it crashed over the iron railings. Across the road, they went through the bowling alley, prowled the free areas of the Tower Building and wound up on the first stretch of Golden Mile where they gave their last leaflets to a bunch of Brummie delegates after affirming that they were not from the Communist Party, Militant or the SWP. They also found Lee and dragged him away from the machines.

'You're just handing your money back to the Capitalists.'

'It's just a bit of fun, Tony. Anyway, my luck was turning.'

'Who wants what luck would bring?' said Simon, suddenly remembering the line from some DH Lawrence novel he'd read at university.

'The workers, for a start,' said Lee. 'It's all they've got sometimes.'

By 8 o'clock that evening, almost sixty people had turned up for the Left Caucus meeting and squeezed into the upper room of the Grapes public house. Maloney sat at the top table with Sandy and Joe. Simon and Lee sat on a window sill counting them in. Mullins and Parrish sat together nearby and McLeod appeared for the first time and slipped into a back row seat.

'Good turnout,' said Simon. 'The landlord said no more than fifty though. Fire regs and all that.'

'He won't mind a few more. He's doing well out of it. Look at all the glasses...'

Ronnie had turned up with three of his SWP mates and Simon recognised a few Broad Lefters including portly Bob Armitage who gave him a half wave, half salute. At five minutes past, Maloney started the meeting.

'Welcome, brothers and sisters to this Conference meeting of the Left Caucus. The Caucus was formed after last year's Conference when, as you know, the Left narrowly retained control of the union. As you also probably know, the left in this union is dominated by

149

that alliance of CP and left Labour supporters who call themselves the Broad Left. There is also a Militant presence within the Broad Left and an SWP presence who work outside it. So, no shortage of active left wing groups. Why therefore do we need another? The answer to that question lies with the way these various groups function. The basic problem with the Broad Left is that it's a reformist organisation, concerned only with getting what it can out of the current system and only too ready to compromise when the going gets tough. It would like to see a genuinely socialist society, but it's not prepared to take the actions that would be needed to achieve that. As a result, it rarely even wins battles, let alone the war. The problem with Militant and the SWP is that while they do argue for recognisable socialist policies, their main concern in this union is to build their own organisations. They are fronts.'

'Not sectarian. are we?' a woman called from the middle of the room.

'No, not sectarian, comrade. Just truthful. This is a very basic analysis, I admit. But there are certain realities we have to be open about at the outset to avoid fudging and muddle and confusion. The Left Caucus is an independent group of activists within the union. Some of us are members of revolutionary socialist groups, some are not. We are all active in our workplaces and in regional union bodies. We are completely open in election addresses about any organisations we belong to and what our policies are. We don't hide under anyone's else's banner. What unites us is a common desire to see a total transformation of society in which power will rest with the many, not the few, with the rank and file, not the bosses, with all men and women, blue collar and white collar, who are exploited under capitalism.'

There was applause at this point, mainly from Caucus supporters.

'All my own words,' Simon whispered to Lee.

'Genius.'

'That's what we fight for within the unions,' went on Maloney. 'Not for deals which forever let the bosses off the hook. Now you can find all our basic policies on the back of this leaflet or in our newsletter which you can take away after the meeting. But this evening, I want to concentrate on one issue: the Tory cuts and how we should respond to the pact agreed between our NEC and full time officers and a Tory government which despite what the opinion polls may say is still running scared of calling an election.'

'*Pact*,' growled McLeod from the back row. 'Total fucking sell out...'

There were mutterings elsewhere and one of the Broad Lefters turned around.

'And what would you have done, *comrade*?'

'Whoa, whoa,' said Maloney. 'It *was* a sell out in our view, but there'll be time for discussion later. What's certain is that the cuts will still go ahead, just on a smaller scale. And if Thatcher does manage to win the next election, the "pact" will be dead and buried and the cuts will simply get worse. The knife will be replaced by the cleaver.'

Simon looked at Lee, raised his eyebrows and tapped his chest.

'The union leaderships will sigh and say - "we did our best". And launch another timid campaign to try and mitigate the worst of whatever the Tories plan to do. And what will happen to those who demand real opposition? As you know, those of us who protested against this deal back in January by occupying HQ were threatened with expulsion from the union. Can you believe that? Expulsion for protesting against the abandonment of a policy agreed at last year's Conference. They drew back from that, but we now face a motion of censure at Conference to be moved by a Broad Left NEC, supported by the right wing - a blatant attempt to damn us in the eyes of the whole membership. Of course, we'll give as good as we get in the war of words, but where do we go from here?'

'The Tories aim to roll back the years, to privatise as much of the public sector as possible, to protect their own class rather than the common good. They've already shown they don't give a damn about poverty and families on the breadline. Their attitude to the working class is classic divide and rule. Let the better off workers buy their own houses, buy private medical care, buy in to Tory selfishness and greed. The rest can go to the wall. The Tories will never win their votes and don't need them if the rest of their scheming goes to plan.'

'Our task as socialists is not to waver. Not to look for excuses in talk about a "downturn". That's just defeatism. Our task is not to sit back and wait until we think the tide is turning. Our task is to carry on organising, to carry on holding meetings, publishing bulletins, making and remaking the arguments. Our task is to carry on building

151

real opposition based on a cast-iron set of principles and hold to those principles whether the next government is Tory or Labour. Labour talk about presenting an "alternative". Brothers and sisters, I don't like that word. People do have a choice, obviously. But we don't present the *truth* as an alternative to lies, exploitation and deception - take it or leave it. We present it as the moral and right way to go about building a new society and ensuring justice and equality for all. And we present it as something that is achievable. How *can* the few hold down the many? With the right will, they can't.'

'Too fucking right.' McLeod again.

Maloney spoke for another ten minutes and received applause from most of the audience that was solid rather than heavy, though swollen with overhead clapping and a few whistles from Caucus supporters. Sandy Reed seemed nervous at first and held her notes with a slightly shaking hand but grew more confident as the audience listened in silence and the Caucus heads nodded at her.

'Comrades, sisters and brothers...when socialists talk about the people, the masses, or particularly the *working class* - what do they see? What do they visualise? Well, let's be honest. If they're male, they'll see men mainly - perhaps with a few women scattered amongst them. But mainly, overwhelmingly, men - because men and work are virtually synonomous. And anyway only men have the strength to throw off chains, don't they? Sadly, if they're female, they might see men mostly as well - it depends on their background and perhaps their education. I come from round here originally, from a cotton town in East Lancashire. I also went to university in Manchester, or Cottonopolis as they used to call it, where Engels lived of course and wrote *The Condition of the Working Class in England* and where he and Marx worked together in Chetham's Library. And I studied the history of the Industrial Revolution. I read a lot of books but I also found a lot of old archive film. You may have seen some of it yourselves. The people, the masses, the workers emerging from the factories at lunchtime or hometime and staring in wonder at the camera. And you know what? I saw plenty of women amongst them. Groups of women in their shawls, chains of women linking arms, often looking more comradely than the men. Yet their work was seen as secondary, supplementary - by socialists as much as anyone else. The Chartists, for example, only demanded the

152

extension of suffrage to adult males. And consider the famous last sentence of the Communist Manifesto. *Proletariat aller Länder, vereinigt euch!* That's what Marx wrote in 1848. "Proletarians of all countries, unite!" What did that become in the translation by Samuel Moore forty years later? Well, here's my battered old Penguin copy. It says "Working *Men* of all countries, unite!" Of course, Marx was dead by the time that appeared, but Engels wasn't and he approved it.'

'The fact is that sometimes the majority of workers in the 19th century textile mills were female. They could do the work and, more importantly, could be paid less than the men. But women worked in many other industries as well, often doing heavy manual labour. This is something we seem to have forgotten in the 20th century. Except during wartime, women have been pushed back into the home or into "women's jobs" which often echo their domestic roles. Doormat jobs, dogsbody jobs, "ministering angel" jobs, hostess or "bit of skirt" jobs, etc. Yet there's one clear link between the mill workers of yesterday and ourselves today in the public sector. And that is the high number of women workers. In the civil service, in education, in health and so on, many vital jobs are carried out by women. In fact, if current trends continue, women workers will soon outnumber men in our sector.'

'Yet how is that reflected in the organisations that are supposed to be fighting for us? In the Labour Party, in the union movement? Look around Conference tomorrow and ask yourselves why most of the top table are male and why 70% - if not more - of the delegates are male? In fact, look around this room. I make it an 80-20% split. The Left Caucus was very keen that we should have a female speaker this evening addressing "women's issues". But you know what? I'll tell you an embarrassing fact. There are very few women members of the Left Caucus and there are only three of us here tonight. But if we want to build a mass working class movement, comrades, how on earth are we going to do it without a mass involvement of women?'

'Thatcher's a woman,' someone called out. But Sandy wasn't put off. She'd had this piercing insight thrown at her before.

'Comrade - if you are a comrade - Thatcher is a freak. The female gender throws up freaks from time to time just as the male gender does. In saying that we're equal to men, just as good as men, I'm

153

saying by definition that we're not perfect. There are various psychological analyses that could explain Thatcher, but she is not a *sister* and is not representative of our gender at all.'

She went on to talk about the Matchgirls' strike, the Women's Trade Union League, working class women active in the suffrage struggle, the different treatment meted out to Lady Constance Lytton and "Jane Warton" and more recently the Ford Sewing Machinists strike, Jayaben Desai's leadership of the Grunswick strike and the part nurses had played in the Health Workers action the year before.

'We are still slowly emerging from centuries of patriarchy when male dominance was thought to be "natural". Today with more women in the workplace than ever before, we have a key part to play in the struggle for workers' control. There can be no "better world" or "new society" - whatever you want to call it - without womens' full involvement at all levels. It's time that the socialist and labour movement stopped paying lip service to such an obvious statement and started to do something concrete about it and to set an example. After all, if you can't implement equal opportunities and equal rights in your own ranks, how on earth can you do it within the new society? Comrades, sisters and brothers - thank you for listening.'

This received a response equal to that given Maloney's speech, though some of the clapping was dutiful rather than enthusiastic. Joe rose to make the last top table contribution.

'Brothers and sisters, I'll try to follow on from Tony and Sandy. To start with the bleeding obvious, we're here at the beginning of another annual conference. A conference at which the Broad Left could lose its majority on the NEC. A conference at which some of us on the left could be censured. And we face a general election at some point in the next year, maybe sooner rather than later, which could result in at least four more years of attacks on the labour movement. It's not the best of times, is it? "One step forward, two steps back" is how Lenin put it. I sometimes wonder if he underestimated the number of "steps back" that are taken. But we know from our own day-to-day involvement in our union branches that there's still a great deal of fight left in the ranks. Our members are not willing to throw in the towel just yet. And as Sandy has just reminded us, that applies to women members as well as men. We know that millions of people out there are not fooled for one minute by Tory propaganda, nor by the constant right wing media attacks on Labour and the unions.'

'This week, we all know the Conference motions that need to be won and those that must be defeated. Of course, the bloc votes - and as you'll see from our leaflet, the Left Caucus is opposed to bloc voting - may already have decided the fate of some motions. But we still need to make the arguments. The debates will be published. Minds can be changed - if not this year, then next year. It's important to try and win the censure motion against the NEC and that's going to be a strange one with some right wing and some left wing branches voting in a quite unpredictable way. But again let's put forward the correct arguments. We're moving and seconding the motion and we can set the terms of debate. There's also the censure motion of course against those comrades - including myself - who took part in the so-called "occupation", which we'll fight tooth and nail, but to be honest it's not critical. If it's carried, it won't be overwhelming and we'll survive.'

One of the Broad Lefters sang a snatch of *I Will Survive* and there were titters.

'Very funny, mate. But actually we'll do more than survive. What ever happens in the next few days here and the next few months nationally, if we *are* defeated this time around, let's remember the famous words of Joe Hill - "Don't mourn - organise!" To give up in despair is just what the right want us to do. Or alternatively, to carry on but in sheep's clothing, compromising our ideals, allowing ourselves to be sucked into the mire of reformism. Some of you may remember that old Sixties saying - "Don't let the bastards grind you down". Compromise is just as bad as defeat. The Left Caucus won't accept either. We're going to carry on organising and fighting. In some ways, our politics aren't radically different from most of the left. A fair day's pay, ie. pay us - men and women - the true value of our labour. We oppose all cuts and job losses imposed from above. We demand equal status and equal opportunities for all irrespective of gender, race and sexual orientation. We want open reporting - the right to know what management are saying about you and your job performance. And in the union nationally, an end to bloc voting and the adoption of workplace voting which involves and inspires the membership far more. We do differ from the Broad Left there, of

155

course. And we differ from all the other left groupings in that we don't have to follow a party line.'

'Luxury!' said Ronnie to the amusement of those around him. Joe heard but ignored it. He finished with a brief exhortation.

"In the Left Caucus, we have open, democratic and dare I say it - intelligent discussion and democratic voting on policy decisions. If you're interested, read our Newsletter, come along to our monthly meetings and talk to us. Or talk to us after this meeting. If you don't want to join us, at least work with us towards those common aims that we all share. Only by forming a genuine united front can we defeat the forces of compromise and reaction.'

There was less applause than for the previous speakers, despite the strenuous efforts of Caucus supporters. When Tim Parrish came forward to chair the discussion, it seemed that the SWP contingent and some of the Broad Lefters did not appreciate being painted as unintelligent, undemocratic, slavish hacks. The word "sectarian" soon surfaced again. It was a lively session.

Downstairs at the bar afterwards, Simon found himself standing next to Bob Armitage. He got the twinkly smile and the husky Yorkshire voice.

'How's it going, mate?'

'Yeah, not bad. Good to see you here.'

'Well there's fuck all else happening.'

'We filled a void.'

'Maloney's a bit relentless. but Joe's a good guy. Some of those people calling him sectarian - well, it's the pot calling the kettle black, isn't it? As for your feminist, she was spot on. The women can be deadlier than the male when it comes to industrial action.'

'I'll go along with that. Cheers!'

'Cheers.' Bob wiped some foam from his lips. 'Talking of women, how's that lass you were with?'

'Who, Molly?' said Simon, slightly taken aback. 'Blimey, you have got a good memory, haven't you. She's fine...but we don't see each other so much now.'

'Split up?'

'Yep.'

'That's a shame.'

'Though actually, we're going on holiday next week with some friends. It was arranged months ago - South of France. I would have

156

dropped out but Ronnie - you know Ronnie Acland? - can't find anyone else and I think he needs my petrol money. He may have some idea that it'll get us back together again as well.'

'Could be a romantic reunion. Or it could just confirm that you or she did the right thing.'

'She.'

Bob shrugged.

'I know what it's like, pal. That's what drove me over the top. That and the pressures of politics and union battles...'

'How's the drinking going? said Simon, nodding down at Bob's half-empty glass. 'I thought you were giving it up?'

'I have given it up. This is just light refreshment.'

Simon shook his head.

'I like you, Bob. Don't fucking kill yourself.'

'My doctor said "Either stop drinking or die". I could tell he was trying to frighten me. I had to explain that I would lose my mind if I stopped drinking, in which case life wouldn't be worth living anyway. We agreed on a gradual reduction. I'm down to six pints a day. Three in the afternoon, three in the evening.'

'And you've never felt better?'

'Never!' He thumped the bar.

'If I drank six pints a day, I'd be dead in six months.'

'That's because you're a southern softie, Simon. In the People's Republic of South Yorkshire, beer is part of the staple diet. The peasantry drank beer all the time because the water was so foul.'

'So I've heard. Those were the days, eh?'

'Those still are the days for some of us. We're still fucking peasants and we still drink ale. I've no idea what water tastes like.'

He peered over Simon's shoulder.

'Oh there's Fordie, just arrived. I'd better go over and join them. I'm supposed to be chairing our meeting tomorrow night.'

Simon turned around as Bob made to move away from the bar. Ray Ford, legendary leader of the Broad Left, was standing by the door, smartly suited though tieless, his hair neatly trimmed and sleeked back. Tall enough to scan the pub, his face was almost expressionless except for a glint of scorn in the eyes. Jon Elder, his steely lieutenant, stood next to him and scowled. They were a frightening pair.

'Good luck, mate.'

'I'll tell 'em the Left Caucus don't like bloc voting,' said Bob as his parting shot. 'That'll go down well.'

Simon lifted his pint from the bar and moved slowly through the crowded pub. There was no sign of Sandy or Joe and Kathy, but near the stairs, he found Maloney, McLeod and Lee standing with Mike Lincoln and Jess Jones of the SWP. The conversation was obviously about the censure motion against the occupation. Lincoln was listing on his fingers some of the branches he'd spoken to who were abstaining on the issue.

'It's all over the place. Anything could happen,' he said.

'How the *fuck* can you abstain?' said McLeod. 'Surely they can make their minds up. You either support what we did or you don't.'

'It's more complicated than that,' said Maloney. 'Some branches don't support what we did, but don't want to vote for a formal censure motion.'

'It *was* the beer talking though, wasn't it?' said Lincoln. 'Let's be honest. There was a pub across the road and the occupation began right after closing time.'

'You weren't there,' said Jess Jones.

'No, but that's how most people will see it.'

'I certainly wasn't pissed,' said Jess. 'I went along with it to try and keep those who were drunk under control.'

'No-one was staggering around drunk,' said Maloney. 'No-one was harmed. No damage was done. We left at five. It was a token gesture.'

'It was a wasted opportunity,' said McLeod.

Simon felt tired. He yawned and turned down the offer of a last beer just before 10.30. The landlord allowed a generous amount of drinking-up time, but eventually he rang the bell again.

'Time, gentlemen, please. Or I'll get my own union on to you.'

'Which union?' someone shouted.

'The NLVA, of course.'

'Whooo?'

'The National Licensed Victuallers Association.'

'They're to the right of Genghis Khan,' said Maloney. 'In fact, they're even to the right of the NFU.'

They milled for a while on the broad pavement outside the pub, talking, listening, saying temporary farewells. Someone knew a hotel where the bar would be open until the early hours and some, including Maloney, were heading that way. Simon didn't fancy it, nor did Lee. The clock of a nearby church was striking eleven - a reminder that Conference would be starting in ten hours time. They decided to head back to the boarding house.

'Let's go via the promenade,' said Simon. 'Sober up a bit.'

It was windy and chilly on the front, though calmer than earlier in the day. A few gulls wheeled overhead despite the late hour. They crossed the tram tracks to the far edge of the promenade and looked over the iron railing. To Simon's surprise, the tide was out and the sand extended before them.

'The lone and level sands stretch far away,' he said.

'What?'

'Shelley. Percival Byshhe.'

'Well they don't stretch that far. I can see the sea.'

'Shall we?'

'Why not?'

They found a set of steps which led down to the beach and walked out towards the tide. The lights behind them and the moon above diminished the darkness. As they went on, the sand became hard and rutted in parts and they had to walk around shallow pools of water. No-one else could be seen either to the left or the right. At the sea's edge, nothing could be seen ahead of them other than the gently shifting water - no ships, no lights, no buoys.

'It's like the sands at Crosby,' said Lee. 'My mam used to say if you could draw a straight line across the sea from Crosby to Ireland, it would end up at Swords - that's the town where she grew up. Whenever we went to Crosby beach when I was a kid, she would always end up at the edge of the sea staring west. I didn't think about it at the time but I suppose she was pining for her lost youth or something...'

Simon let the water lap at his toecaps. All he could think about as he gazed at the vast expanse before him was Molly. She'd talked once about coming to Conference with him. If that had happened, she'd be standing here next to him now. There was all the difference in the world between being alone and being with someone else...

'I need a pee,' said Lee.

'That's an idea.'

They peed close to the tideline and watched as the frothing water slid forward to cover the stained sand.

159

'A drop in the ocean,' said Simon as he zipped up.

'Quite a few drops actually.'

'What would your mam think?'

'She wouldn't be happy. But then she never is.'

They walked back across the sands in an erratic, slanting fashion, close at hand like the Walrus and the Carpenter, but with little to say. The end of the day had settled in their bodies. They kept a watch on the soaring Tower ahead and the cream-bricked Woolworth building alongside it until reaching dry land at last they set their course for the haven of Sea View.

10. The Lions' Den

Next morning they breakfasted like kings. Corn flakes and toast were followed by scrambled eggs, two sausages, two bacon rashers, baked beans, mushrooms and fried bread with a pot of coffee each.

'We can add black pudding tomorrow if you like,' said Gail.

'What's that?'

'It's a Lancashire delicacy, love. Made with pigs' blood.'

'We might have to think about that.'

Simon had heard Maloney banging around next door at two am and expected to see him hungover, but he appeared looking no worse than usual and ate as hearty a breakfast as his table mates.

'I've never seen anyone eat so fast,' said Gail.

They reached the Winter Gardens entrance at eight forty and joined the gauntlet of leafleters and paper sellers that all delegates had to pass through. The Left Caucus Conference Newsletter consisted of six stapled A4 pages with comment on What To Vote For, Who To Vote For and Women's Issues. The front page article by Maloney screamed CENSURE THE NEC - NOT THE RANK AND FILE! Most delegates took one and the headline elicited such trenchant replies as 'we'll censure the whole bloody lot of you' and 'rank and file, my arse.'

They packed up just before nine and hastened through the long foyer to the Ballroom where the President's voice boomed crisply around the auditorium, welcoming everyone to Conference 1983. As an observer, Lee had gone to the Balcony and his feet could soon be seen resting on the front rail.

The main business began with motion after motion debated in accordance with the official programme. Movers, seconders and speakers came to the rostrum from the floor or spoke from the NEC top table. The little traffic lights on the rostrum changed from green to amber to red in line with laid down time limits. There were good speeches, poor speeches, rousing speeches, flat speeches, funny speeches and corny speeches. Hands went up and down when the President called the vote. From time to time, Maloney disappeared to do the rounds of hall, corridor and tea bar. Simon imagined him huddling and accosting, urging and arguing with activists of various stripes, gathering information and building up a picture. Five minutes before the Cuts censure motion was due to be heard - the last motion of the morning - he slid back into his seat.

'Ford's going to oppose the motion on behalf of the NEC.'

'What - not the General Secretary?'

'Nah, he'd just say - I did what the NEC told me to do. They're putting the Broad Left on the spot, basically.'

'Hmm, interesting. Are you going to try and get in?'

'Maybe, but I don't think he'll choose me given that Joe's moving. You might have a chance.'

'Me?' Simon felt a stab of anxiety in his chest.

'Yeah, I know you like to have your speeches all neatly written out, but just jot down a few points while he's speaking. You know all the arguments. The more spontaneous you sound, the better.'

Simon sighed. He'd spoken at Conference for the first time two years ago. The prospect had seemed unreal and the night before was entirely sleepless. He had turned and turned again on a hard hotel bed while a thousand delegates crowded into his mind and sat there to watch and judge him. But come the morning, it had gone reasonably well. The Branch's motion on workplace creche facilities had been near the start of business. The microphone had carried his voice easily around the hall and seemed to lend it an extra authority. The President - that reformist fucker in the Big Chair at the centre of the top table - had been a reassuring presence behind him. He was there to quell any mockery or abuse and allow anyone other than uniformed Nazis the right to say their piece. Even when Simon's speech had overrun and the red light had gleamed before him - even then, the President ("Wind up now, please") had given him extra seconds to leap over two paragraphs and cobble together a conclusion. And there had been solid applause. Now he was unprepared, but knew he had to rise to the challenge or Maloney would never let him forget. With luck there'd be many arms in the air and he would not be among the chosen.

'Fuck.'

He pulled a notepad from his bag as Joe stepped up to the rostrum. It was difficult trying to listen while scribbling down a few choice phrases of his own.

'Our campaign against the cuts was right,' said Joe. 'Our campaign against the cuts had real momentum and was gathering widespread support in the public sector and with the public.' His confident East

End voice reached every corner of the hall. *Importance of dissent,* Simon wrote down. 'Our campaign - which surely was the campaign of all of us here today and of the members in our branches - was not just a campaign against the cuts and poorer service to the public.' *Real voice of the public must be heard. Standard bearers.* 'Our campaign was a campaign against job losses, against more people being thrown out of work and consigned to the human scrapheap that the Tories are building.' Applause. *Helping the Tories break the unemployment record.*

'And then what happened? Capitulation. Even worse - capitulation disguised as victory. No, let me be fair. It's important to be fair.' Ironic laughter from some quarters. 'It was "partial victory". "The best deal that could be achieved". Brothers and sisters - how can a deal resulting in 10% job losses ever be described as some kind of victory?' Moderate applause with cheers and whistles from some quarters. *Fact that job losses = vol redunds irrelevant.* 'The NEC know perfectly well what game the Tories are playing. Start with a high-level threat, then lower it and let the troops think they've won something. Lower it so the Tories can say - "Look, we're reasonable. We've listened to your concerns".' *Line should have been drawn in ground. No retreat.* 'Does the NEC really think that rank and file members don't understand that trick? "You can only fool some of the people some of the time" as Abraham Lincoln once said. And what are the Tories now saying to themselves? "A 10% cut will do very nicely, thank you - for now".' Scattered applause, two cheers.

Joe continued up to the amber light and raised his voice for the peroration.

'Brothers and sisters. No-one likes to censure our Executive Committee. But a door has been wedged open and the Tories will be back for more. Our fight for jobs must therefore be taken seriously. A clear message must be sent from us and our membership. No more deals! No more cuts! There *is* power in a union. We can fight and we can win. Support this motion!' The applause was moderate with some cheers, whistles and foot stamping. Maloney stood to applaud and a few others did around the hall. Simon was too busy scribbling to join in. *NEC must represent will of the members. Use our power. Serious fight for jobs and future prosperity.*

'Oh, shit,' he whispered. He'd forgotten there'd be a seconder. He'd have to listen to her as well. And *God* - Ray Ford replying on behalf of the NEC. He gripped his pen.

The seconder was an SWP member who read from sheets of paper and rarely looked up. Her voice was a monotone, stumbling over sentences that evoked little response from the hall until somebody yawned loudly and there were titters of amusement.

'The deal was a sell out, plain and simple. Our members have been betrayed. Wheeled out to demonstrate on the front line, then shoved back in the box when it suited the NEC.' *What point the No Cuts slogan?* 'The result of this so-called victory is more job losses, fewer promotion prospects and, as the mover of this motion said, the door is now open for more.' *Wheeling and dealing - thought of winning never occurred.* 'Brothers and sisters, we need to trust our rank and file members. They know when they're being screwed. We need to show the Tories we mean business. But right now, we need to send a clear message to our membership' - 'Wind up, please' - 'that we want action, not words, victory not collaboration. Please support this motion.' Mild applause, except from the usual quarters. Simon put his notepad down and joined Maloney in some enthusiastic clapping.

'Ray Ford will reply to the motion on behalf of the NEC,' said the President.

Simon watched as Ford stood before one of the microphones on the top table. In a slim fitting suit, white shirt and maroon tie, he looked smarter than both the President and the pipe-puffing General Secretary. The usual expression of contempt was softened, but the sense of comfortable confidence was manifest.

'Brothers and sisters, we have many important issues to debate at this conference and I won't take up too much of your time with this effort. Frankly, this is a contemptible motion moved and supported by elements in this union who are stuck in the student politics of the 1960s.' Strong applause. 'They are not part of the long and genuine tradition of the labour movement that we cherish and wish to continue serving. They are Johnny Come Latelies who naively think there are short cuts to the victory of the working class. I've been a union member since I left the School of Hard Knocks at the age of fifteen and I know there are not.' Applause.

'Let me just give you three facts about the Cuts Campaign. Firstly, the membership was not solidly in favour of industrial action. That was reflected in the Branch voting and the turn-out on 19th January. There was a majority but not as big as for last year's pay strikes, for example. And the bosses knew that. Unfortunately, some of our members think cuts are necessary to support economic recovery. We still have work to do in convincing them that the opposite is true. Secondly, the Tory government was not bluffing with its demand for 20% cuts. They produced a paper which worked out how those cuts could be achieved. I've seen it. And let me tell you, if we'd let those cuts go through, we'd deserve to be censured. But we didn't. We used every tactic at our disposal - not just the sledgehammer of strike action - to ensure that the majority of those cuts were averted.' Applause. 'Thirdly, despite the cuts that we did have to agree to, not one single member of this union - in fact, not even one single non-member - will lose his or her job as a result of the agreement that we negotiated.' Loud applause and whistling.

'In conclusion, let me say this. A general election is due within the next year. I hope that the Labour Party with its bold new manifesto will be returned to power. But we just don't know. The Tories are like one of those alien races in Doctor Who who keep on returning to earth' - widespread chuckles - 'who seem to have a mesmerising effect on some folk and may yet cling on to power. But if that happens, we are ready. By keeping our powder dry, by not throwing every egg at the overlords, we are ready to fight again.' Applause. The amber light came on. 'This motion supports what Trotskyites in their better moments call "adventurism". This motion seeks to undermine our solidarity. This motion is disloyal, divisive and insulting. Conference, I call on you to show our loyal membership what you think of it. Throw it out!' Loud applause and cheers.

Simon realised he hadn't noted down a single word. And Maloney had disappeared again.

'Shit!'

Arms arose on all sides. A Broad Left branch activist was chosen and came forward to oppose the motion. Hardly listening, Simon stared down at his notepad. After some reflection, he crossed through his previous notes and wrote down half a dozen words in a column. Then he tore out the page. When the next call came, he thrust his hand in the air but someone else was chosen. When the next call came, the President pointed straight at him. Startled, Simon pointed a finger at his chest and mouthed 'me?' The President nodded. The world seemed unreal again, but he walked rapidly to the rostrum and placed his single page on the stand. The green light came on. Remembering his past experience, he gave his name and branch, took a breath and began.

'Brothers and sisters.' His voice was quavering slightly and he paused to take another breath.

'This is a democratic trade union and any branch should be able to challenge the NEC without experiencing the condescension and belittlement that we've heard just now from Ray Ford.' Scattered applause. 'He used the word "loyalty". How dare he accuse the members in my branch of "disloyalty" because they weren't impressed by the deal agreed by the NEC? My members have supported this union through thick and thin. And if they're all so-called "Trotskyites" by the way, they've been keeping it very quiet.' It was very quiet in the hall.

'My members agreed to support this motion at a well-attended branch meeting. They've been on the picket line every year in all the struggles we've been through. But they're tired of seeing the agreed aims of the union that they've marched for and chanted on the streets being abandoned. They're tired of endless compromise. They didn't fight for "only 10% cuts". They didn't chant - "What do we want? 10% cuts! When do we want it? Now!"' Applause. Some laughter. "And of course, Ray has said nothing about the cut in promotion prospects that a 10% cut means.' Nodding of heads. An undercurrent of assent. Simon began to feel more confident.

'Ray tells us there was only a small majority in favour of strike action. How often have we heard that before as an excuse? Perhaps if the NEC really showed that it meant business, more members would respond. How could they *not* when we're facing obviously the most anti-working class government in living memory? He paused. 'Now I remember seeing Ray at the Conference disco last year. He was - I won't say *dancing*, but certainly *moving*. And he's quite a nifty mover in all sorts of ways. And what was he moving to? Let me spell it out. "*Get* up. *Stand* up. Stand up for your *rights*." Applause and a cheer from the usual quarters. The amber light came on. 'Not *get* down, *sit* down and *negotiate away* our rights.' He paused again. There was silence.

'Conference, this is getting serious. If the Tories get back in, they will go to town on the trade union movement. We will have to take

166

action purely in self-defence of a sort that hasn't been seen since the 1920s. I ask you therefore to support this motion. Not in a negative manner, but as a wake-up call to the NEC. No more shadow boxing. We need to draw a line in the ground and fight before it's too late. Thank you.'

He walked back to his seat amid polite applause with a few louder surges, but all of it sounding some distance away like a retreating ocean tide.

'Well done,' said Maloney. 'Good speech apart from one thing.'

'What?'

'A bit too personal with regard to Ray Ford.'

'Oh for fuck's sake. The guy's a cunt.'

'I know. But if we're serious about building the Left Caucus, we have to build bridges with him and the Broad Left. Otherwise, we'll stay in the same old cul-de-sac with the SWP.'

Simon thought about this.

'I wasn't that critical of him.'

'That stuff about him at the disco. You were trying to make him look silly. It was too clever, Simon. We just need to make the arguments.'

Simon felt angry, but didn't know whether it was with himself or Maloney.

After another opposition speaker, the President picked a well-known member of the Sunlight Group who supported the censure motion. Simon groaned as the man dragged out a familiar stock figure.

'This NEC has behaved like the Grand Old Duke of York. They've marched the members halfway up the hill and then said: "Wait here a minute. We'll just nip up to the top and see what's going on." When they've returned, they've marched them back down to the bottom of the hill saying: "Don't worry, lads and lassies. It's all sorted out."' Mild applause. 'Now Conference, I'm not one who supported strike action on this issue. I only support strike action as an absolute last resort and we were nowhere near that point. What the NEC have achieved could have been achieved without strike action in my view and a lot of people back in the branches have lost pay for nothing.' Applause. 'But if you *are* going to take that step, then you should at least be prepared to follow it through. Instead, the NEC have treated what Ray Ford calls "our loyal membership" with contempt. For that

167

reason, I and my branch support this motion though for different reasons than the mover and seconder.' Jeers. 'The NEC deserve to be censured because the whole sorry saga merely reflects their total incompetence to lead this union. I urge you therefore to support this motion.' Loud applause from the usual quarters. Boos and jeers from the usual quarters.

'I'm worried now we might win this motion for the wrong reasons,' said Simon. Maloney shook his head.

'The right wing are split on the issue. Some oppose the motion because they don't like where it's come from. Others support it for the reasons that twat gave. But the Broad Left will now say we're working hand in glove with the right.'

The final speaker from the floor was a veteran Broad Left sympathiser who denounced the motion as a 'straightforward assault' on the NEC which would have 'disastrous implications for our credibility as a strong union' if passed.

The President looked at his watch, then at Joe who was standing beside the rostrum.

'Right of reply?'

Joe nodded and moved to the microphone.

'Briefly, Mr President, I just want to say that this motion is not an attack on the character and politics of the NEC as all the opposition speakers have made out. The fact is this government - in very simple terms - is out to get us. It's out to destroy the trade union movement and the working class communities we represent. We have to fight back even more strongly than they're attacking us. The era of deals and compromises is over and you're letting the wool be pulled over your eyes if you think any differently. Finally, I would like to disassociate myself and my branch from the speaker before last. He and his branch may support this motion but for entirely the wrong reasons. Thank you.'

As Joe left the rostrum to scattered applause, the President tapped his fingers on the elevated desk before him and spoke.

'I'll let that go this time, but can I remind movers who wish to exercise their right of reply....that you may only reply to points raised in opposition to your motion. If someone speaks in support of your motion but in terms you don't like, that's just too bad I'm afraid.' Loud applause with Ray Ford raising his hands aloft at the top table.

'In view of the contentious nature of this motion, we'll go straight to a card vote. Tellers, please!'

A buzz of voices spread over the conference floor. The tellers appeared beside seat blocks with special badges hung around their necks.

'All those in favour of motion 65, please raise your green card.'

Maloney raised the branch card and Simon stood to look around. A fair proportion of cards were in the air. When the vote against was called, it looked as if a larger number of arms rose up. Everything depended on how many votes those arms represented.

'We're not going to win, are we?'

'Of course not. The Broad Left will have enough right wing branches voting with them to sink the motion.'

'I think we can now adjourn for lunch,' said the President after consultation with the Chief Teller and the Chair of Standing Orders. 'Can we recommence at one forty five please when the result of the card vote will be announced.'

Simon felt confused and depressed as he and Maloney joined the crowd shuffling slowly out of the hall.

'What was the point of submitting that motion?' he said. 'It was never going to be carried and half the votes in its favour will come from the other side. It's turned into a big deal in the wrong way.'

'Are you serious? It's helped to establish the Left Caucus as a presence in the union and it's made a crucial point. You don't build a fightback against *this* government by deals in back rooms. If the Tories win the next election, there won't *be* any more deals. They'll just tell the unions to fuck off.'

'Yes but now we're associated with the right wing.'

'So what? The Broad Left will only defeat the motion with the help of the right wing. Anyway, Conference isn't everything you know. The important thing is whether this influences the Broad Left in future and whether it makes the membership think about tactics.'

Simon shook his head.

'The Broad Left'll carry on just as they always have,' he said.

'We'll see.'

They emerged into the long foyer and started threading their way towards the exit. Two people who Simon didn't know said 'Good speech, mate' and an SWPer said something similar. He was hoping to avoid anyone who was influential in the Broad Left, at least until

169

he had a couple of pints inside him. Unfortunately, as they detoured around a group of delegates huddled in discussion, they came upon the most influential of them all with several of his henchmen and women.

'Good afternoon, Tony,' said Ray Ford. 'We were just discussing the future merger of the Left Carcass and the Sunlight Group.'

'Your banner could say *Where the Sunlight Don't Shine*,' said Jon Elder.

There was mocking laughter from the group with a few looks of contempt thrown in. Simon was relieved that Bob Armitage wasn't among them.

'Very funny,' said Maloney. 'That would be the same Sunlight Group whose votes you need to defeat the motion.'

'I can tell you now that the motion has been defeated,' said Ford.

'Really? Now how could you *possibly* know that?'

'Oh, not because the tellers are all corrupt Broad Left members. No, it's because I've got the knowledge. Up here. I can look at arms raised in the air and work out very quickly how many votes they represent.'

'Ah, the good old bloc voting system that gives you your power. Something else you've got in common with Sunlight...'

'Bloc voting gives the *union* power, Tony. Anyway, you're right about one thing. None of this is very funny, is it Jon?'

.No, Ray, it isn't. And as for your smarty-pants friend here' - Elder glared briefly in Simon's direction - 'and his witty comments, I'd keep him under wraps if I were you. For his own protection.'

Simon's heart was beating fast. He tried to take a deep breath without it being too evident. *Say something? What?*

'Is that a threat?' said Maloney.

'It's advice. From the People's Advice Bureau.'

'Okay, we'll get back to you when you're in a better mood. It wasn't meant to be an anti-Broad Left motion-'

Ford interrupted.

'It was though, Tony. It was. But we're in a perfectly good mood, thanks all the same. Anyway we have to go now and feed the inner man. After all, there is another important censure motion coming up this afternoon.'

170

'Can I just say one more thing, though,' said Jon Elder as if a serious thought had occurred to him. 'And it's only a suggestion. But why don't you all just...*fuck off back to the SWP*.'

And laughing, they turned almost as one and moved off towards the exit. Maloney followed without adjusting his stride but looking away from them. Simon trailed after him. Outside on the pavement, they found Joe leaning against a lamppost with Kathy and Tim Parrish.

'The Yorkshire Soviet went that-a-way,' said Joe.

'Well let's go this-a-way.'

'You saw them?'

'We met them inside. They told us what they thought of us.'

'Oh dear. Not good?'

'They threatened me while hardly bothering to look at me,' said Simon.

'He's to be terminated like some irritating insect,' said Maloney.

'Oh, thanks.'

'I've heard they turn extra nasty when they come to Lancashire,' said Joe.

'Where's Mad Dog McLeod?' said Simon.

'Oh, he only came for the weekend,' said Maloney. 'His branch didn't elect him as a delegate. That's how much influence he has with the rank and file.'

'Thank God. Where's Lee?'

But nobody knew.

'He'll turn up,' said Joe. 'Let's go and get some medicine and have a proper chinwag. We may not have got things *quite right*, you know.'

They walked up Church Street and found a grand old corner pub which provided at least some of the sustenance their bodies and souls needed.

When they got back to Conference, the card votes had been counted and the President announced the result. The motion was defeated by some 25,000 votes, not a huge margin but substantial enough. Clearly, some right wing branches had voted for it, along with the Left Caucus and SWP branches and probably a good swathe of the DE Section where Joe was a popular figure.

'Could have been worse,' said Maloney.

171

The occupation censure motion was scheduled for around three pm. Maloney sat reading and annotating his scribbled notes with furrowed brow. They hardly listened to the debates but their arms went up and down routinely when votes were called. At one point, Simon looked round and saw that Lee was once again resting his feet on the balcony rail. After an hour or so, Simon went to the toilet to retrieve the pressure of lunchtime beer. When he returned, the General Secretary had just risen to his feet to move the motion. A tall stick of a man in a buttoned-up suit, he recounted in a lilting voice 'more in sorrow than anger' the basic facts which had led the NEC to submit this motion.

On the morning of 27th January, a group of about 50 members had picketed an NEC meeting at Union HQ called to discuss 'the terms agreed in principle between the Employer and the Union's full time officials for concluding the industrial action in respect of the proposed economy measures.' The picket had led to some strong arguments with arriving NEC members which had delayed the start of the meeting. At eleven am with the meeting underway, the picket had disbanded. At three pm, shortly after the conclusion of the meeting, about 25 members had returned and entered the reception area of the building. They had discovered from departing NEC members that the government's terms had been accepted and that the industrial campaign would be called off. The protestors then moved into the main ground floor admin offices, sat down and declared themselves to be 'in occupation.'

Despite the best efforts of AGS Peter Lerner and *Public Servant* editor Steve O'Neill, the protestors refused to budge. Eventually, the admin staff had to be sent home and the switchboard closed. The protestors then demanded that he, the GS, came to meet them. 'Conference, I refused point blank to address people who were occupying our building and disrupting our work.' Applause. Instead he had offered to address them outside in the forecourt. The protestors refused to accept this offer. Finally, 'to cut a long story short', a compromise was agreed. The protestors left the admin offices and assembled in the reception area where he had outlined the reasoning behind the NEC decision. After a long and difficult discussion, the protestors had left the building at five fifteen pm.

No members of staff were abused during this episode though some intemperate language was addressed at Peter, Steve and himself, 'but we have broad shoulders.' No damage was done to property. Nevertheless it could not be regarded as 'just a storm in a teacup.' A line had been crossed. Legitimate dissent was 'one of the hallmarks of this union', but this sort of behaviour was unacceptable. Word had got out 'within the movement' and the union had been embarrassed. The NEC therefore felt that Conference had to fire 'a warning shot across the bows' and strongly censure those involved. Expulsion from the union could not be ruled out if such a thing ever happened again, though that was the last thing he wanted to happen.

There was strong applause when the GS sat down but Maloney looked puzzled.

'Hmm...not quite as thunderous as I expected.'

'He's a wimp.'

'He can be a nasty little shit when he feels like it.'

The motion was seconded by Len Fawcett, a leading Sunlight member whose voice flowed with irritating smoothness out of a short rotund body. He added 'a little more detail that delegates may not be aware of.' The 'so-called protestors' - in reality, the 'usual far left extremists' - had spent the hours between eleven and three in 'a local hostelry.' They had entered the HQ building as a 'drunken rabble'. They may not have abused any of 'the ladies' on reception or in the offices, but their language was 'loud and unrestrained'. One of them had climbed out of a window and urinated on a flower bed. And delegates who found that amusing should be ashamed of themselves. They had insulted and abused Peter, Steve and the GS who had shown great restraint throughout. Had it been him, he would have told the mob 'exactly what to do with themselves'. To cap it all, a journalist from the Evening Standard had arrived. Luckily, the protestors had left by then and the HQ officers were able to persuade her that there was no story. Otherwise, this 'whole outrageous affair' could have 'sullied the reputation' of the entire public sector trade union movement.

The red light came on and Len wound himself down. There was loud applause from the usual quarters, but little from elsewhere. Maloney had already sprung to his feet with arm raised and the President summoned him. Simon watched as he strode confidently to the rostrum. The green light came on and he began.

'Someone said to me at lunchtime that if I got the chance to speak, I'd be like Daniel in the lions' den. Really? It feels more like I've

173

wandered into a circus. How does that song go about sending in the clowns? They're already here, or something? You can't expect a Trotskyist to know the exact words.' Scattered laughter and applause. 'So thank you Len Fawcett and no doubt there are a few more clowns waiting in the wings. And we've had two versions of what happened on 27th January. The official version from the GS who at least was there. And the fevered imaginings of Len Fawcett who was nowhere near the place. But the question is - why are we having this debate? It's absurd. As Ray Ford said this morning, there are far more important issues that we need to discuss.'

'As a union representing working people, we face huge challenges. If the Tories get back after the next election, those challenges are obvious. If Labour get back in with such a radical manifesto, the bosses and the media will attack them from every angle. In fact I wouldn't rule out a military coup.' He paused. 'And yet here we are focusing on a minor incident in which two dozen members occupied HQ for two hours. And if it's true that a journalist turned up at that event, well there are journalists here today, so how hypocritical is that? Our little jaunt could have besmirched the reputation of the entire trade union movement, says Len, so let's publicise it all again and give the press another chance.' Applause. Some laughter. The amber light came on.

'Conference, let me briefly set the record straight. About fifty members did indeed turn up at HQ on 27th January to picket the NEC meeting. At eleven o'clock, we went to the pub across the road and during the next few hours, alas, consumed more beer than food. Whoever heard of such a thing in this great and glorious movement of ours?' Laughter. 'At three pm, about 25 of those members including myself went back to HQ to find that the meeting had finished. We met the last two departing NEC members who told us that the industrial action had been called off. A decision was taken on the spot to enter the HQ building and demand to see the General Secretary. This turned into a two hour "occupation" while we waited. Do we regret it?' The red light came on. 'No. It was a justified protest over the ditching of a Conference decision. I regret that we'd been drinking because that's fuelled all sorts of slanderous misrepresentation.' 'Wind up please.' 'But no-one was hurt, no damage was done and the flower bed, I understand, is recovering. Conference, oppose this motion!'

'Motion of order!'

The loud Yorkshire voice from the back of the hall ensured that the applause died almost before it had begun. Some delegates looked confused and there was a buzz of speculative discussion both on the conference floor and at the top table. Simon turned around to see Bob Armitage marching down the central aisle and then mounting the rostrum while the President sat back in his chair.

'Conference, I think we've heard all we need to hear. The basic points have been made but to continue is to waste valuable conference time and is not, I submit, in the best interests of this union. I move next business.'

The buzz got louder as delegates conferred. The President spoke briefly to the General Secretary and then to the Conference.

'I accept the motion of order that we proceed to the next item of business. Could I see all those in favour? Those against?'

Instinctively, Simon had voted in favour, but from where he sat it looked very close. After a slight hesitation and glance at the GS, the President spoke again.

'The motion is carried. We'll move to the next item on the agenda.'

'Card vote!'

The President scanned the hall quickly.

'There aren't the required number of delegates on their feet as far as I can see. And let's not be silly about this. As the mover said, both sides of the case have been put and I think the general feeling is to move on.'

And they did so with a wave of applause from the floor and Ray Ford nodding his assent from the top table.

'Er, what happened?' Simon asked as Maloney returned to his seat.

'Elementary, my dear Hayes. I suggested it to Bob last night in the hotel bar while you were sound asleep in bed. It turned out the Broad Left had already been thinking about it. They don't want to piss us off entirely because things are so close now between left and right they might need our votes one day. On the other hand, it wouldn't do their credibility much good if they were to openly support a bunch of ultraleft loonies. Sweeping it under the rug therefore was the best way forward.'

'But Ford seemed to indicate at lunchtime that they were looking forward to censuring us.'

175

'He was just keeping us on the rack a bit longer. I didn't know whether they were going to go for it or not.'

'And why was Elder telling us to rejoin the SWP?'

'Oh, he's just a hardcase who can't restrain himself. Ford and Armitage are wiser men.'

The rest of Conference 83 went by in a welter of speeches, drinking sessions and meetings in smoke-filled rooms. There were many hoarse voices by Thursday morning when, as half-expected, the Sunlight Group won a small majority in the NEC elections. But no-one seemed too despondent about this. It was assumed that the pendulum would swing back again next year and the Left would return triumphant and renewed.

On the train back to London on Thursday afternoon, Maloney harangued Lee who had frequently gone missing during the last few days.

'You've joined *what*?'

'The Labour Party Young Socialists.'

'Come on, be honest. You've joined fucking *Militant*, haven't you?'

'I'm thinking about it. They're very impressive.'

'They are if you're very impressionable. They turn out so-called revolutionary Marxists on a conveyor belt, all yapping the same limited policies.'

'They're doing great things in Liverpool. They're really going to take on Thatcher if she wins the next election.'

'Yes, but they're not up to it. They're not capable of doing what really needs to be done. It needs a broad front - a *socialist* broad front - and they're not interested in building that. They're even more deluded and sectarian than the SWP. It will end in tears, believe me.'

They were all weary and Simon fell asleep soon after Rugby, waking only as the train jerked into Euston. Their goodbyes were brief and perfunctory. On the tube, Simon stood in a dull trance amid office workers absorbed in their Walkmans and the black and white pages of the Evening Standard. At Finsbury Park, traffic roared through the streets and the shops and cafes were doing business as usual. Nothing had changed. On Stroud Green Road, he realised what was happening. He was coming down from an adrenaline high. He was falling to earth.

11. Gorges du Loup

When Simon met Molly outside Victoria Station on Friday evening, it was the first time he'd seen her since that bright day near the beginning of March when their relationship had finally expired. He'd told Maloney first, simply because he saw him every working day. He'd told Lizzie and Matt during a long intense evening over beer and curry which had ended with a taxi back to Matt and Anna's flat in Battersea and an overnight stay - Simon on the sofa, Lizzie in the spare bedroom. The next day being a Saturday, they'd gone to a local pub at lunchtime, then returned to the flat and spent a jolly hour accompanying the Chieftains on spoons and other kitchen utensils, much to the annoyance of neighbours. After that, Simon had somehow found his way back to Stroud Green, collapsed on the bed and cried himself to sleep until the wee small hours. From then on, he'd told people as casually as possible and met their sympathy with a tough guy shrug. And now here was Molly again, looking more or less as she had on the first day of their relationship, but as distant as that memory and unsmiling.

'There are twin beds in our room, right?' she said as they stood on the tube escalator.

'As far as I'm aware. I've explained the situation to Ronnie.'

'If we have to share a bed, Simon, it had better be a very big one.'

'We're staying at a hotel en route for a night and I think Ronnie might have had to book a double for that.'

They reached the platform and Simon went through the details as they waited for the train.

'Ronnie wants to be back by the Friday after next, so it'll probably be about 11-12 days.'

'Uh-huh.'

'The house belongs to his mother and her partner. His parents separated when he was at university. She's a doctor and he's in advertising or something like that. Anyway they're loaded...I don't think they even let this place out.'

Molly sniffed and said nothing.

'I think it's a nice place, but Ronnie's been vague about the details. I think he sees it as too bourgeois and, you know, doesn't go there very often.'

'More fool him.'

They didn't talk on the tube. At Brixton, there was no sign of Ronnie outside the tube station. Simon pulled a piece of paper from his pocket on which he'd scrawled a crude map.

'What shall we do? He said it's about half a mile.'

'Don't you have a phone number.'

'Yes, but their phone's not always working.'

'Well why not try it and see. I'm not walking half a mile with this.'

The phone box further along the road was occupied. They went and stood outside it with their suitcases, watching the busy to-and-fro of people and cars. At last, the man came out of the box and Simon went in. He dialled the number, listened to the ring tone and waited nervily with his coin pressing against the slot. But then came a loud rapping against the glass...What was it? Outside, Molly was turning away to give Ronnie a hug. He put the receiver down and went out.

'Evening all.'

'I was just trying to phone you.'

'What for? I'm here.'

'I thought you'd forgotten.'

'Oh ye of no faith. The car's just around the corner in - dah dah - *Electric Avenue*...'

Simon was familiar with the car, a four door estate called the Avenger with a capacious boot in which they dumped their luggage.

'Wow, this is big,' said Molly. 'How long have you had this?'

'It's on loan from my dad. He can't quite bring himself to give it to me because he thinks I should be doing more with my life. You know, get a private sector job, earn more money, etc. Made by Chrysler. See the badge?' He patted the boot lid. 'It's called the puckered arsehole. Not by Chrysler, of course.'

Molly looked at it.

'Oh, yes.'

Ronnie laughed.

'Always cracks me up. Hey, no pun intended! Anyway, how are you two?'

'Oh, fine,' said Simon.

'I'm well, thank you,' said Molly. 'Can I sit in the front?'

'You can but you'll have to belt up.'

They settled into the car.

'Oh God, I've never used one of these before.'

'Here, look. Pull it out and push it in till it clicks.'

He started off and drove them smoothly through the back streets of Brixton.

'Yeah, made by Scottish workers at Linwood this car. Usual story. Badly managed factory, passed to the multinationals - Chrysler, then Peugeot - who played around with it. Closed two years ago. You probably remember?'

'Fraid not,' said Molly.

'Thousands of jobs lost. Dead now, Linwood. A ghost town. Hugely successful at one time. They made the Hillman Imp there - you must have heard of that?'

'Oh, yes...I think my sister had one of those. Second hand.'

'British Rail used to run a special train to bring them down south. Hundred cars at a time. Absolute fucking tragedy. Of course, Thatcher had a hand in it.'

'She usually does,' said Simon.

'Here we are.'

Ronnie turned into a short street with a terrace of flaking Victorian houses on one side and a crumbling brick wall along the other. Waste land could be seen through gaps in the brickwork. A huge message had been whitewashed across part of the wall...

LILAC ROAD MASTURBATES WITHOUT FEELING GUILTY

'Who did that?' asked Molly.

'A rival gang of street squatters,' said Ronnie. 'We added the last word.'

He led them into one of the houses. The hall was empty and bare other than posters and a house noticeboard. Someone had scraped away a large patch of wallpaper to reveal different layers beneath. Simon and Molly left their suitcases in a back room where they were due to spend the night. It seemed to be used as both dumping ground and crash pad. Boxes and stuffed bin bags lay around the sides, a bicycle was propped up against a wall and in the centre was a double mattress.

'I've put a clean sheet on it,' said Ronnie.

He gave them a tour of the ground floor. The big front room had two sofas, assorted armchairs, a large striped rug and an old TV set in the corner. The bathroom had missing floorboards but was relatively clean. The kitchen was narrow but long with a scuffed

179

pine dining table at the rear. It had a hole in the floor too but with a plank placed across it. There was a pot of chili on the hob, a pot of rice next to it and a stack of plates. Following Ronnie's example, they helped themselves and sat at the table with cans of beer that Simon had brought. They were joined by a jolly blonde woman called Mel who'd been minding the food.

'They'll be up from the meeting soon,' she said.

'Aren't you two supposed to be at the meeting?' asked Simon.

'No, it's for those who aren't working. Or officially working, which is most of the people in this house.'

'It's about changes to UB rules and social security entitlement,' said Ronnie.

'We'll join them on the demo, won't we, Ron?'

'We certainly fucking will, Melanie.'

It turned out that Mel was a social work assistant in Lambeth. She regaled them for a while with case stories she'd come across.

'This old couple were living in a time warp, they dressed like Victorians, didn't seem to understand modern English at all, I've never seen anything like it...this family, the father'd had a heart attack, lost his job and was on medication, the mother had a hip problem and hobbled round everywhere and their daughter was mentally disabled and had recently scalded herself in the bath...the wife had succumbed to Alzheimer's which is basically where you lose your mind and can't remember things and the husband had covered it up...I was thinking of training to be a proper social worker so I could help more, but I don't know - it's a challenging field to work in...'

There were footsteps on the basement stairs and voices getting louder and then six or seven people were milling about in the kitchen, glancing at the visitors, peering at the food and still talking.

'I'm still not sure that's the right approach.'

'Has anyone seen my tablets?'

'Jake and Ros - it's your turn to wash up tonight.'

'We know, we know.'

'We'll get out of your way,' said Ronnie after introducing Simon and Molly.

'Can't we wash our plates to help out?' said Molly.

'No, just leave them on the side,' said Ros. 'If you're guests of Ronnie, you're guests of the house.'

'Well thank you, whoever cooked that. It was delicious.'

'You're welcome,' said Hector.

They went into the living room. The TV was on with volume turned low. Ronnie and Molly sat on the brown leather sofa, Simon sat in a matching armchair.

'We found these on the pavement just off Brixton Road,' said Ronnie. 'It was a complete three-piece suite, but one of the armchairs was a little bit manky so we left it. We've got standards, you know.'

'Must be something wrong with them,' said Simon peering at the sofa legs.

'Nah, we turned them over and had a good inspection. No woodworm, nothing. This whole neighbourhood is like one big furniture exchange sometimes. I heard a massive rumbling sound the other day and looked out the window. Two guys were pushing a wardrobe on casters along the pavement.'

People drifted in and out of the room and the only time anyone watched TV was when M*A*S*H came on. After that, Hector settled on the other sofa and read one of his latest poems.

Our fire lights up the beach
a glowing circle in the night
glints on beer bottles
white bones on tawny sand
darkness deep around us

and when my song is done
in shadows of flickering flame
we make love for the first time
and it is so beautiful to feel
my essence flow into your body

and lying together afterwards
my arms enfolding you
we hear the wash of the sea
as the new meaning of life
swells within us

'Wow, that was cool,' said Mel. 'Sex on the beach. But does that last bit mean you got her pregnant?'

181

'Fortunately, no,' said Hector. 'It's about losing your virginity and coming out of adolescence. A rite of passage. Starting to see life in a different way.'

'Simon's an English Literature graduate,' said Ronnie. 'What did you think, Simon?'

'That was good,' said Simon.

'Shelley's the only poet who means anything to me,' said Ronnie. 'Red Shelley.'

Hector liked Shelley too and quoted the last five lines of *The Masque of Anarchy*.

'That's it,' said Ronnie. 'Fantastic!'

They talked about Shelley for a while and sandy beaches and union conferences which no-one else had ever been to. After that, Ros made some coffee and Sue suggested holding a séance, but that came to nothing. Instead, Jake strummed a guitar and they sang a few songs from the Big Red Songbook. Then Billy the drugdealer called by and stood in the hallway in his motorcycle leathers and helmet. He carried a brown leather pouch from which he drew some little blocks of red leb in cellophane wraps. Simon leaned in the doorway watching the transactions and felt Molly brush past him.

'I'm afraid I need to go to bed, Ronnie,' she said. 'I'm tired and if I have any of that stuff, I'll feel even worse.'

She disappeared into the bathroom and Simon hesitated, but knew he wouldn't be wanted. He subsided into the brown leather sofa, watched the spliff being rolled and passed it on when it came around.

'Are you and Molly okay?' Ronnie asked at one point in lowered voice. 'I mean I know you've split, but are you okay together?'

Simon made the so-so gesture.

'We're okay as can be.'

After a while, he said goodnight to the half dozen people sprawled around the room and went to the bathroom. As he sat, the prim chimes of a church clock announced the midnight hour through an open window. It sounded somewhat incongruous in a Brixton squat of drugs, revolution and holes in the floor.

When he'd done with the bathroom, he opened the back room door as quietly as he could and closed it behind him. It seemed ridiculous that this should feel like a bold move. What else was he supposed to do? He stood still for a few moments to let his eyes adjust. There

182

were no curtains or blinds, but the window faced north and the back of a dark Victorian terrace, so there was only a soft fall of light from outside. Molly lay on the mattress half undressed, covered with blankets, asleep. There were no other blankets, so Simon took his shoes off and lay down fully clothed next to her. They were singing to a guitar again in the living room, but quietly, dreamily. Someone was talking in the kitchen, then there were footsteps on the stairs and on the ceiling and a siren wailing in the streets. And somewhere behind or beyond it all was the soothing hum of the giant hidden dynamo that kept big cities going and could best be heard at night. And soon Simon found himself searching for it with Molly and Ronnie and a shifting cast of other people walking up escalators, hurrying along corridors, gliding on black conveyor belts until he came at last to a slope with steps going down seemingly for some way and started climbing down them carefully until realising that the slope was coming to an edge, a precipice, because someone ahead of him saw it too late and wobbled wildly waving arms, then hung in the void for one brief moment before dropping from sight without even a scream.

The next morning, Ronnie provided a rather conventional breakfast of corn flakes and poached eggs on toast as they sat in the kitchen. When the phone rang in the hallway, he jumped up and went to answer it.

'Brilliant,' he said on returning. 'Dave's ready. We're picking him up at ten outside the library.'

Half an hour later they were on the pavement stashing their bags in the Avenger's boot. It was Saturday morning and everyone else seemed to be in bed.

'Can you two sit in the back unless one of you wants to navigate?' said Ronnie.

Simon and Molly sat in the back. At the last moment, Hector came running out in multi-striped pyjamas and sang *ne me quitte pas...ne me quitte pas...ne me quitte pas* with his hands held together in mock supplication. Mel appeared behind him in a white dressing gown laughing and waving.

'Mad fuckers,' said Ronnie.

The library was in the centre of Brixton next to the Ritzy cinema. Dave stood up from the steps as they approached, stubbed out his

183

cigarette and flung his rucksack into the boot with a thud that rocked the back seat. He slid into the front and turned around as Ronnie made basic introductions. Simon saw wiry black hair, lean cheeks and four o'clock shadow and got a careless nod, while Molly was treated to raised eyebrows and a smile. He looked away and watched the council estates go by as they drove up Effra Road and Tulse Hill onto the South Circular. After a while though, the contrast between blokey chatter up front and empty silence in the back started to bother him and he attempted some conversation with Molly.

'How's your sister these days?'

'Still the same.'

'Still living in Reading?'

'Uh huh.'

She continued to stare through the window. They were on the A2 now and soon on the outskirts of London moving between tame fields of the green belt.

'Hey, lively up you two,' shouted Ronnie over his shoulder.

'Music,' said Dave. 'Let's have some tunes. We can't hit the highway without music.'

'Yeah, music!' shouted Molly. Simon had noticed yesterday how she was deliberately talking to other people as if to say *I'm not with the guy beside me*.

'You've brought some different tapes,' said Dave. 'About fucking time.'

He selected one and slotted it into the cassette player. There were audience cheers and whistles, then the voice of the MC introducing *all the way from Trenchtown Jamaica - Bob Marley and the Wailers!* And the music began.

'My sister went to this, you know.' She glanced briefly at Simon.

'Really? When was this? 75?'

'I wanted to go,' said Dave. 'But I couldn't find anyone to come with me.'

'Aw, I'd have come with you,' said Molly.

'This was when their music was really kicking off,' said Ronnie.

On the M20, Ronnie pressed the car up to 90 mph. Dave entertained Molly with tales of his time as a window cleaner and Simon managed to get her talking about current music for at least two minutes. Beyond Ashford, they gave the music a rest and played Crazy I Spy (tyre dust cap, nostril hair, glorious revolution) and Who

Am I? (Tricky Dicky, Ronnie Kray, Antonio Gramsci, Marilyn Monroe). Then they were driving into Dover and by early afternoon leaning on the rail of the car ferry as the white cliffs sank slowly beneath the horizon. The boat docked at Calais and Dave took over the wheel. They shot south along the Autoroute des Anglais and by nine had reached Troyes and the hotel where Ronnie had booked two rooms. *Deux chambres, oui?* And Simon stood gazing at a double bed and Molly's grim expression as she dropped her shoulder bag onto it.

'Look, I can see if Ronnie and Dave are willing to swap if you want. Their room'll have twin beds.'

'Go on, then. See if they'll mind sharing a double bed.'

'Oh, they won't give a shit.' He turned towards the door.

'Look, let's be clear. Our relationship is over - right?'

'I know it is.'

'Okay, let's just get through the night.'

The hotel manager recommended a café used by local people which would still be serving if they hurried. In fact, the café staff were quite relaxed and served them a three course meal with a large carafe of red wine. A shaggy dog came to inspect them and its owner, an old man at a corner table, raised his brandy to the *messieurs et mademoiselle*. They ordered brandies to return the compliment.

After leaving the restaurant, they felt relaxed and expansive enough to wander through the old town admiring the half-timbered buildings. The streets were almost deserted. At the end of the Rue Émile Zola, they crossed the Place de la Liberation and stood on the bridge overlooking the gleaming river. A stately building stood on one bank and a line of dark trees stretched along the other. Ronnie pulled a camera out of his shoulder bag and took a flashlit picture of the scene. Then Molly took a picture of the 'three musketeers'. Finally, Simon took the camera and as he pressed the button saw Ronnie raising a clenched fist, Molly giving a sultry smile and Dave stonefaced. It was almost midnight as they got back to the hotel.

In their room, Simon and Molly undressed in silence, backs to each other in low bedside light. Simon had slept naked next to Molly in the past, but felt he could hardly do that now. He left his briefs and T-shirt on before getting into bed. The alcohol had taken the edge off his anxiety and he lay on the hard mattress in the dark unfamiliar

185

room thinking of the absurdity of it all and that at least he was in the right country for the absurd. Then a voice came out of the darkness, level and emotionless...

'You can rub me if you want.'

He had wondered if something like this might happen and fantasised about it too. He turned on his side and made to put his arm around her, but she stopped him.

'Just rub me please. If you want to...'

It took only a few minutes to bring her to orgasm and she moaned loudly as she came. He wondered if Ronnie and Dave had heard in the next room and whether it would be a good thing if they had.

'Thank you,' she said. Was that all? No, her hand found his cock and began to stroke. It had never worked.

'I'll do it,' he said after a minute or two. 'Can I?'

She lay still but let him put his arm around her shoulders or at least under her neck. He smelt the familiar scent and pressed his body lightly against her side. As his breathing became more urgent, she groped on her bedside table for a tissue and passed it to him without a word. He closed his eyes and came into it with a whimper. His arm had begun to ache and he pulled it away and lay on his back.

'Thank you again,' she said. 'But this changes nothing.'

He turned onto his other side and let a few tears trickle into the pillow before bringing himself under control. Molly turned away from him and soon he heard the soft regular breathing of sleep.

They left the hotel at nine thirty next morning and barrelled down south along the A6 and A7 to a soundtrack of Toots and the Maytals and Van Morrison. Near Lyon, they filled up with petrol, bought baguettes and coffee and swapped drivers. In Provence they swung eastward on the A8 to Grasse where they stopped at a supermarket and filled two trolleys with jumbled heaps of food and drink. Then Ronnie drove the car up winding hill roads to the little village which stood on the edge of a gorge in the Alpes-Maritimes. Simon saw a sprawl of red-roofed white-walled houses on a gentle slope, an old stone arch that they passed under, narrow streets and a large village square with café and circular stone fountain. Then another narrow street led uphill to their destination.

They left everything in the car and went inside to look around. The house was on three floors with living room, utility room and a large

186

kitchen on the ground floor. Ronnie unshuttered the rear doors and opened them onto a terrace area which had loungers, a table and sun shade. The view looked over rooftops to the other side of the gorge where another red and white village stood on top of the rock face.

'According to legend that village used to be part of this village,' said Ronnie. 'Then somehow the people upset the local giant who stamped his foot and created the gorge, splitting the village in two. It's called the Gorges du Loup now.'

'Wo-ow,' said Dave. 'Are there still wolves around here then?'

'Did you say it's your mother's house?' asked Molly.

'Her and her boyfriend's.'

'It has a woman's touch. Clean and tidy and all the baskets and rugs...'

'They were here at Easter so she'll have done some housework I suppose. You like it then?'

'Definitely. You're so lucky to have it.'

'Hmm. I hardly ever come here. It's a sleepy little place in the mountains - a long way from the real world.'

He led them up to the first floor which had two bedrooms and a bathroom.

'I thought me and Dave could have this floor and you two could have the top floor. Follow me.'

They went up the final flight of stairs and into the bedroom. It had twin beds, though quite close together with a small bedside table between. Simon glanced at Molly's face but it showed nothing. There was a dressing table next to a large pine wardrobe and on the other side of the room, a chest of drawers flanked by two chairs. They inspected the bathroom further along the hallway which was a decent size - 'big enough to swing a dog' - as Ronnie put it and poked their heads inside a small room used as an office.

'Okay?'

'Yes it's lovely.'

'Yep.'

They brought everything in from the car, then Simon and Molly lugged their stuff up to the top bedroom.

'Will it do?' he asked.

'Yes, it will do.'

She opened a window and began humming to herself as she went about unpacking, putting clothes away, arranging make-up on the dressing table. Naturally, she'd chosen the bed on that side. Simon lifted his rucksack onto the other bed, then went to the bathroom. When he came back, he'd been left a few hangers at the near end of the wardrobe and the bottom two drawers in the chest. Without a word, he began unpacking. Without a word, Molly went downstairs.

When he got down to the kitchen, Ronnie and Dave were storing away the food and Molly had put a sliced baguette on the table with some olives and humous.

'Beer? she said. 'Or shall we chill them for a while?'

They took a bottle each and squeezed the rest into the fridge.

'Listen, can we just heat up this onion tart or this quiche tonight?' said Ronnie. 'I don't really feel like cooking after that journey.'

'Cool,' said Dave.

'I can make a salad niçoise if you like,' said Molly.

'Excellent.'

'Oh look - my dear old mum's left a recipe for Provençal beef stew,' said Ronnie, holding up a page torn from a magazine. 'I could do that tomorrow.'

'Are we going to have a cooking rota then?'

'Nah, just take it in turns,' said Dave. 'Whoever feels up to it.'

'What are your culinary skills, Simon?'

'I can do spag bol.'

'Oh yeah, that'll be good seeing we're in France,' said Dave.

You could do a boeuf bourguignon, Simon,' said Molly. 'It's no more difficult than spag bol.'

'I'll find a recipe,' said Ronnie. 'Just use red wine, no stock.'

'Haven't you learnt anything from that creepy landlady of yours,' said Molly.

'I stay out of the kitchen while she's around.'

They opened a bottle of red wine and ate around the kitchen table. Afterwards, Simon loaded the dishwasher, then they began a round of cards and drank coffee. By eleven o'clock, there was widespread yawning and weariness.

'It's been a tough two days,' said Ronnie.

Half an hour later, they went to bed although Simon hung back after Molly and the others had gone upstairs. Cautiously, he opened the front door and stepped outside. There was a small paved garden with large potted plants and a low wall. He stood in the gateway and looked up. A light was on in Dave's room and a glow came from

188

'their' room at the top. Above that, a few stars were visible and a faint aura of moonlight. He looked up and down the street. Dim lights could be seen in other houses, but there was no-one about and deep silence all around. No wind in the trees, no voices filtering out, no sounds of distant traffic, no background hum...and then the high call of a bird came over the rooftops, perhaps from the gorge - a single note repeated several times. And from the other side of the village, the same call as if responding. Then silence again. He went back in and climbed the stairs. After brushing his teeth, he went into the bedroom. Molly was sitting up reading by the bedside light. She had closed the windows and shutters so that it was like being inside a box. He sat on the edge of his bed facing away from her, undressed and slipped under the covers.

'Are you going to read for long?'

'No, not for long.'

He turned away. A few minutes passed, then the light clicked off and Molly settled down in her bed. A few more minutes went by and a clock in the village started to chime. Still wide awake, Simon counted every stroke. After a brief pause, it started to chime again the full twelve strokes as if to make sure. At the end, he waited, then turned in the darkness and whispered.

'Hey, did you hear that? The clock chimed midnight twice!'

There was no response.

In the morning, after breakfast of croissants and jam, Ronnie took them on a tour of the village. They crossed the square, walked along another narrow street and went out under the stone arch. There was a level border of grass, then a steep twisting path which took them down close to the edge of the gorge. As an acrophobic, Simon hung back but could still see the wooded lower slope on the other side with white houses dotted here and there. Light cloud was drifting into the gorge from the east and they heard the distant drone of an aeroplane which Ronnie said came from the airport at Nice. On the way back up, he pointed out a stretch of terraced earth where the villagers had once grown grapes and the old stone baths where village women used to do the washing.

'They were quite well organised then,' said Simon.

'There still is a communal feel to the village amongst the residents,' said Ronnie. 'Not much of a socialist consciousness though.'

189

'I thought you hardly ever came here,' said Molly.

'Half an hour's chat in the café will tell you that.'

'When did your mother buy the house?'

'About ten years ago...after the divorce. I came here for three summers running when I was a teenager. That's when I really got to know the place. Look - along there is old Marteau's farm. I did some work for him before I went to university. I think his son runs the place now. It's mainly sheep, goats and chickens.'

He was pointing down a long dusty lane off the other side of the road where in the distance a farmhouse and outbuildings stood.

They walked back into the village and stopped at the little church with its tiled floor and neat rows of chairs. There was an altar at the far end and paintings on the walls. Next to it was a walled cemetery with some recent headstones and fresh flowers on the graves. Further on at the other side of the village, an abandoned church stood with another little cemetery behind locked iron gates. A similar gate secured the arched entrance to the church which had no doors. A congregation of sparrows could be seen inside flitting in and out through broken windows. Ronnie said the villagers still tended the place and kept the weeds down. A large silver cross stood on a pedestal outside.

On the way back, they passed the tabac which also sold wine and groceries. And just beyond it, they made way for an old lady in a blue and white flowered dress with a cardigan around her shoulders and a faded yellow bonnet on her head.

'Bonjour monsieur,' she said to Ronnie.

'Bonjour madame.'

They watched the thin figure walk on steadily up the sloping street.

'My mother knows her,' said Ronnie. 'She walks around the village every day, once in the morning, once in the afternoon. Greets people with formal courtesy and ignores anything else they say.'

In the square, a dog was sleeping in the shadow of the fountain.

'Too early for a beer?' asked Ronnie, glancing at his watch.

'Don't be silly,' said Dave.

They peered inside the café while Ronnie went to the counter and ordered. The only customer was an old man sitting on a bench which ran the length of one wall. There were half a dozen tables, but they decided to sit outside in the sun. The woman brought their beers out and Ronnie spoke to her. *Ce sont mes amis d'Angleterre.* They

190

exchanged greetings. *Bonjour, bonjour, bonjour, salut!* The dog woke at this and padded over to their table, its tail wagging lazily. After sniffing them, it followed the woman back into the café. A little while later, the old man came out and gave them a wave. They looked on as he moved with infinite slowness across the square.

'Village life,' said Ronnie. 'Can you bear the excitement?'

'It's hard to keep up,' said Dave.

The two of them talked about French cars, films and football. Simon couldn't think of much to say to Molly without fear of being brushed off. And once upon a time he'd talked so easily to her. After half an hour, they walked back via the tabac and bought some goat's cheese for lunch.

'Wow, only two francs fifty,' said Simon looking at bottles of red wine in a large wicker basket.

'I'd go easy on that stuff,' said Ronnie. 'It's deadly, believe me.'

Back at the house they made some lunch, warming up a couple of baguettes in the oven. They ate on the terrace which the sun was slowly reclaiming. After reading and talking for a while, Ronnie decided to wash the car while Dave disappeared to his room. Simon put down the book he'd been reading and looked across at Molly. The sun was now shining fully on the terrace and she was lying on a lounger in shorts, T-shirt and sandals.

'Fancy a walk?' he said.

She shrugged.

'We've been for a walk.'

'I feel like going back where we were this morning on the ridge.'

She glanced at him through her sun glasses.

'Well don't let me stop you.'

He counted five slow seconds, then sat forward in his chair.

'Come on, Molly.'

'What?'

'Let's go for a little walk.' He tried to keep his voice level. 'For old times' sake.'

Her chest rose and fell with a sigh, then she sat up.

'You don't have to if you don't want.'

She swung her legs off the lounger.

'Just give me ten minutes.'

She went upstairs. It turned out to be twenty minutes and at one point he heard her talking to Dave and laughing. Then she came

191

back down with her small brown shoulder bag and they went outside. After a few words with Ronnie, they set off down the street and followed what was already becoming a familiar route around the bend, across the square, along another street and out under the stone arch. They carried on walking for a while on the grass border of the road with farm fields on one side and the slope down to the gorge on the other. The cow parsley was starting to bloom and there were little blue flowers in the grass.

'Is that a cuckoo calling?' asked Molly. It was. After about half a mile, they stopped and sat down in the shade of some trees, resting their backs against a large grey boulder. There was silence for a while as Simon rehearsed what he was going to say and watched the occasional butterfly bobbing over the greenery.

'Come on, the suspense is killing me,' said Molly. 'I know you want to talk about something.'

'Well, I want to talk about us, obviously.'

'Uh huh.'

He tried to keep his voice steady again.

'Can't we give it another try?'

She looked at him.

'I doubt it. You know as well as I do it wasn't working. You can't have been happy and I certainly wasn't.'

'It did work to begin with. It worked for quite a while.'

'Yes but it ran its course, Simon. Apart from anything else - and there were other things - you're just too serious for me. Too involved in politics. I don't share that. I never did.'

He said nothing.

'I finished a difficult relationship before I met you - as you know. I need to be sure before I get involved long term with someone again. For now, I'm happy as I am. I'm not short of friends, you know.'

'Can't we just start talking to each other then? Can't *we* be friends? You ignore me most of the time.'

'Well this is an odd situation, isn't it? We've broken up but we're on holiday together. We've broken up but our host doesn't seem to fully appreciate that.'

'I've told him.'

'I believe you. I haven't been talking to you very much because I don't want you to get the wrong idea. But yes - we can be friends.'

He shrugged.

'Okay. That's better than - well, that's better.'

She leaned over and gave him a kiss on the cheek.

'But remember - a kiss is just a kiss.' And she laughed.

'We saw that film,' he said.

'I know.'

'I was going through my Humphrey Bogart phase.'

They both laughed.

When they got back to the village, Ronnie and Dave were sitting outside the café again.

'Had fun?' said Ronnie.

'We just went for a walk,' said Molly. 'It's lovely out in the countryside. We heard a cuckoo calling. I've never actually heard one before.'

'Yes. And the crickets'll be singing soon,' said Ronnie. 'You don't hear much of that in Brixton.'

'I'm an urban dude,' said Dave. 'The countryside's just scenery as far as I'm concerned. Beaches are good though, especially if they're attached to a town.'

They talked and argued and drank beer for an hour or so, then stopped at the tabac on the way back. Simon bought six bottles of the cheap red wine. The plump old proprietor in the black beret said something to Ronnie.

'He says are you having a party?'

'Oui. Er...un bon temps.'

'Il va passer un *très* bon moment.'

Back at the house, Ronnie got started on the beef stew which took three hours cooking before it was ready. They nibbled bread sticks, cheese and olives, drank some wine and played cards, then ate the stew and played cards again. After half an hour of that and despite some coffee, Simon began to nod off at the table. When they started a new game, he took a glass of water and climbed the stairs unsteadily to bed. Later, something woke him and he sat up tense and fearful. His brain scrambled to remember where he was and how he'd got there. The shutters were still open and moonlight was slanting into the room. Molly's bed was empty. And then he heard again the sound that had woken him.

12. Sounds of Passion

Next morning, Simon thought he should talk to Ronnie. He had fallen asleep again eventually and woken with only a mild hangover. The other bed was still empty. Down in the kitchen, he poured out a large glass of orange juice and took it with a bowl of corn flakes onto the terrace where Ronnie was just finishing his breakfast.

'There's some croissants in the bread bin.'

'I know. I'll have one later.'

Simon gulped down half a glass of juice while Ronnie examined the blue sky.

'There's usually some rain here in the spring, but I think we're going to be lucky.'

'Ronnie, I did tell you Molly and I are no longer a couple, didn't I?'

'Yeah, you did. Of course you did. It's just that I wasn't quite sure if it was still an on/off sort of thing.'

'We broke up several weeks ago. She still wanted to come on this holiday though.'

There was a noise from the kitchen and they looked round. Molly in her dressing gown had got two mugs out and was starting to make coffee. She waved through the glass door. Ronnie waved back, Simon turned away. They talked vaguely about plans for the day.

'She seems to have slept with Dave last night,' Simon said when Molly had gone.

'Oh right...'

'But we've broken up, so...how can I complain? It's just a little bit awkward, that's all.'

'Yeah, I can see that. Sorry, but Dave's a sort of 'anything goes' guy. He doesn't consider other people's feelings very much. I can have a word-'

'Nah, leave it. I don't want him to know that I'm - oh, never mind. The fault's just as much with her.'

'To be honest, I put you both in that top room partly because I thought you might get back together...and partly because Dave and I would have to share it otherwise. And although we're good mates, I didn't fancy that for a fortnight.'

Simon shrugged.

195

'I'll tell you one thing. If she carries on making the sort of noise she was last night, you'll have the neighbours knocking on the front door.'

And with that, he went back upstairs and left Ronnie to ponder.

In the afternoon, Ronnie drove them to the village on the other side of the gorge. Nothing was open and there was hardly a soul on the streets, but they wandered around.

'It's a summer seasonal place, really,' said Ronnie. 'No sheep farming economy like our village.'

He pointed across at what he said was their house, but everyone was tired and no-one was talking much. Things improved at the next stop - a fabulous fairytale village perched high on a ridge. The views of surrounding slopes and gorges were spectacular and there were glimpses of the sea on the Mediterranean shoreline. They looked round the perfume and souvenir shops and Simon thought of buying some postcards, but what would he say on them?

They drove to one more town for a beer and a look at its church which had a medieval painting of a *danse macabre*. The devil had the face of a science fiction alien and with a bow and arrows and some little black demons was driving the dissolute nobles into hell through the gaping jaws of a monster. Molly turned away from it, but Dave thought it *fantastic*.

'Literally,' said Simon.

'Yeah, literally,' echoed Dave somewhat sardonically.

As no-one could face cooking that evening, they stayed and ate in a restaurant where the food and beer were good and the conversation went well until flagging over coffee. It was dark when Ronnie drove them back to the house. They watched French television in the living room for a while, then Molly said goodnight and went upstairs. When Simon followed a little later, he was relieved to find her asleep in 'their' room.

The days went by slowly, the nights too. Molly slept soundly in her bed and Simon began to feel better. Then they had an outing to Grasse and when she went off to look round one of the perfume factories, Dave had his arm around her. Simon wandered up and down the narrow streets with Ronnie and had lunch outside at a bar, but resisted the temptation to pour out his soul. They did another supermarket shop and drove back. The next day while Molly stayed in bed with a migraine, Ronnie and Dave repainted the window frames at the front of the house as Ronnie's mother had requested. Simon came out while they were sanding the wood.

'Want to help?'

'Well, I've never actually painted before.'

He went for a long walk instead, further out along dusty winding roads in a landscape of rocks and scrub, feeling like an exile in the wilderness. Back in the village, he sat outside the café with a beer and listened to a song thrush singing in the distance. That evening with Ronnie's help, he cooked the boeuf bourguinon.

'I don't know,' said Ronnie at one point. 'You've barely cooked before, never painted, never driven a car. You've hardly lived!'

The bourguinon, however, was excellent. Molly said so. She was feeling much better and slept with Dave again that night. But the sounds of passion that reached the top bedroom were a little gentler.

They had agreed to visit Antibes the next day. Simon woke around eight and had a quick crap and bath. He went down to the kitchen and sat for a while eating croissants, yogurt, drinking coffee. No-one else appeared. Going back upstairs, he heard low voices coming from Dave's room and Ronnie la-la-la-ing in the shower. In the bedroom, he opened the wardrobe door to take out a shirt and there hanging on her side of the rail was a dark orange blouse that had been one of his favourites. Behind it was the brown Afghan waistcoat with yellow leaf designs that she'd bought in Camden Market soon after they'd met. It had cost a lot of money, yet she'd bought it to please him. Behind that, her favourite blue and white flowered dress that she'd worn many times and a couple of 'peasant' skirts. At his feet in front of the wardrobe lay her blue bedroom slippers, so familiar he had to turn away. On the dressing table a bottle of lavender water she'd bought in Grasse and anointed herself with the previous evening. It's odour had still been in the air when he came up to sleep. He pulled the stopper out and smelt it now. On the bed lay the white V-neck sweater that she'd worn last November when... Footsteps on the stairs. He put the bottle down and moved quickly around the bed, struggling into his shirt at the same time. Molly came into the room and frowned.

'What have you been doing?'

'Nothing. Just getting dressed.'

'Why is the wardrobe door open?'

197

'I just got this shirt out.'

She slammed it shut, put the stopper back in the lavender water bottle and looked at him.

'I was thinking of trying a bit myself,' he said in a jocular tone.

'You know you're really beginning to piss me off.'

He pulled a pair of socks on, trying to keep his balance. He wanted to remain at her level and not sit down.

'You're getting to be a real drag. I'm going to have to do something about you.'

'You're already doing it, Molly,' he said.

She shook her head.

'When we get back to London, you'll never hear from me again. You can go back to your meetings and your political friends.'

'I thought we were going to be friends.'

'I should never have said that. It's over. Get used to it. Stop pulling faces and hanging around me.'

He picked up his trainers and left the room.

They got to Antibes just after mid-day. The temperature was around 21°C and the sun shone on dazzling white buildings, palm trees and English voices on the esplanade. They had lunch outside a brasserie in a large square. The man at the next table turned out to be a lorry driver called John who told them stories as if eager for an audience after lonely hours in the cab. First off, he wasn't really called John but had changed his name to get the lorry-driving job after a run-in with the police. He'd managed a pub back home in Brum, but had to raid the till to pay people. He used to do some small-time drug smuggling but they had sniffer dogs at Calais these days. He was thinking of teaming up with a mate now and importing wooden lanterns. You soaked the cases in sulphur and water, scrubbed them with wire wool and flogged them to the dodgy antiques trade and the souvenir shops. You never knew - he might be able to import them back to Blighty. They liked John and went down to the beach with him to dip their feet in the sea and stretch out on the sand. As they sat talking, a loud explosion came out of the blue and they jerked their heads round almost as one.

'What the fuck was that?'

'The sonic boom,' said Ronnie. 'A jet out over the Med.'

'Jesus, I thought it was all over.'

'Yeah...scared the shit out of me when I first heard it.'

After a while, they stood up to go though Simon lingered for a minute, struck by the different shades of blue in the sea. When he caught up with the others, a word floated out of the conversation.

'*Topless*? Where?' he said.

The beach was busy and some people were sunbathing.

'Didn't you notice?'

'You must be blind,' said Dave.

'It's a bit early in the year but there might be a few people on the naturist beach if you want a look,' said John. 'You'll see the fellers as well though.'

'Anyone want to have a look?'

'No,' said Molly. She was wearing the dark orange blouse.

After a couple of hours sightseeing and a visit to the Absinthe Museum, they walked back to the car park. John didn't have to pick up his lorry until next day. He'd intended to hitch back to Marseilles and sleep in the cab overnight, but in a spirit of bonhomie, they took him back to the village.

'The sofa's very comfortable,' said Ronnie. 'We'll get you back to Marseilles tomorrow.'

It turned out that John had worked as a chef at some time in the murky past and as they found flour, yeast and tinned anchovies in the cupboard, he made them a pissaladière with salade verte. There were still three bottles of the tabac wine left and Simon drank without counting the glasses. He had felt progressively wounded during the last few days and needed to do something about it. Gradually, he became ensconced behind a sensory barrier, barely able to follow the conversation around the kitchen table and sitting out the card games.

'It's nearly midnight,' he heard somebody said. And then he was outside on the street 'going for a walk'. After a minute or so, he realised that John was with him.

'Hello,' he said. 'Are you coming for a walk too?'

'Well they're worried about you, Simon. And someone's got to keep you away from that gorge they've been talking about.'

It was amazing how *distinctly* he could hear John.

'Oh I'm not going anywhere near that fucking gorge, mate. That fucking gorge might...swallow me up. I suffer...I suffer... from vertigo, you know. Amongst other things...'

199

'Oh well, there's a double risk then. You're drunk and you suffer from vertigo.'

Simon stopped and took a deep breath. They were on the far edge of the square.

'I'll be fine. Listen...'

The clock was striking.

'It strikes midnight twice, you know John. Just listen.'

John listened as they walked on.

'Only once, Simon.'

'It's not working properly. Where's the clock winder?'

'Simon, don't do that. They'll chase us out of town.'

'Well that's where we're going anyway. Out into the countryside, under the stars.'

'Simon, don't do that.'

'Listen, do you know any songs?'

'Quite a few. Are you suggesting we sing?'

'Absolutely. How about the Inter-nasha-narlay...'

'Don't know that one, but at least it sounds French.'

'It was French, it was. But I do the American version.'

He started off, but it was a struggle even in his inspired state. After a few lines, he fast forwarded to the chorus.

> *'It's the final conflict*
> *Let each stand in his place.*
> *The international working class*
> *Shall be the human race...'*

'Hang on, hang on. I know...The Red Flag. You join in.'

He sang the first verse while John dee-dee-deed along.

'That was the official version. Now this is *our* version.

> *'The people's flag is deepest pink,*
> *It's not as red as you may think.*
> *But workers still can stand and cheer,*
> *The Labour Government is here.*
> *We'll change the country bit by bit*
> *So nobody will notice it.*
> *And just to show that we're sincere*
> *We'll sing the Red Flag once a year.'*

'Ah, that's a good one, Simon. I like that.'

Simon sang it again with John joining in. By now they were walking along the road outside the village.

'I say, I say,' said Simon. 'Let's go and have a look at the farm. This way!'

And he plunged into the nearest field. Afterwards, all he could remember was ploughing towards an abandoned car and climbing onto its roof and then his remarkable feat of strength in picking up the rear axle and throwing it somewhere while John stood and watched. And moonlight glinting on the windows of an old hut.

Such were the memories that came back to Simon next morning as he lay low and dry beneath a layer of blankets. He'd half-woken a few times, but what finally made him stay awake was the sound of voices at the front door below. It was a loud conversation in French between Ronnie and another man. Shortly afterwards, Ronnie clomped upstairs and into the bedroom looking unusually flustered and grim.

'That was Denis, the Marteaus' son. He said you were at the farm last night pissed out of your skull. He said you've damaged a car he was repairing, broken a window in one of their outhouses and trampled on some crops he was growing.'

'Oh, shit.'

'He lives on the other side of the village and didn't hear anything, but he says Madame Marteau got out of bed and saw you and another man - presumably John - through the window. She was too frightened to do anything. Great, eh? Old Man Marteau's in hospital in Nice, it turns out - so this is the last thing they need.'

'I'm sorry. I can barely remember...'

'My mother isn't going to be too thrilled about it either when she hears. Nor her partner. Apparently some of the villagers heard you shouting and singing. You were knocking on doors too. It won't go down well.'

'Sorry.'

'You'll have to pay them damages. He was talking about 270 francs.'

Simon did a calculation as best he could.

'Bloody hell.'

201

'I told him you were in a bad way today, but we'd go over and see Madame Marteau tomorrow. Apart from paying her the money, you'll have to make a formal apology.'

'I will, I will,' Simon groaned. The first thing he'd done on waking was to look at the other bed and now he looked at it again. It hadn't been slept in.

'Where's Molly and your best mate?'

'They're driving John back to Marseilles.'

'Are they? What's the time?'

'Eleven.'

'Jesus. I feel absolutely awful. In every sense.'

'I warned you about that wine.'

'Yes, you were right. Everybody's right about everything except me.'

'I'll make you some coffee if you want, but you'll have to come down and get it.'

A few minutes later, Simon forced himself out of bed, went to the bathroom and shat comprehensively. Then he went down to the kitchen. Ronnie had gone back to his room, but had left a half-full cafetière on the table with a sheet of folded white notepaper propped against it. He opened the note and read.

Simon. Sorry I haven't been able to say goodbye. I hope you feel better soon. Don't worry - I'll let Molly know how you feel about her like I promised. And thanks for that version of the fucking Red Flag. I wrote down what I could remember before going to sleep last night and I'll sing it in my cab tonight! Here's to Maggie! John.

'Oh, fuck,' said Simon.

He went upstairs and lay on the bed, but there was no chance of sleep again. Eventually, he had a shower and got dressed.

'I wouldn't go outside today if I were you,' said Ronnie, back down in the kitchen.

Simon had never felt less like going out in his life. He spent a restless hour or so on the terrace drinking tea and trying to read. When Ronnie went to the tabac, he climbed the stairs to Dave's bedroom. The door was ajar and he stepped inside. A knotted condom was visible in the waste basket. Clothes including some of Molly's were strewn around the floor and her nightdress was on the bed. Simon kept the tears back, but some salt leaked out and stung.

202

He remembered saying to John last night *she's the love of my life.* Oh, Jesus! What would John say to her? Would he say it in front of Dave? A large bottle of pills sat on the bedside table. He resisted the temptation to read the label.

It was almost dark when Dave and Molly got back. John had paid for lunch and paid for petrol, then gone off to sleep in his cab before driving back to England. They'd had a look round the Old Port, then driven back.

'Five fucking hours there and back,' said Dave.

'I'm hungry' was all Molly said. It felt as if they might have had a row.

Ronnie had put a chicken in the oven and they ate that with saute potatoes and courgettes. Simon managed a plateful - the first food he'd eaten all day. He sipped water with it. They played a few lacklustre card games, then sprawled out in the living room and watched television. Simon decided to go to bed and Molly came up not long after. Nothing happened, nothing was said, but he drifted off to sleep a little more happily.

Next morning, Simon went with Ronnie to the Marteau farmstead. They saw hardly anyone in the village. On the lane leading to the farmhouse, he rehearsed his apology. A black car was jacked up on the far edge of the field to their left. Further away, a cuckoo was calling again from a copse. The farmhouse door was opened by the son, Denis, a plump balding man who moved awkwardly as if embarrassed. He led them into the living room. A huge rug covered much of the tiled floor and a low fire was burning in the grate. Madame Marteau was seated stiffly and impassively in a hard-backed armchair. She wore a black dress and cardigan and her grey hair was tied tightly in a bun.

'Bonjour, Madame,' began Ronnie. He gestured at Simon. 'C'est le méchant qui est responsable.'

'Mais oui.'

Simon bowed.

'Madame, je suis vraiment désolé.'

The old lady inclined her head solemnly and waved her hand at two dining chairs which had been arranged facing her. They sat down. Ronnie spoke some more to her in French and Simon thought he had got the gist.

203

'Oui,' he interjected. 'C'était le vin Français. C'est très' - he searched for a word - '*formidable*!'

And he mimed the act of knocking back glass after glass. Denis chuckled behind him, Ronnie laughed rather nervously and Madame Marteau smiled.

'Mais oui,' she said. 'C'est très formidable parfois.' Then she signalled to her son who picked up a piece of paper from the big mahogany sideboard and passed it to Ronnie.

'Ah, yes. This is the itemised bill.' He showed Simon the total which was 276 francs. 'I'll pay it now and you can owe me. Then we don't have to come back.'

Madame Marteau accepted the money gracefully and signalled again to her son. To Simon's surprise, small glasses were produced and an amber liquid poured into them.

'C'est le peach brandy,' said Denis. 'Fait maison!'

'Home made,' said Ronnie. 'I think it's to seal the deal and pronounce your forgiveness.'

They raised their glasses.

'Santé!'

Madame Marteau spoke again to Ronnie with sharp amusement in her eyes.

'She says that you'd better only have one glass. And that the local wine turned out to be more expensive than you bargained for.'

Simon gave a Gallic shrug.

'C'est la vie!'

'No, no,' said Ronnie. He spoke to the lady of the house in French.

'I've told her you've learned your lesson. Now drink up fast and let's get out of here while the going's good.'

That afternoon, they drove into Grasse where Simon drew out the money to repay Ronnie. They ate in a restaurant and made the most of it as time was running out.

'I'd like to start back on Wednesday if that's okay,' said Ronnie. 'It's another two day trip and I have to be at this wedding on Saturday. My favourite uncle has decided to get married - fuck knows why. He's the only member of my family whose views could be described as left wing.'

'That's fine,' said Molly.

'Yeah, time to get back to Brixton,' said Dave with a drum roll on the table. 'We've done it justice here.'

'It's been great, Ronnie,' said Molly.

'Sure,' said Simon.

They spent the last day cleaning the house and packing, having a picnic lunch on the old grape terraces, a few beers at the café and a last meal and round of card games in the kitchen. Molly slept in 'their' bedroom again that night.

Next day, they set off at ten and drove back along the same route with stops for petrol, toilets and food. It was late and almost dark when they reached Troyes and Ronnie hadn't booked rooms. The hotel they'd stayed at before was full. The next two places they tried were also *complet*. Then they saw the dimly lit sign of a small pension in a narrow side street. The patron said he had only one family room free, but could fit them in and provide a meal. He led them upstairs to see the room. It had a double bed, two singles and a small shuttered window.

'Cosy,' said Dave.

'It'll do, won't it?' said Ronnie. 'Just to get our heads down for the night.'

Molly nodded.

'Nous le prendons,' said Ronnie to the patron.

Simon felt dismay but said nothing. He knew no-one would want to look elsewhere. They dumped their overnight bags and went to the dining room where a rather rubbery coq au vin was served. The conversation sounded forced and superficial to Simon and he wondered if the same thought was lurking behind those careless faces around the table. The question was answered when they returned to the bedroom and Dave and Molly sat down on either side of the double bed. Without hesitation, Simon sat down on the far edge of the bed next to them and Ronnie stretched out on the other single bed in the corner.

'Well I'll just go to the bathroom,' said Molly. And she took her nightdress and toilet bag down the corridor.

'Who's going next?' asked Ronnie.

'Moi,' said Dave.

'You go after that, Simon. I'm just going to read for a while.'

'Sure,' said Simon, pretending to look for something in his bag.

Eventually, they were all in bed with the lights out. Simon lay on his back in what seemed to be deep darkness at first until a faint light crept into the room through a transom window above the door. Soon he could see knobs on the end of his bed and the dull outline of a wardrobe against the wall. Then whispering started from the double bed and Molly giggled and then the kind of silence brought about by fingers on lips and holding of breath. And he told himself he didn't care less what they did so long as he couldn't see it or hear it. He tried the corpse posture - something Di had taught him when they were 'Si and Di.' You did a mental scan of your body from scalp to soles and relaxed any muscles that were tense. It was surprising how many muscles you could keep tense without realising. He tried taking deep regular breaths, counting them, counting something else. Sheep? Never worked. Pebbles on the shore? Madness. Waves on the incoming tide? Cat's eyes on the road? Windows in twenty storey buildings? The chimes of a clock...midnight again? You can't relax the mind...

The double bed creaked and all his muscles tensed again. *Whispers and wet pecking of lips*. His breath hung suspended. *Soft talking, body shifts, rustling covers*. Fear and anguish flowed along the neural pathways of his body. *Soft exclamations. Here! This way! No-oh! Ouch!* Half-suppressed laughter...then Ronnie spoke from the corner.

'Hey, can anyone join in?'

Molly's voice answered.

'Yeah, come on then.'

Simon lay on the rack.

'Now - or after?'

'After what?' *Dave's sardonic voice.*

'You know what.' *Molly's moist voice.*

'What about Simon?' *Ronnie's cautious voice.*

'He's asleep.' *Dave's contemptuous voice.*

Breathe. The soft voices went on. I'll give it a minute. Soft voices still. Breathe. Is Ronnie out of bed? Soft voices again. One more minute. Soft voices - what's happening? Breathe... Simon couldn't take it any longer. He sat up in bed and spoke.

'Ronnie, could I take your keys? I'll go and sleep in the car.'

But his words were partly drowned by a scream from the double bed.

206

'Oh God, you gave me a fright.'

Simon pushed away the covers and put his feet on the floor.

'What did you say, Simon?' Ronnie was still in his bed. 'We're just about to go to sleep.'

'I doubt it.' He began to pull on his jeans. 'I said give me your keys and I'll sleep in the car. I can't stand any more of this crap.'

'Oh, dear. Someone's sore,' said Dave.

'Shush,' said Molly.

'Simon, don't be ridiculous. We're going to sleep.'

'Ronnie, *this* is ridiculous from my point of view. In any case, you can do whatever you want. I just don't want to be part of it. If you can't understand why...'

'What d'you think's going to happen, Simon?' said Dave. 'Nothing. You're imagining stuff. We're just having a bit of fun because we can't sleep.'

'You were right first time, Dave. I'm sore, I'm a bad loser. So just fuck off.'

'Oh dear,' said Molly.

'Simon...' Simon was dressed by now. He stood up.

'Keys or not? If not, I'll just go and find a bar or walk around town until you've had your fun.'

'A bar - that's a great idea. Let's go out again and find a bar. We could even have a bar fight, me and Simon, just to round off the holiday.'

'Oh don't be so fucking stupid, Dave.'

'Why's everyone fucking swearing at me?'

Molly giggled.

'Simon, we will go to sleep,' said Ronnie. 'Honest. I swear on the Communist Manifesto. I swear on the Collected Works of Marx, Engels, Lenin and Trotsky. Especially Trotsky. They're going to stop pissing about. Aren't you?'

'Yes,' said Molly firmly.

It all seemed so pointless to Simon. He lay back on the bed fully clothed. A couple of minutes went by in silence, then Dave whispered.

'Is he still here?'

'Dave,' said Ronnie. 'You've always been a mate of mine. But if you don't shut the fuck up, I'll get dressed, I'll take Simon, I'll take

Molly if she wants to come and I'll drive to Calais without you. I'll leave you to find your own fucking way home. Is that clear?'

'Oka-a-ay,' said Dave irritably. But apart from a brief bit of whispering and shifting about, that did the trick. There was peace in the darkness and Simon turned on his side feeling much relieved. He had made his point. He had stood up for his rights. And Ronnie had stood by him in the end. *I'll take Simon and I'll take Molly and I'll drive back to Calais without you*. Simon almost smiled before drifting gently into sleep. A sleep so sound, in fact, that he never heard the beast in the double bed wake the beauty by his side later in the night and quietly fuck her with his hand over her mouth.

Part Four
July 1983

13. Aftermath

It was a small gathering in the Chapel. The family had introduced themselves beforehand while they waited to enter. Now the mother and sister sat together at the front while the cousin, his wife and a small overawed child spread out further along the row. Simon, Lesley, Bashir and Maloney were three rows behind them. On the other side of the aisle sat a pair of hairy podgy young males who had squeezed themselves into suits for the occasion. Another duo of similar age, grey-clad and almost hairless, sat two rows behind them. Four work colleagues from the Institute sat at the back.

The Minister said a few words of welcome and gazed solemnly at the coffin which lay on the catafalque at the front. Then without warning, a familiar harmonica refrain emerged from the speakers and the sound waves of 'He Ain't Heavy, He's My Brother' filled all the space around them. On the front row, mother and daughter clutched each other in grief. Simon couldn't help whispering to Lesley.

'But he *was* heavy!'

She smiled, but when he glanced at her a little later, she was crying.

After the longest four minutes twenty seconds in history, the music ceased and the Minister began his eulogy. Vince had been a loving son and brother, an enthusiastic supporter of the 'Red Devils', a lover of music and a longstanding member of the Sealed Knot. A track by Turmoil then thundered out, though the volume was quickly reduced. Simon watched the hairy guys to see if headbanging would be part of the service, but there was no movement. Vince's sister then stood and read in quavering voice a poem which began 'Death is nothing at all.' The cousin spoke of Vince's good work for charity and how proud he had been to serve as godfather.

They stood for the committal which was brief and which Simon found rather moving:

> *To every thing there is a season, and a time to every purpose under the heaven; a time to be born and a time to die. Here and now, in this final act without fear, in love and appreciation, we commit the body of Vincent Duane Leggett to be cremated.*

Dark red curtains closed around the catafalque and they filed out of the Chapel to the strains of 'Let It Be'. Outside, the few floral tributes were arranged in a semi-circle for inspection. As well as a wreath of white lilies from the union branch (inscribed 'One for All and All for One'), there was a red rose sheaf which Simon and Maloney had clubbed together to buy. For ten minutes or so, they stood talking to the family, to Vince's colleagues and to the other mourners. Simon's assumptions about the latter proved incorrect. It was the almost hairless guys who were the heavy metal fanatics. The podgy hairy guys were from the Sealed Knot and, in a few weeks time, were going to help Vince's sister and cousin scatter his ashes on a suitable Civil War battlefield, probably Roundway Down.

'I remember him telling us how he'd once played the part of a blood-stained corpse in some film re-enactment,' said Simon.

'Oh, we've all done that one time or another,' said one of the hairy guys.

'Aye,' said the other. 'There's always a big demand for corpses in the Sealed Knot.'

Lesley drove them back to London with Maloney helping to navigate. Simon sat in the back seat with Bashir.

'That was about right, really,' said Lesley. 'Quite moving at times.'

'Are you okay?'

'Yes, I'm okay. I just can't help thinking about how he was found. Alone in that place, living off takeaway food apparently. Beer cans everywhere. I know he was only twenty seven, but it's no wonder his heart gave out.'

'He was mixing alcohol with drugs - uppers and downers. I think that's what did it,' said Simon.

'Well, maybe. But when you get down to it, we didn't really know him at all, did we?'

'We knew what he chose to tell us,' said Maloney. 'No-one ever really wanted to probe any further. But if he'd ever said he needed to talk, I'd have listened.'

'Well, we all would.'

'It's surprising though, how much you can find to praise somebody for at their funeral,' said Bashir. 'When it's too late.'

'That's quite true,' said Simon. 'When they're no longer around to be a pain in the arse.'

'Yes, but he was a decent chap underneath,' said Bashir. 'He wouldn't have harmed anybody. That's really important...'

'He harmed himself instead,' said Lesley.

'I agree,' said Simon. 'I was just being a tad cynical.'

'I thought of asking them if I could say something about his union involvement, but I don't think the family knew much about it,' said Maloney.

'Well at least you didn't try and sell any copies of Workers' Struggle,' said Simon.

'Thanks, Simon. I'm not entirely a two-dimensional cardboard cut-out, you know.'

'They could have just mentioned it though,' said Lesley.

Maloney shrugged.

'He probably kept it to himself. He wasn't really an obvious working class hero, was he?'

'They did seem a bit surprised when the four of us turned up,' said Simon.

'He did his bit. He carried out his union duties, he supported the cause,' said Bashir. 'He never crossed a picket line like that other fellow.'

'Precisely,' said Maloney, half-turning in his seat. 'And just so you know, I didn't go to his funeral out of some sense of duty. I went *because* he did his bit for the cause. And *because* the silly fucker should have talked instead of endlessly joking about his problems. There's no shame in asking for help.'

He looked away through the window.

'Oh, Tony,' said Lesley. 'Don't say things like that. You'll get me all emotional again while I'm driving. Where do I go here?'

'Second exit, then stay in the inside lane.'

'How's your little boy, anyway?'

'Lev is beautiful. And healthy.'

'And Wanda?'

'Healthy. And beautiful...'

The traffic was heavy through Croydon and it was almost an hour before they were driving through Brixton and Simon had a brief glimpse of Lilac Road, the street of squats. At the Elephant, they turned north and on Waterloo Bridge both he and Maloney gazed upriver and saw the union flag flaunting itself over the Houses of Parliament. They drove on past the Aldwych and up Holborn Kingsway.

'I know where I am now,' said Lesley.

She'd managed to book a space in the little car park at the rear of the Institute. Simon had not been round there since the day of the strike which seemed a long time ago. The same security guard was sitting in the glass-fronted kiosk and after consulting his clipboard, he raised the barrier and let them through with a little wave at Lesley. They parked and went their respective ways. The Records Office was deserted apart from Mary. Simon didn't bother asking where everyone was after receiving a tart 'good afternoon' in response to his 'morning'. He made a couple of phone calls, shuffled some papers and went to the Staff Restaurant to reconvene with Maloney.

'Caucus meeting tonight, then,' he said over cottage pie and chips. Maloney nodded and yawned.

'Kid keeping you up then?'

'Lost two hours last night.'

'Oh dear. Listen, I'm meeting Lizzie in the Fountain at six. Just wanted you to know.'

'Okay. I'm going to our Centre first, so I won't be there till seven at the earliest.'

'Okay. Well I don't know if you'll overlap but she won't stay long.' Maloney shrugged.

'That"s fine. She came to some Workers' Struggle meetings when we were having our fling. She doesn't anymore, but I still regard her as a comrade. We'll start being friends again at some point...'

They finished the meal and returned their trays to the servery.

'I'm going up to the Union Office to have a nap,' said Maloney. 'Never done that before.'

'I'll wake you if the revolution starts.'

Lizzie was at the bar when he got to the Fountain that evening.

'Hello, Brother Simon. What do you want to drink? Shall we sit outside? It's a gorgeous evening.'

They sat at a little table on the side pavement. Lizzie tossed her hair back and stretched out her legs.

'I've got something to tell you,' she said.

'Sounds ominous.'

'I'm buggering off for a while.'

'What?!'

'Going travelling for six months. All agreed at work. Unpaid leave.'

'Wow! Where are are you going?'

'Well, first of all I'm going to see an old friend who lives in Ireland. We're going to walk the McGillicuddy Reeks.'

'The which?'

'Mountains. In Kerry. You know the song:

As I was going over
the far-famed Kerry mountains

'We're doing part of it on horseback. Can you imagine?'

'Fantastic!'

'Then I'm going to the States with another friend. I've got relatives over there in Ohio, she's got relatives in Long Island which'll be fantastic for New York. When we've had enough of that, we'll hire a car and drive down to San Francisco, maybe Mexico as well.'

'Holy horsepower! You'll be *on the road*.'

'Oh yeah, that Kerouac book. I'll be - what was his name? Dean...'

'Moriarty. You will as well. Don't drive like him though...'

'Don't worry. I'm not on some fucking death trip. Anyway, this is not till September.'

'Six months though. How're you going to afford it?'

'Remember my grandma died just after Easter? Well she left me *five thousand pounds* in her will. Can you believe it? I'm still going to work all the hours I can though before I go. I'm not splashing it all on America. I'm thinking of trying to buy a flat when I come back. God, it'll be *1984* then. It's been coming for so long... Still at least things aren't that bad.'

'They're bad in a different way. Anyway, what will you do about your room in the commune?'

'I'll leave. Move out. Haven't told them yet, but I've had enough. All the meetings and rotas and the lack of privacy and the moaning and the tedious monologues. Actually, most of the women are fine and I'm close to Julie as you know, but there're one or two who are a total pain. Anyway I want out. I want to be in charge of my own life.'

'And I'm stuck here in this fucking dead end job.'

'Simon, do something about it. Ever since I've known you, you've talked about saving up and going travelling, or else going back to university and doing an MA. Stop talking about it, stop dreaming, do it! Do both! Nobody is ever stuck these days unless they want to be or are too lazy or frightened.'

'Yeah, I will. I will. I do feel I'll be abandoning the struggle though.'

'The struggle will still be there. What we're having to abandon is the idea that the revolution is just around the corner. That it would happen within our youth, not just within our lifetime. That was the spirit of '68 - you know? We thought people would listen to us and agree with us. Well, you've seen what's happened. One of the reasons I'm taking this break is because I'm so fucking disillusioned with the working class. I could just about forgive them for electing Thatcher once, but to do it twice is just blind stupidity.'

'Hmm, I don't know. They've been bamboozled by the right wing media and the Falklands War and led astray by the SDP.'

'Those are just excuses. They've shown no desire to throw off their chains, have they? In fact, most of them don't even realise they're in chains. The writing was on the wall when the Longbridge workers abandoned Derek Robinson. I know he was an arrogant CP bastard and supported all that "workers' participation" crap, but he was their elected leader. To let him be thrown out of his job...that was shocking.'

'Well, that was one of the worst episodes, but there have been some great fightbacks, some great displays of solidarity. The power is still there.'

'I agree. Like I said, the struggle will go on. Blatant injustice can't last for ever. But it's going to take a lot longer than we ever envisaged. It'll still be there when you've done your MA or whatever. The next target will be the miners, it's obvious. They've made it clear by putting McGregor in charge - the butcher of British Steel. That's going to be the next major battle and I think Thatcher will find that's a bridge too far.'

'I hope so. Something's got to stop them, otherwise they'll be in power for years.'

Simon looked at his watch.

'You are aware that Maloney's coming here?'

'Yes, you told me. That's all right. I'll be going soon, but if I see him, I see him. I'm not going out of my way to avoid him. Apart from going to America, that is.'

They laughed.

'Have you had any contact?'

'No, it'd be pointless really. It's over. It was just a fling - on his part.'

'Oh I don't know. I think he was struggling to decide at one point.'

'Well, he made the right decision...for the sake of his child. I sent him a congratulations card - him *and* Wanda actually. To his work address...'

'I was there when he opened it. He didn't say anything other than it was from you, but I think he was quite touched by it.'

Lizzie was silent for a moment.

'He might have left Wanda, you know...if she hadn't become pregnant. But whether we would have lasted...the thing is, you become attached to somebody despite the imperfections you find when you get close to them. When you've slept with them a few times, when you've watched how they deal with mundane domestic things and how they relate to strangers like your friends and workmates. Tony did spend a night at the house and at least three different friends' places. We even spent one night in the nurses' home at the hospital. I know a student nurse who was going away for the weekend and she lent me her keys. We slept in her three foot wide bed - how close is that?'

'Tell me about it.'

Lizzie hesitated and lowered her voice.

'He wasn't bad in bed, given my experiences with some supposedly enlightened socialists. He didn't just - well, no. Perhaps I'd better not tell you about it.'

'I didn't mean it literally,' said Simon, uncertain if he was disappointed or relieved.

'Beyond that though, he has no real interests other than politics. He's actually quite practical and fixed a plumbing problem that one of my friends had, but things like that are just a distraction to him. I think I'd find that tedious and limiting after a while. Anyway, enough about me and him. How about you and Molly? Is that completely over too?'

217

'It was completely over before we went to France. And even more over afterwards. She slept with somebody else in the house while I was there.'

'Oh, God. Really rubbing your nose in it...'

'I don't think it was vindictive. Heartless and insensitive, perhaps - but she was just thinking logically. I've finished with Simon. Here's an attractive guy who's interested - I'll sleep with him. Why not? Ronnie tells me they haven't seen each other since then, so I suppose it was just a holiday fling. Very awkward for me though.'

'I can imagine. Were you hoping when you set off that it might be reignited?'

'A very faint hope, but that was extinguished pretty fast.'

'Oh, dear. If only we had the courage to admit when a relationship isn't working and leave it, but we linger on in hope, don't we? We're just so desperate to have a partner, to have a stable loving relationship with another person. That was the norm for our parents' generation, but it's become like the holy grail for us. Who wants to be living on their own? Or living with other people just for the sake of it?'

'Yeah, I suppose. But apart from all the awkwardness of that, I was made to feel like a spare part in general. I can't drive, I can't cook apart from one dish, my practical skills are almost zero. Actually, it did wake me up. It did make me realise I've got to move on and develop.'

Lizzie picked up her bag.

'I'd better go. Listen, you'd better come round to the house sometime soon. I'll try and arrange it when the dreadful duo are out. I can show you how to cook a chicken curry - that'll be a start, won't it. And I'll make some hash cookies.'

'Lizzie, you're the greatest woman I've ever known. Even greater than my mum.'

'Really? I've never been compared with anyone's mum before. Perhaps I'm getting old.'

'Would you like to be a mum?'

'One day. I hope that's not a proposal?'

They hugged. Lizzie wore no perfume, but the smell of her hair and skin was sweet. Her body was firm and soft and alive.

After Lizzie had gone, Simon moved back inside the pub and found a table. He took the *Guardian* out of his rucksack and leafed through it for a while. Caucus members arrived one by one. First Albert who bought him another drink, then Sandy clutching her crash helmet, then Joe who looked weary and Maloney who'd recovered his usual impatient energy.

'Who's leading off?' asked Joe after the small talk had dried up.

'Well you organised the meeting.'

'Okay, well first of all this is not a meeting - okay? We've got a meeting on the 18th. This is just a few of us having a drink. I don't want to set up a caucus within the Caucus, or a drift within the tendency or a splinter within the fragment-'

'Yes, yes. Get on with it,' said Maloney.

'-but I didn't get round to inviting Mick or Paul. I tried to get hold of Tim but he's off sick apparently. So this is just a social occasion - okay?'

'Cheers,' said Albert.

'Okay, so what's the feeling within the branches?' asked Maloney.

'Resignation,' said Sandy. 'I don't mean they're resigning from the union. I mean that most members could see it coming, even if we tried to persuade them - and ourselves - that it wasn't going to happen.'

'It's the sheer scale of the Tory victory that's depressing,' said Simon. 'That's a real kick in the teeth.'

'I couldn't believe it,' said Albert.

'It's a combination of things,' said Maloney. 'The Labour campaign was crap, there was no simple summary of the manifesto for people to read, Foot didn't come across as a leader - too mild, too much the right honourable gentleman, the Labour right wing undermined him, the tabloids passed themselves off as the voice of the common man, the SDP split the vote...'

'Yes, but the result is that Labour has lost part of the working class vote,' said Joe. 'What does this mean for the future?'

'Well, obviously it means Labour will move back to the centre if not the right to try and recapture those votes,' said Sandy.

'They're talking about Kinnock now as favourite to be new party leader,' said Albert. 'He's not right wing.'

'Kinnock is soft left,' said Maloney. 'That means he'll shift to the centre if the wind blows that way. And Labour centrism is effectively right wing.'

'So after all these years of struggle,' said Simon,'we're back with a right wing government and a right wing opposition. '

'One step forward, two steps back,' said Maloney. 'Lenin, 1904. *We have already won a great deal and we must go on fighting, undismayed by reverses*.'

'But logically two steps backward for every step forward means you're really going backwards all the time.'

'Yes, I can add and subtract as well, but you can't apply simple maths to this. Everything depends on the size of the steps and the one step forward was massive. It shook the foundations worldwide. It pulled the wool away from people's eyes and exposed the real nature of global capitalism and the state.'

'You're talking about 1968?'

'I'm talking about the re-emergence of militant anti-capitalism in the later 1960s. You can centre it on 1968 if you like, but 1968 has become almost too symbolic. There was a far wider struggle over a longer time period. The two steps backward were inevitable. They're the reaction of monopoly capitalism which is huge and powerful and still there ruining our lives.'

'The two steps backward are partly a result of the left failing to unite,' said Sandy. 'All the different strands of left political thought - socialism, communism, Eurocommunism, Maoism, Trotskyism. All the liberation movements and single issue campaigns. We get in the way of each other and actively fight each other a lot of the time instead of fighting the real enemy. It saps our energy and our impact...'

'Just a minute,' said Albert. 'What are the two steps backward that you're talking about? The last two elections?'

'No no no,' said Maloney. 'Two steps backward is just a blanket term for the fact that a certain amount of reaction has set in against the working class struggle. And I'm not just talking about the UK. We have Reagan in the White House as well as Thatcher in Downing Street.'

'But the working class are partly to blame for that,' said Simon. 'They've rejected any kind of left wing alternative and voted these people into power.'

'Comrades,' said Joe. 'This is all very interesting, but getting us nowhere. Let's get back to specifics. Within the union, we have a right wing NEC and we can't just assume the pendulum will swing back next year as some people seem to think. And instead of being led by a left wing Labour government with the most radical agenda since the Levellers, we're stuck with the most right wing gang of scumbags since God knows when. Well, certainly since before 1945. So where do we go from here?'

'I think the first and most important thing is simply to say *we're still here*,' said Maloney. 'We're not going to give in or give up or go away. Look!' He tapped the front page of a newspaper which someone had brought. '*Lawson announces £500 million spending cuts*. It's exactly what we said would happen - they'd be back for more. So we're right and we'll continue to fight.'

'Hear, hear,' said Albert.

'In one sense, you can even say we're better off because we're shed of the illusion - which was an albatross around our necks - that a radical Labour government was going to come along and sort everything out,' said Maloney. 'The fact is in present circumstances, it's almost certain there'll never be a radical Labour government. So we're thrown back onto our own resources, but we're also in control of them. Any temptation to compromise has been removed. We just need to carry on arguing and campaigning within the union branches, the regional meetings and so on.'

'One good step would be to say exactly that. The fight goes on,' said Sandy. 'That could be our headline for the next Newsletter.'

'It won't be very original,' said Simon. 'Every left wing or socialist or revolutionary group will be saying the same thing. Some already are.'

'Well that's okay,' said Sandy. 'All groups will be in agreement.'

'I haven't given up on the idea of a radical left-wing Labour government,' said Joe. 'Realistically, it's the best chance we've got of introducing real change. Any other ideas are just pie in the sky at the moment - and in the foreseeable future.'

'Fundamental change is what's needed,' said Maloney.

'Okay, but sticking to what we can do in the Left Caucus, I agree that we need to reiterate our basic policies,' said Joe. 'Including our willingness to build a broad operational front within the public

221

sector union movement and to report on and support all struggles against the government.'

'Exactly,' said Maloney. 'Nothing changes.'

'Except maybe the timescale.'

'I give you that, Simon,' said Maloney. 'It's going to take longer.'

'In which case,' said Joe, 'whose round is it?'

They broke up around eight thirty and went separate ways. Simon had drunk three pints, enough to inoculate himself against the minor challenges of street life, but not enough to be drunk. There was a fine flush of setting sun between buildings to the west. He walked to the tube via Russell Square remembering as he always would that autumn evening with Molly. A blackbird was singing from one of the plane trees in the plangent tone that blackbirds use at day's end. It could be an elegy for lost love or for all sorts of hopes that had faded, but of course it wasn't. He stopped and looked for the bird amongst the branches and watched its yellow bill opening and closing as it sang, listened and sang again without concern for the affairs of humans grounded below.

At the tube station, he went down in the lift and ran as he heard the train coming in. The carriage was half empty and he sank into a reverie as they roared through the darkness. Was it just the beer or was he coming out of a depression? One good thing about disasters, whether personal or political was that they released you from false hopes, from yearning for what was not going to happen. They freed you to 'start over' as the Americans said, as Lennon had sung. Not much could go wrong when you were rebuilding your life, at least not in the early stages. And one good thing about friends was that they kept you up to the mark. He could not be sitting in a pub with Lizzie next year when she was back from her travels and admit that he had done nothing to change his life.

At Finsbury Park, he came out onto Wells Terrace and stopped at the Cypriot cafe to buy a doner kebab. A white dove perching on girders watched him as he walked past the buses and turned into Stroud Green Road. The sun had set, but it was still daylight and as he walked along the familiar streets, he felt a knot of resistance at the thought of just going back to his room. There was unfinished business to consider away from the everyday rut. Behind the houses to his right ran the embankment of a disused railway line. He had seen workmen up there recently and heard they were converting it into some sort of public pathway. On impulse, he turned off down a side street and came to one of the old bridges. Just before it, a set of crumbling steps led upwards and disappeared behind leafy saplings and scrub. With a flutter of trepidation, he walked up the steps and followed them out of sight to a gap in the fencing which let him through onto the embankment. For a moment, he was startled by an abrupt screeching sound, then saw a bird shooting away into the bushes. He calmed himself and looked around. The railway tracks had all been removed and the surface was smooth enough to walk on. He wandered forward. Here and there, the workmen had piled up branches, foliage and brambles, bricks, stones and general waste. The sides of the embankment were lined with trees and bushes, but with gaps in between. It wasn't that high, slightly lower than the house roofs, and he could see little of the surrounding district. Eventually, he sat down in one of the gaps on a grassy mound and began to eat his kebab. The steep slope ran down to garden fencing and he realised that just to the right was Anne-Marie's back garden which he'd sat in once or twice earlier in the summer. There were no lights on in the back windows. Alex was abroad and Anne-Marie would be in her living room or the front bedroom. Looking down at the house, it felt as if he'd stepped outside his own life. And as he chewed on pitta bread and juicy meat, the cogs slackened by alcohol began to turn again. What was he going to do?

As if in answer, the cogs began to throw up ideas. He would look around for somewhere else to live and move by autumn at the latest. Should he travel like Lizzie or study for an MA? Why not both? He had to leave the Institute at some point soon or he would end up staying there for ever. He would save to go travelling next summer. Spain to begin with because he'd never been there, then maybe across to Italy and Greece. He would apply to do an MA next year as well, starting in the autumn. Part time or full time? Look at the options. How would he survive financially? See previous answer. What would he do after that? Fuck knows. Teach? Write? It was all too far away. Find a new girlfriend? Wait and see. It seemed unlikely at present and there were issues in the back of his head that he had to sort out.

So, one more year at the Institute. One last birthday celebration when he hit thirty in October. Only three months away and how different it would be with Lizzie in New York and no Molly. After that, a few more months of meetings and cases and causes, then he would stand down as Chairperson at the AGM. He didn't see why Maloney should be surprised. Maloney who scorned him as a 'liberal'. He wasn't really giving up. As Lizzie had said, the struggle would still be there. Let others carry it on for a while.

Dusk was setting in now and he had the embankment to himself. Or did he? Birds were still flitting about and, surprisingly, he heard the quavering hoot of an owl from further along the path. He'd heard it before while lying in bed at night, but it had always seemed distant and mysterious as if from some other realm. And there was a fox living along here somewhere which according to Anne-Marie had almost got into her chicken coop. What else might be living in these wild places in the heart of the city? He stood and scrunched up the greasy wrapping paper, then stuffed it into one of the workmen's piles. There was nowhere else for him to go now but back to his room.

He squeezed through the broken fence again and went down the steps into the street. As he turned the corner and approached the house, he saw Anne-Marie's light glowing on the second floor. Her 'friend' was probably up there with her. Even Anne-Marie had a lover. He opened the garden gate and let it swing shut behind him. After a side glance at the laurel bush, he turned his key in the lock, stepped inside and closed the door.

A few seconds later, a dim light came on in the front room and a silhouette appeared in the window bay. Its arms rose in the air for a moment as if celebrating victory against the forces of darkness. Then its hands gripped and jerked the curtains together stage by stage until they met finally in the dead centre.